D1927866

ONCE UPON A VOW

JESSIE CLEVER

SOMEDAY LADY PUBLISHING, LLC

Published by Someday Lady Publishing, LLC

ISBN-13: 978-0-9984192-7-5

Cover Design by The Killion Group

There have always been three women in the Black family who inspire: Lady Jane, Nora, and Jane.

There have always been three women in my family who inspire me: Grandma Irene, Mom, and Gigi

This story is for them.

CHAPTER 1

When her thoughts turned to arson, Jane Black knew it was going to be a very long season.

It was only the invariably delightful personality of Madame LeFevre that had Jane discarding ideas of burning down the woman's dress shop as a means of escaping another season.

Or more specifically, the Marquess of Evanshire.

Unfortunately it was the dreadful incident at the Brownlow ball that had saved her from the previous season. And then it had only been a temporary reprieve. One captured at too great a cost.

Her eyes roamed over to her new sister-in-law, sitting as straight as her ever increasing stomach would allow as she surveyed the gowns Jane modeled. It was just short of a year since her brother, Samuel, had wed Penelope Paiget while the two had chased after the also invariably delightful Professor Xavier Mesmer after the professor's assistant was murdered by an unknown entity attempting to steal the professor's telescope discovery.

And Jane had been left in the care of the Marquess of Evanshire for safekeeping.

Austin.

She blinked and ducked her head into her shoulder as heat swarmed her cheeks. She darted a glance at her mother and Penelope, sure they saw the blush caused by her traitorous thoughts, but they chattered on about the Gigot sleeves and whether there should be covered buttons or pearl buttons gathering the cuffs. Jane heard none of this as the forbidden name ran around her brain.

Austin. Austin. Austin.

She believed she had done a rather fine job feigning disinterest in the man. Or at the very least, a polite amiableness. But her true thoughts had her pushing a hand to her stomach and ducking her head into her shoulder again.

"Miss Black!" Madame LeFevre snapped. "I cannot fix this sash if you will not stand still. Young ladies, isn't it so, Mrs. Black?" This to Jane's mother, Nora, who was momentarily distracted from her conversation with Penelope. "They are all atwitter for their young beaus."

Jane squeaked, all eyes in the small sitting room turning to her. She pressed her hand to her stomach again, dipping her eyelashes in false demure.

"It's just a little tight," she said, running her fingers over the sash Madame LeFevre was so ardent about fixing.

Madame huffed. "Too many lemon squares at the balls, Miss Jane?" She tutted a finger at her. "You mustn't let yourself get carried away. You must win a fine young man this season, no? It is your second season after all."

Jane closed her mouth and looked away. It *was* her second season. Two seasons too many, but no one had asked her for her input. Or rather, they hadn't listened when she'd given it without invitation.

She had already picked out a suitable man to marry. Mr.

John Smith, a perfectly reasonable second son of the country baron who made his home not more than three miles from Eaton Park, her father's estate in Kent. Mr. Smith had always been kind to her at the local assemblies. Asking her for the first dance. Fetching her lemonade. He had extraordinary insight on crop rotation and fertilizer that he planned to use when he became of age and inherited the parcel of land his grandfather had left him.

Jane had grown so comfortable around the man, she'd even revealed her terrible secret to him. That it was, indeed, herself who kept the accounts at the estate and not her father. Such an untoward thing for a woman to manage, but there was nothing about Mr. Smith that would suggest he would find disfavor in the thing. So she'd revealed it to him.

It was all very comfortable and...known. There was nothing about Mr. Smith and his agriculture ambitions that Jane could not surmise at the outset.

Not like when she looked at the Marquess of Evanshire.

Not when he cast that grin at her. The one that lit his brown eyes until the delicious pain in her stomach became too much to bear.

Not like when his hand slipped into hers, leading her onto a dance floor. Not like when he pulled her close. Not like when she could smell the vanilla of his soap. The mint on his breath.

She squeaked again.

"Really, Miss Jane, it is not at all that tight," Madame LeFevre admonished, sitting back on her heels with another huff. "I should think that will do for today."

Jane trailed a hand down the skirts of the gown, their luxurious fabric reminding her that this was all a terrible, unneeded expense. The money for her gowns could have gone into the building of Eaton Park's gristmill, which would have been a far better investment. She eyed her mother but was met with the same stern expression she had since the first time Jane had balked at the idea of a season.

For Jane's seasons were not at all about Jane. They were about her cousin, Lady Emily Black. Emily was beautiful and refined. Everything a gentleman would seek in a wife. Not at all like Jane.

But Emily's beauty and her natural way of enticing the gentlemen meant she required extra chaperoning. That came by way of her plain cousin, Jane, and Jane had been forced to debut with Emily. Attend the same balls. Dance the same dances. Smile at the same gentlemen. All in hopes of keeping Emily in line.

But as Emily had become firmly affixed to the Marquess of Evanshire, Jane had had very little actual chaperoning to do as Emily's attention was rather narrowed.

The pain in Jane's stomach now had nothing to do with the memory of Austin's grin.

Austin.

She bit her lower lip, swallowed the disappointment that rose up at the thought of Emily and the marquess, and stepped down from the dais where she had stood while Madame LeFevre adjusted the gown. It needn't matter. It shouldn't matter. She was determined to marry Mr. Smith after all.

And the excuse of chaperoning Emily gave her leave to fulfill her other plan. A vow really. One she'd made in secret and was now struggling with learning how to bear.

"I will help you out of the gown, ma cherie." Madame LeFevre pushed to her feet, brushing a strand of her silver hair from her forehead and back into the cap she wore perched high on her head. "With all the pins in the bodice, you are likely to get stuck like a Christmas pig!" The French woman's laugh tinkled through the room, but Jane could hear the rasp of age under it.

Jane studied the woman more carefully, noting the lines around her dark eyes, the creases at her mouth. But more, the swollen knots that were her fingers.

Jane smiled, resting a hand on the woman's arm. "I would appreciate your assistance, madame."

The modiste shooed away her attentions. "Of course, my child." She turned to Nora and Penelope. "Would you like some fresh tea, my darlings? Perhaps another tray of the scones?"

Penelope pressed a hand to her rounding stomach. "Oh, lud. I am certain the baby would enjoy two more trays of scones with that decadent cream you have, madame, but I'm afraid my dresses will just not forgive me for it."

Madame LeFevre laughed her raspy laugh once more. "Oh my dear, but that is not at all a problem for me." She swept the room with her splayed hands. "Merely step up on my dais, and I shall solve that little problem for you."

Penelope laughed, her wide, almond-shaped eyes crinkling in her happiness, her hand massaging her belly. A twinge sparked in Jane's chest, and she rubbed a hand absently at the spot. But when she hoped the pain would go away, her mind only saw the Marquess of Evanshire's face. She turned, carefully picking up the skirts of her gown to retreat back to the changing room where madame would help her into her regular things. Jane only had to remember her vow and get through this. It would all be over soon.

A knock at the door stopped her.

"Madame, the gentleman is here," a young seamstress said with a curtsy to Madame LeFevre.

"Already?" Nora looked about her. "Whatever time is it?"

Jane's hand clenched into the fabric of her gown. "Gentleman?"

Nora nodded. "Your brother sent Evanshire to collect us." Her gaze slid to madame and back. "After the excitement of last season, he wanted to exercise a certain degree of caution."

Austin.

He was here.

Now.

Just on the other side of that door.

The pain blossomed through her chest and into her stomach, driving the air from her lungs. She dropped her gaze to the floor, shuffled her feet back toward the changing room.

"Come, child, before you ruin all of my hard work. We must get you out of that gown." Madame LeFevre chased after her, shooing her into the adjoining room and snapping the door shut behind them with a sudden burst of unusual excitement.

This space was smaller but equally as appointed in lush fabrics and gilt mirrors. Jane's regular things hung on hooks along the wall, and their familiarity and serviceable, plainness quelled the rush of emotion inside of her.

"I have never met a woman so fidgety, my child," Madame LeFevre mumbled as she undid the back of the gown. She slid it away from Jane's small shoulders and carefully eased it down her body until Jane could step free. "Just a moment, and I'll get you back into your things, love."

Jane stared at herself in the mirrors. She was too thin. Too tall. Her bones protruded from her unusually long limbs. Her corset hung loose about her. Even it was no match for her thinness.

Her nose was too big. Her forehead, too, but at least that she hid under a generous spray of fringe. The spread of her petticoats made her appear as though she were a duster, ready to flail across the floor.

She was certainly no match for Lady Emily Black.

Jane ran her hands up and down her arms to abate the sudden chill that spread over her, letting her gaze move up the mirror to Madame LeFevre's reflection to see where she was with Jane's regular gown.

Her eyes froze on the reflection of the modiste. The woman held an indigo blue glass bottle in one hand and a rag in the other, dumping the contents of the bottle onto the rag while keeping her face carefully averted. Jane kept very still, her hands frozen on her arms as she watched the modiste set the indigo blue bottle back on a table, keeping her hand with the rag carefully extended away from her body.

"Just a moment more, child," Madame LeFevre cooed. "And then we shall be all done."

The modiste turned, keeping her eyes on the rag, and approached Jane from behind. Although much older than Jane, the woman was also much bigger. Taller. Wider. Thicker. Stronger. Jane's hands clenched on her elbows. Her body preparing for flight as she knew she didn't stand a chance at fight. Not like her father, the great spy for the War Office. Not like her brother, the revered detective inspector for the Metropolitan Police Force.

She was just little, plain Jane Black, who hoped to one day marry a farmer and live a quiet life in the countryside. But madame kept coming closer, the rag held high. Three more steps.

Jane's mind raced, searching for a way out. A weapon. Something she could use to protect herself. The gown she had just tried on hung on a hook beside her, the soft light of the room glinting off the pins along the sash.

Two more steps.

Jane spun and plunged toward the gown, her fingers slipping over the pins before catching one. She wrenched it free and turned, her arm swinging where she thought the modiste had stood.

Flesh met flesh, and she heard the rasp of the woman's cry just as Jane screamed the only thing she could remember.

"Austin!"

* * *

AUSTIN PEREGRINE, the Marquess of Evanshire, had never been in a modiste's shop. He wasn't sure what he had been expecting. A great deal of frippery perhaps. Cakes and teas and fainting couches. As he stood in the receiving room of Madame LeFevre's, he realized his expectations were not too far off the mark.

There was frippery.

There were tea cakes.

And there were fainting couches.

Only, he believed the fainting couches were likely referred to simply as settees by the clientele. They were, after all, quite an adaptable piece of furniture.

That there were no other ladies waiting in the receiving room was not a cause of concern for him. In fact, it was more of a reprieve. The season was once more getting underway, and he found himself, once more, in the difficult position of fending off mothers with daughters of a marrying age. He never thought of himself as a catch, but it was obvious from the motherly contingent of the ton that he was. The situation was made only more difficult by his abject refusal to engage in such social expectations as marriage and family.

He shifted on his feet, his eyes scanning the room from one end to the other, noting all of the possible exits. Possible because he inventoried the windows as well. He wasn't at Madame LeFevre's for pleasure. No gentleman would claim such a thing about a visit to a modiste's shop. He was here on duty. A duty granted him by Samuel Black, a man who demanded Evanshire's utmost respect and dignity.

Jane.

The name passed through his mind like a whisper or the creak of a stair tread. Heard but not quite.

Jane.

Such a simple name for such an extraordinary creature.

He cleared his throat although no one was about to witness his sudden discomfort. While he may not pander to the idea of marriage and family, his thoughts had taken a wayward turn when he'd learned of Jane's return to London. The winter months had been long and dull. While he did not pursue the ultimate result of a wife, he had never been one to shy away from female company.

That was until he'd encountered Miss Jane Black.

She had wormed her way uncomfortably through his thoughts until he could do nothing except think of her. He had never developed such an infatuation with any of the women he'd encountered in the years since he'd left Peregrine Hall when he had become of age, and he wasn't certain what to do about it now.

Jane was not the type one dallied with and yet there was no alternative for him.

He shifted again but for entirely different reasons, the echo of his past making his eyes seek out the clock across the room. The ladies should be finishing up by now, and the young woman who had greeted him had been gone for quite some minutes. Surely the members of the Black family would be ready to depart. He didn't like having them exposed as such in an unfamiliar place. Not with the threat to their lives still lingering after what had happened last summer.

With the remembrance of the Brownlow incident, Evanshire straightened and fastened his gaze on the far door where the young seamstress had disappeared. He had no business letting his thoughts run to the more interesting nature of Jane Black or what he planned to do about her.

Especially when Jane screamed his name.

It was a breath before he realized she'd screamed his given name. Austin. He didn't even know she knew his given name.

By the time this thought solidified, he was through the door where the young seamstress had disappeared, vaulted over a startled maid in the resulting corridor, and crashed through an opposing door where he thought he'd heard Jane's scream.

This was a sitting room much like the receiving room he'd left. Remnants of a tea cart lay scattered about the crimson carpet. Sounds of a scuffle interlaced with the wheeze of his own labored breathing, and he turned about the room until his eyes settled on a door at the opposite end, slightly ajar and teeming with outraged cries of injustice.

He was to the door in two strides, throwing it wide to find a scene his brain could not process. Mrs. Penelope Black, his dear friend Samuel's wife, sat on a chair, her hands pressed against the walls of the adjacent corner to push herself more fully into the chair. Mrs. Nora Black, Samuel's mother, stood next to Penelope and wrestled with something between her hands.

It wasn't until Penelope spoke that the image righted itself in his mind. "Oh, hello, Austin," Penelope said with that wide smile she was quick to use. "We seem to have encountered a spot of trouble.

Penelope's almond-shaped eyes were wide in her bright face as a smile spread across her lips as if she were not sitting in a chair, using her substantial girth to hold another woman hostage in said chair. A woman with whom Nora Black struggled to remove something from the woman's hand.

The captive woman let out a raspy cry. "Get off of me, you cow!"

"That's rather overdone," Nora replied, yanking whatever the item was from the woman's hand.

They were in a dressing room. Mirrors hung on the walls, hooks stuffed with garments. Penelope. Nora.

Where was Jane?

His eyes swung about. Where was Jane?

"Austin."

This time it was much quieter, but he knew without hesitation whose voice spoke his name. His eyes dropped, and there she was. Huddled into a corner, her knees drawn to her chest. He fell more than bent, scooping her into his arms without listening to her protest that she was fine. Two strides carried him back to the outer sitting room.

He sat directly on one of the sofas, not bothering to set her down. Not bothering to realize she was underdressed. Indecent. He was being indecent. He had no claim on her person and yet his hands roamed relentlessly. Up her arms, down her shoulders, across her back. His fingers unable to stop until he had touched all of her. Every last inch.

"Are you hurt? What's happened?" And then because he hadn't given her enough time to speak, he merely dragged her against him, his arms closing around her until he felt the whole of her pressed against his chest.

She was so still. It was unnatural and yet so natural. So like Jane. To encounter whatever it was that had happened to her and not fall trembling into the arms of her rescuer.

Was he her rescuer?

Vaguely, he thought he heard more complaining from the dressing room, but he bent his attention to Jane. He cupped her cheek, pushing back the dark hair that had fallen loose from its pins, nudged her chin up until her eyes flickered open, and he could finally see their warm, brown depths.

"What happened?" He asked it more calmly this time, sucking a breath to keep from trampling her answer.

"I think she tried to poison me." The words didn't make sense at first, and he shook his head.

"Poison you?"

"Madame LeFevre." There was the slightest catch on the woman's name. Not in fear. But rather, incredulity. "I think she tried to poison me with something. She had a rag and a bottle and—" The air evaporated then. He watched it disappear as her mouth opened but no sound came out.

He tucked her head back into the crook of his neck, trying hard not to think about how natural it felt. How normal. How quickly he could get used to the feeling of Jane in his arms.

Mrs. Nora Black appeared from the dressing room then, and Austin felt every shred of comfortability flee at the look of concern cast over him.

"She's all right," he said as quickly as he could get the words out. "Fetch a constable. He'll send for Samuel." If there was one thing he'd learned about Nora Black, it was that the woman spent very little time on demonstrations of theatrics. Give her a job to do, and she was quickly your ally.

She nodded and left. The sound of an outer door opening reached them followed by the rumble of traffic beyond. His eyes studied the dressing room door, imagining the scene beyond as more disgruntled cries erupted.

"You are strangling me!"

"I'm doing no such thing, you evil wretch! And to think I complimented your cream!"

"I'm no wretch. Ye lot come in 'ere and expect to be treated like queens. Well, I'll give you the treatment ye deserve!"

Jane's head came up so quickly it nearly clipped him in the chin. A line had formed between her brows, and her eyes creased as she looked to the dressing room door.

"She's not even French," she whispered in disbelief.

Austin felt a devious bubble of laughter creep up, which brought Jane's gaze to him when he was unable to stop it.

The puzzlement on her face vanished when her eyes met his, and his stomach clenched in anticipation.

He looked at her, remembering that day nearly a year before when he'd sat across from her in a carriage. When she'd absently stroked the line of the scar along his cheek. She stared at him much the same way now, and he wondered again what he was doing with her.

Quiet, beautiful Jane.

Footsteps in the hall alerted him to Mrs. Black's return, but he couldn't move. He couldn't let go of Jane even though propriety demanded that he do so.

A constable soon arrived, and Austin nodded in the direction of the dressing room. "She's in there. Under Mrs. Black."

The constable was rather young, likely a new recruit, and at hearing the name Black his face lost what little color it had.

"Aye, sir," he said, touching his cap before ducking into the dressing room where another melee quickly ensued.

Penelope emerged seconds later, her hands cupped protectively around her middle. "Well, that was quite unlike any fitting I've ever attended." Her right hand twitched madly against her belly, and Jane seemed to deflate against him.

"You're going to put this in a book," Jane said, the line of worry reappearing between her brows.

"Obviously." Penelope smiled, and Austin knew he'd be reading that adventure of Penelope's alter ego, the novelist Miss Melanie Merkett.

Pounding footsteps off the corridor announced the arrival of more constables. Austin's grip on Jane tightened without him consciously being aware of it until Jane's startled gaze swung to him. Her brown eyes were so wide in her face, and he realized suddenly that she'd grabbed hold of him. Her hands were twisted in the lapels of his jacket. He had just to dip his head and—

Samuel Black came through the door, his arms extended to his wife before he'd even noticed the other persons in the room. Penelope waved him off with a protest that she was fine.

"I sat on her, Samuel," Penelope cried triumphantly. "You should have seen it. I knew this bundle would come in handy." She patted her stomach once more.

Samuel turned a concerned gaze on his mother. "She's putting this in a book, isn't she?"

Nora tried to hide a smile. "So she says."

Only then did Samuel's eyes turn to Austin and Samuel's nearly naked sister sitting on his lap. Samuel Black had not come to be a detective inspector in the Metropolitan Police Force on the good graces of the Black family name. No, he had earned it through a steely grit and unerring determination. Both of which he turned on Austin just then. Along with a good deal of stark brotherly protection.

"She's fine," Austin rushed to say.

"That's wonderful," Samuel returned. "Would you mind letting go of her so she can put her clothes back on?"

CHAPTER 2

Even though she was fully clothed now, her body could not forget the feel of Austin's hands pressed to her bare skin. How big they were. How easily they cupped her, drew her closer without making her feel trapped or caged. She'd simply felt…safe.

Her teacup rattled in its saucer, and she quickly set it down on the table in front of the sofa in the Lofton library where she sat with her mother and Penelope. Her mother put a hand to her arm, bending forward to look more closely at her in the concerned way she had that never felt smothering.

"I'm all right. It's all just a little overwhelming." Jane tacked on a smile to make her statement ring with more truth than she felt.

Her mother's expression indicated she clearly did not believe her.

"It just doesn't make sense." This was from Penelope, who was seated in a chair opposite them.

Samuel and Austin had taken Madame LeFevre into custody. She'd heard the woman screaming the entire way out of the shop. Something about the injustice of a working woman's fate. Slaving at the needle her whole life with nothing to show for it. Jane recalled the woman's knotted, arthritic hands and felt a stab of sympathy. Even if the woman had tried to poison her.

"How so?" Nora asked, her hand still on Jane's arm.

Penelope shook her head, her attention on the biscuit that sat on the saucer she had perched on her belly. "I would think they would at least still be going after me. I mean, after what happened last year."

"You don't believe whoever it is, is still after the professor?"

Penelope shook her head. "He must, wouldn't you say? He never did get the technology he sought. And he's already lost so much. He seems quite determined to reach his end."

A shiver passed over her at the words. The man in question, although his identity was unknown, was very real to Jane. She'd seen him attack Penelope the previous season at the Brownlow ball and still remembered the man's hands at Penelope's throat. Enclosed around her sister-in-law's slim neck. Pressing in. Cutting off the air.

For a moment, Jane saw Madame LeFevre's reflection. The soaked rag in her hand.

The image was shattered when the library door opened, and Professor Mesmer himself strode in. The professor was an unexpected person. When one thought of an academic, one thought of smoking jackets and ink stained fingers. White wigs and pipes. Mesmer was none of those things. He was young for starters, with soft brown hair that fell over his brow, and a way of walking that suggested he was in a perpetual hurry. Jane liked him a good deal and smiled as he approached them.

"I am so very sorry, Miss Jane," he said in greeting.

She waved a hand at him. "This is hardly your fault.

Whoever we're up against attempted my kidnapping long before you became known to us."

Nora gestured to an empty chair in their grouping, and Mesmer absently sat.

"I can still feel a measure of guilt, I'm afraid." Nora handed him a cup of tea, which he accepted with the same obvious degree of absent thought. "I had hoped this entire mess would be resolved by now. But to have this menace reappear after nearly a year." He peered down into his tea but did not drink it.

"He must have been healing from the injuries he sustained at the Brownlow incident. Lying low until he was ready to attack again."

Jane marveled at Penelope's outward calm when speaking of her own near abduction and possible murder. She wished she were as brave. She returned her gaze to the professor who still stared into his cup. "I would think you would wish to return to America," she said in hopes of pulling him from his obvious guilt.

He looked up at her words. "Yes, I do. My studies are waiting for me, but I cannot leave with a clear conscience until Bobby's murderer has been found."

Bobby Egemont was the professor's assistant who had been murdered when whoever it was went after the professor's telescope discovery.

"I'm so very sorry," Jane whispered.

The professor's direct gaze landed on her, and for a moment, she realized he was quite a handsome man. Not unlike her brother, Samuel, or Austin.

She swallowed convulsively. She really must stop thinking of him as Austin or she was likely to make another improper slip. She only hoped her mother and Penelope had forgotten her earlier cry in the modiste shop's dressing room. Or perhaps, at least, had chalked it up to nerves.

"Thank you," Mesmer said then and finally took a sip of his tea.

Samuel and Austin's—Evanshire's arrival was predicated by a lot of stomping and Samuel's aggravated voice in the corridor before the two men burst into the library.

"We have no such evidence she should even receive the pay out she was promised," Samuel was saying as he entered. "We cannot put Jane in harm's way like that."

"I wasn't suggesting that we should," Evanshire replied. "But we could use another operative for the stand in. Make them think the job's been done and lure the man out."

"What's this?" Nora asked, her fingers curling around Jane's arm.

Samuel came to an abrupt stop in front of them. "Madame LeFevre was too happy to talk in the hopes of receiving leniency. She was to receive a significant sum for the safe capture and delivery of Jane."

Jane sat back, her spine suddenly losing its strength.

"Whatever for?" Penelope asked.

"She didn't know. She said she was approached in The Bent Broom, that coffeehouse down Marlborough. A gentleman offered her a sum if she were to effectively kidnap Jane."

"What kind of sum?" Nora asked.

Jane peered at her mother, but her mother only raised an eyebrow in return. "It would indicate what class of gentleman we are dealing with. If he offered a significant sum, he would need to have a means of acquiring it."

Her brother shifted momentarily on his feet. "It was enough to allow Madame LeFevre to give up her shop entirely. For the rest of her life."

Jane swallowed so hard her tongue was in imminent danger of disappearing.

"But if she were to be taken unharmed, why was Madame LeFevre trying to poison her?" Penelope asked.

Now Evanshire stepped forward, his gaze uncomfortably focused on Jane, and for a moment, she thought this interest in her extended beyond the case. But that was ridiculous, and she closed her heart against the absurd thought.

"Chloroform," he said. "It's a poison designed to render a person unconscious." His gaze drifted to the professor. "It's a recent development from an American chap."

Mesmer raised his eyebrows and shrugged. "Bloody American chaps," he murmured.

"How interesting," Penelope breathed.

"No," Samuel said quickly and with a pointed finger no less.

Penelope adjusted the saucer on her belly, all innocence. "I was just thinking."

"That is precisely the problem," Samuel mumbled.

"You're saying whoever is trying to steal the professor's discovery attempted to have Jane kidnapped?" Nora interjected.

"Yes, that's it exactly," Evanshire replied, but his eyes were on Jane.

Jane twisted her hands into the napkin she'd forgotten was in her lap, forcing herself not to look away from him. To for once have the strength to hold his gaze. To not be such a coward. To simply be more like the rest of her family.

Until the library doors banged open and she jumped with a debilitating shriek. Her mother's hands were on her shoulders instantly, but her heart still raced. Even when her father, Nathan Black, came striding through the doors, his arms outstretched for her.

"I'm fine," she said, pushing to her feet as he reached her.

Her father's arms closed around, and she let her eyes close in some semblance of peace. Although she may be of marriageable age and fully out for the season, there was nothing more comforting than the feel of her father's arms around her. For a moment, she felt like a little girl again. Happy to sit in her father's lap as he let her go through the sums in the ledgers with him.

Her father straightened, his expression stony as he turned to Samuel. "All right, who the bloody hell tried to nab her, and what the hell are we doing about it? This isn't making any sense. First Jane, then Emily, and then the professor and Penelope. This villain appears almost irrational, and we're no closer to figuring it out."

But before Samuel could answer, Jane heard herself speak. "I'd like to help."

As all eyes turned to her, no one was more surprised than Jane herself. While she may have grown up in a family of spies, she could not be more unlike them. If she didn't have her mother's eyes and nose and her father's smile, she would have been utterly convinced she'd been adopted.

"Terrific!" Penelope said, pushing to her feet when the remainder of the room still stood in stunned silence. "I've been wanting your help in going through the guest lists once more. I think you may remember something that I don't."

Nora stood next to Jane. "That's a wonderful idea, Pen. Let's set up here in the library. We'll need more tea."

"The guest lists?" Jane asked, suspicion that she was being coddled pressing against her neck.

Penelope nodded as she took Jane's hand. "Remember I knew my attacker. I'd danced with him at some point last season. I've been going through all the guest lists Samuel and his men acquired from the hostesses last season, but nothing is jumping out at me. Perhaps there is something you can remember."

Jane recalled now Penelope's determination that she

knew the feel of her attacker's hands. "Yes, that is a wonderful idea. Let's get started."

Samuel stood. "Evanshire and I are going to The Bent Broom to see if anyone remembers the gentleman who came in that day to offer Madame LeFevre the bribe."

Mesmer surged to his feet. "I'm coming with you."

Samuel cast a knowing glance at the professor, and Jane knew all too well his understanding of the professor's determination to see Bobby Egemont's murderer captured. But his expression softened when he said, "We need your help with something entirely different."

"What's that?"

"Cousin Lady Emily—" was all he managed before Mesmer immediately resumed his seat.

"I take it back. I'd better stay here."

Samuel attempted to conceal his grin as he said, "Aunt Sarah says she's gone for her regular walk in the park. She needs to be fetched and brought back to the house while things are so uncertain. Can you manage it?"

"I'd rather manage an American grizzly bear," the professor muttered but reluctantly slipped from the room.

Samuel turned to their father next. "Can I ask you to stay with Jane? Keep a vigil on the house?"

"I will always keep an eye on Jane." Her father's voice was even, but oddly enough, it was an unusually icy glare he cast in Evanshire's direction.

* * *

XAVIER SUPPOSED this was what the Brits called spring, but to his American bones, it still felt closer to winter.

He missed home. What little of it he still had. His quarters at the college in Boston had always been enough, but now? Now after a year of living with the Black family, his rooms in

Boston seemed a little less while also being more. Smaller. Quieter. Lonelier.

And worse, he was technically in hiding with the Blacks. Although, he couldn't have called his time spent wintering in Kent as anything subtle or covert. Nathan Black's estate in Kent was sprawling and lush even during the dormant winter months, and he'd traipsed the whole lot of it, hauling his telescopes and journals with him. He'd mapped more of the Kent countryside than he'd ever mapped of the Massachusetts shore.

The developments in his reflecting telescope technology were progressing faster than he had expected. He was much closer to a working prototype than he had anticipated he would be at this point in his research.

The thought made his gut clench.

Bobby should have been there to see it. Bobby should have been there to help him build the damn prototype. But his friend and mentee had made the ultimate sacrifice for him. Xavier. Now Bobby would never see the development of their work.

This drove Xavier's feet into the frosty grass of the park with greater force, propelling him in the direction Sarah Black, the Duchess of Lofton, said Lady Emily often took her afternoon constitutional. His determination to find Bobby's killer spiked hotter in him at the thought of Jane's near abduction that morning. Whoever was after them hadn't given up. He'd merely been buying his time through the winter, and he was clearly ready to finish what he'd started the previous season.

Xavier rounded the bend onto a smaller path that led into a thicket of trees and nearly collided with a stream of ladies headed in the other direction. They were all equally flounced and bonneted, and he scraped to the side to allow them to pass. But they didn't. Bloody British and their manners. Each lady in turn stopped to give a polite nod of her head, some let out a silly, little twitter of laughter, some batted eyelashes, one bold lady even blew him a kiss.

He stood, his arms relaxed at his sides, only his eyes moving to assess the progression of the gaggle. He knew what he looked like. He knew his appearance drew unwanted attention. It was a damn nuisance in Boston when he would attend lectures and dinners to enlist the support of benefactors for his research only to find himself dripping with the attentions of unmarried ladies.

At first, he had done his best to repel the attention, but he had learned it only made it worse. Indifference was a far more effective weapon.

Eventually the ladies filed past him with a final call of greeting, and he proceeded down the path, his eyes scanning either side for the copse of trees and the bench where Lady Emily supposedly spent time in the afternoon. Her mother had said something about the young woman enjoying the sound of the stream in this part of the park, but he had had the unfortunate consequence of enjoying Lady Emily's company far too often in the past year when she'd visited Kent, and he quite safely determined she did not at all care for something so simply exquisite as the sound of a stream.

Rounding another bend brought him deeper into the thicket, and the sound of a stream became apparent.

Along with the sound of voices.

He halted his steps, killing any sound that may have given away his presence.

Two voices.

One belonging to Lady Emily.

One most definitely belonging to a male.

He straightened, putting his hands to either lapel of his jacket as he waited. He was very good at waiting. Some of his best observations had occurred as a result of his profound ability to wait.

He didn't care for Lady Emily Black, but then, not many people did. Even her own family members. The young woman was dangerously selfish, yes, but what bothered Xavier was her extreme naivety. He had always found such a trait in anyone to be irksome. As his mother was always quick to say, Xavier did best with people ten years his senior. Then they would be much closer matched in temperament. As Lady Emily was already nearly ten years his junior and then more in deportment, he found her simply vexing.

But as the villain had presented himself once more, Xavier understood the danger the young woman was in being out in the park, unprotected by the steel bulwark that was her family. While he was not happy to fulfill Samuel's request to return her to the house, he also understood the necessity of it. It was a task he was happy to take on after so many months of waiting.

But now.

Now having caught the young lady in an indelicate situation, this made the task all the more intriguing.

He wasn't the type to prescribe to blackmail, but in the matter of Lady Emily, he knew having a pawn in his pocket would be valuable. Whatever should arise.

He edged closer to the sound of the voices, carefully keeping a screen of trees between himself and where he thought the voices originated. The sounds grew more distinct, and soon he was able to decipher words.

"Oh, I don't know why they expect such things from me. It isn't my fault she's plain."

Lady Emily's voice rang through the thicket now, each word dripping with the young woman's ubiquitous narcissism. The volume at which she spoke demonstrated her lack of discretion when it came to illicit rendezvouses as this was clearly what was occurring here. Her partner demonstrated no such fault as his response was muffled and whispered.

But then Lady Emily again—

"I certainly hope they don't expect me to cart her around this season. I did plenty of that last year. To think the number of gentlemen with whom I tried to encourage a bit of interest in her. She should really thank me for it. Even if she's my cousin. I deserve it."

Xavier looked up at the trees. It was still fairly early in the season, but most of the trees were sporting a new lush of leaves. He concentrated on those until his pulse stopped thrumming at Lady Emily's heartless words.

Her partner's murmured response was unclear.

"That is it precisely. Oh, Harlow, I'm so glad you understand me. Why doesn't anyone else see how much I've done for her? To think I've spent so much time on a plain relation. I should be lauded."

Lauded indeed. He sucked in a breath. He'd had enough.

He retraced his steps to the path, ensuring he was a good few yards away before turning and tromping back a few paces as loudly as the early spring ground would allow him.

"Lady Emily!" He bellowed it. Bellowed it so loudly any genteel lady would be appalled by his manners. "Lady Emily, your mummy is looking for you!"

A shriek erupted from the thicket he had just vacated. He tromped farther down the path until his way was impeded by a frazzled, disheveled, and most obviously irate Lady Emily as she tumbled through the thicket onto the path before him.

"Excuse me!" she railed, sticking a finger in his chest until he bounced against it. "The nerve, Professor Mesmer."

The tone with which she said the word *professor* was likely one she also used to lament getting dog poo on her slipper.

"You're needed back at the house, Lady Emily. I've come

to fetch you." His tone was exactly as it always was because modulating it in anyway did no one any good and expended unnecessary energy.

Her eyes darted to the side, and he bent forward, peering through the thicket.

"Someone in there?" he asked.

She shoved him away. "I am enjoying my afternoon constitutional. Mother knows that. I need this to maintain my glowing appearance, which I must have if I am to catch a duke this season." She fluttered her hands at him. "Now go away. Shoo."

He cocked an eyebrow at that. "I'm not a varmint you can scare away, lass."

Her gaze drifted to the thicket again.

"Where is your maid?" he asked.

Her eyes shot back to him.

"She had a smudge on her apron. I couldn't possibly be seen with her in the park so I dismissed her." Her nostrils flared, and her hands clenched against her skirts.

"Of course not," he mumbled. He nodded back the way he had come. "All right now. Let's go. I promised to bring you home, and I shall."

"No." The blonde curls framing her face bounced beneath the rim of her bonnet as she stepped back toward the thicket. "I shall return when I am done."

Very rarely did he feel the need to straighten to his full height to intimidate another, but just then he did it more reflexively than on purpose. His six foot two stature towered over the diminutive Lady Emily, and the rebellion in her eyes was quickly replaced by unease.

"I said I shall bring you back to the house, and I will. Now."

The unease was still there when she put her hands to her hips, sticking out her chin. "No."

"Do not make me force you, lass."

She raised that hand again. Extended that finger. Poked him in the chest.

"No." The unease in her eyes gave them an unnatural spark when mixed with her defiance. For all of her shortcomings, the girl had verve. It was too bad she had attempted to use it on him.

He seized the hand she had just poked him with. "Have it your way, lass."

He slid his hand to her wrist just in time to watch her eyes go wide, and then he bent and hoisted her up until he cradled her nicely over his shoulder.

"You bloody fecking bastard! Put me down!"

She'd clearly learned that from her mother.

She beat at his back, but her small fists were ineffective against his large frame.

"Put me down this instant. Do not—no, please. Stop. I'm sorry. I'll go with you!" The words cascaded so quickly from her mouth, he heard very little of them distinctively as he rounded the bend back onto the main path of the park.

And into the crowd of members of the ton enjoying afternoon pleasantries.

"Good day, ladies," he said with a brush of his fingers to the brim of his hat.

Lady Emily screamed now. Her legs kicking wildly so every patron of the park that afternoon saw her petticoats.

He kept going, back out to the street and then across. Gentlemen and ladies, boys and girls, all stopped to see a flailing Lady Emily Black as he carried her back through Mayfair to Lofton House. It was a reasonable walk, but the streets were crowded at this hour with the ton paying calls on one another and going about their usual business.

It had been a long time since he'd smiled, but right then, he was feeling quite a many reason to do so.

He strode up the steps of Lofton House just as the butler opened the door. As soon as he crossed the threshold, he dropped her. Directly on the floor. She fell in a puddle of wrinkled skirts, shifted bonnet, and far too many petticoats.

"I said I would bring you home, and I did. " He peered down at her.

Footsteps drew his attention upward to find Alec Black, the Duke of Lofton coming down the hall, followed closely by his wife.

"Mummy!" Emily cried, scrambling to gain her feet but finding her boots trapped in the swarm of her petticoats. "You won't believe what this horrible man did!"

Sarah looked from Emily to him, clearly trying to hide a smile as Alec came up to his side and leaned in.

"You wouldn't by chance be on the market for a wife?" he asked.

Xavier cocked an eyebrow. "I'd rather suffer castration."

CHAPTER 3

The Bent Broom was a respectable coffeehouse on Marlborough. As respectable as coffeehouses went. They tended to lure in a certain rabble, which usually carried radical ideas leaving a dangerous air in its wake. But for the most part, there was nothing exceedingly seedy about the Broom.

Which made Austin all the more cautious.

They chose a table near the back, taking the seats on one side so their backs were to a wall. A young girl brought a tray bearing an urn of coffee and two cups. She didn't speak. She didn't make eye contact. But Austin knew it wasn't to do with any sort of rudeness on the young girl's part.

He'd seen her eyes under the wilted edge of her soiled white cap. They were tired and weary. Perhaps wary. Her pupils darted from side to side as if she couldn't trust her peripheral vision. Or more, she couldn't trust what might sneak into it when she wasn't paying attention.

He didn't observe any noticeable marks on her person though, and he wondered if it wasn't the proprietor that caused her such fear but the tendencies of their clientele.

"Been to many coffeehouses?" Samuel spooned sugar into a cup.

"Can't say that I have." He held out his cup for Samuel to add sugar as well. "Although I believe you and your lady wife have a history of frequenting such establishments."

The smile came quickly to Samuel's face. "It was only once, but it was enough to never allow anyone to forget it."

Something in Samuel's expression spoke of his place, securely snug in the bosom of a wide and loving family. It tugged at Austin, and his mind drifted away for just a moment. To Peregrine Hall and the family he had not left behind. Because there was no family to leave.

"I'll be sure to remind you of it often." He poured coffee into his cup and took the opportunity to scan the few patrons in the place.

None of them appeared particularly seedy, but Austin had come to realize in the past few years he had worked with the Metropolitan Police Force that appearances carried very little weight. The most cunning criminal could just as easily be a member of the peerage, bedecked in the latest fashions from Paris and tailored to painful exquisiteness, as he could be a dock worker dressed in rags and smeared in filth.

"Recognize anyone?" he asked as Samuel filled his own cup with coffee.

"No." Samuel set down the urn. "But it doesn't mean someone hasn't recognized us."

"Do you think we should just wait then?" He took a sip of the steaming liquid, finding its bitter taste strangely comforting.

In his travels with the army, Austin had had the opportunity to sample foods and drinks from various cultures across the continent, but none had stuck with him like that of his first taste of Turkish coffee while stationed on the Greek peninsula. The coffee he sipped now was nothing like that of

Turkish coffee, but as he hadn't sampled the stuff since his return to England, the memory came flashing back to him with stark clarity.

And with it, his remembrance of how much Mrs. Rowling would have loved the stuff.

He set down the cup and pushed it away.

"I think the presence of a known Metropolitan Police Force inspector is likely to draw some attention in an establishment such as this," Samuel said.

Austin relaxed in his seat, dropping his hands to his lap even as his eyes remained on the cup of coffee and the reminder of its taste.

"And I think while we wait, we should discuss your intentions with my sister."

Austin looked up at this and met Samuel's stare. It wasn't an icy stare, but neither was it welcoming. In the years they had worked together, Austin had found their relationship rather brotherly, something for which he pretended he had no need, but in the end had drawn a measure of comfort.

"My intentions?" he decided to say, but Samuel was not deterred.

"You seem to have taken a remarkable interest in her person."

He raised an eyebrow. "What makes it remarkable?"

Now Samuel relaxed back in the seat. "I have known you for a good number of years now, Austin, and in that time, I've seen any number of mothers with marriageable daughters throw their offerings at your feet."

"I think that is the consequence of being a marquess and nothing more." He tried to sound glib as he said it, but even he noted the strained tone in his voice.

"I would tend to agree with you only you didn't react to these mothers as a beleaguered marquess would," Samuel went on.

"And how would that be?"

"Well," Samuel paused and took a sip of his coffee. "I'm afraid to say it, chum, but you've rather acquired the reputation of being a rogue."

Austin stared at his friend. "I'm sorry?"

"You treat each mother and marriageable daughter with an excessive amount of patience and even kindness." Samuel shifted in his seat, leaning in closer to Austin. "You even listened to that one girl sing for God's sake. What was her name? The flighty girl with no chin?"

He could have pretended he didn't know what Samuel was speaking of, but it would do no good.

"Lady Abigail Moore." He set down his cup. "She's the Earl of Harton's daughter. I was being polite."

"That's precisely what I'm saying. Your exhibit of politeness to these girls has garnered you with the label of charmer."

"Charmer is a far cry from rogue," he pointed out.

"Yes, but it's your infallible escape from the marriage noose that has earned you the other term. You can charm young women and then not pursue them with honest intentions."

"I haven't been on the market for a wife." The rebuttal came swiftly now, having been honed for so many years.

The whole suggestion of a wife. The resulting family.

The return to Peregrine Hall.

His stomach clenched as the words paraded through his mind once more.

Peregrine Hall.

It was just an edifice. An estate in the vast array of Evanshire holdings.

And yet it had the power to send him across the world into a war he needn't fight.

He was shaken from his thoughts at a sharp elbow from Samuel.

"Two gents by the door are eyeing us." The words were mumbled as Samuel took a sip from his coffee.

Austin allowed his gaze to drift but kept the motion slight so as not to alert the gentlemen in question.

They were watching. They had a tray of coffee and such before them as well, but they clearly had forgotten it was there as their eyes remained fixed on them.

They weren't workers. Not like those found at the docks or in the warehouses. They were perhaps clerks or tradesmen. Their clothes suggesting an occupation that involved a certain level of engagement while their lack of filth elevated them in class. However, Austin didn't miss the ring of grime around their collars, marking the white linen as not quite clean.

The gentleman farthest from them was dark in complexion while his companion sported a red shock of hair and generous beard. It was this chap that stood and made his way over.

He nodded politely as he approached. "Good day, gentlemen. Ye be the Duke of Lofton's nephew, isn't that right?" The man's coat was threadbare along the cuffs and lapels, and at this closer distance, Austin noted the dullness of his boots.

"I would indeed be the Duke of Lofton's nephew. Who might you be?" Samuel asked as he eyed the man.

The man sat without replying, taking the empty chair opposite and scooting in as close to the table as possible. He leaned forward, crossing his arms on the table.

"It doesn't matter who I am. I knows why you're here, and I don't want to cause no trouble or nothing, but I could do with a coin or two. Not for me, of course, but for the missus. We've got the babes to feed, ye see."

Austin patted his coat pocket. "You can be assured a coin is at the ready if the information deserves it."

The ruddy man blinked his wide eyes and licked at his thick lips. "Oh, right, it'll be worth it, gent. Yous wondering about ye sister, eh?"

Samuel belied no expression in his reply. "What is it you have to say concerning my sister?"

The man licked his lips again, quicker this time. "There was another gent in here. Not a week ago. Asking around for favors. Said he needed someone delivered to him that wasn't willing to come. Said he would pay well."

"Who was this gentleman?" Austin watched as the man's knuckles turned white where his hands gripped together on the tabletop.

The man shook his head, his shock of red hair crackling. "It's not that, ye see. It's what he said when he asked around. He said—" He licked with abandon now as if whatever he had to say repulsed him. "He said any degree of force like wasn't a problem, so long as the girl was alive when she was delivered."

Austin wanted to drive his fist into the man's ruddy face if only to release the surge of anger that pushed through him then. But he was only the messenger. There was someone else deserving of Austin's anger, and he was damned sure he was going to find out who it was.

"Who was it?" Samuel's question gave no room for argument, but the man just shook his head harder.

"That's just it. The man gave a name, but I knows it's not his real one."

"How do you know that?" Austin clenched his hands in his lap to keep from reaching across the table and dragging the man to his feet and shaking the answers from him.

"He was a right fine gentleman."

Austin couldn't stop the look he gave Samuel.

"Like a member of the peerage?" Samuel asked.

The man nodded, his hair crackling madly. "That's exactly it. He claimed to be some sort of solicitor, but wes knew right off, he wasn't nothing of the sort."

"A solicitor?" Austin asked. "Did he use the name Jencks?"

The man stopped licking his lips so abruptly Austin feared he'd bit off his tongue. "That's him all right." His eyes darted between Samuel and Austin. "Do ye know him, lad?"

"Not yet." Samuel stood and reached for the man's hand. "Your service is appreciated."

The ruddy man peered at Samuel's hand as if he didn't know what to do with it, but finally he clasped it with his own.

"I just think about me own daughter. Such a sweet lass. I couldn't live not telling you what's what."

Austin stood and taking the man's hand into his own, he pressed a guinea to the his palm.

"Thank you," he said as he held the man's gaze.

He shook his head, and spittle splashed from his agitated tongue. "But sir, I wasn't expecting such as this." His hand had closed around the guinea even as he denied wanting it.

"It's not for you," Austin replied. "It's for that daughter of yours."

They were nearly to the door when the man stopped them again.

"There's one other thing, chaps," he said, rushing up to them until he could lower his voice. "This Jencks fellow. He's a rather odd one, isn't he?"

"Odd?" Samuel asked.

The ruddy man nodded furiously. "All stiff and such. Almost like he'd been in the army or something. It was just so strange, he was."

"Military?" Austin asked, the muscles at his neck bunching. "As if he worked for the government?"

The ruddy man snapped his fingers in the air. "Oh aye, that's it."

* * *

"I DON'T KNOW what it is we're looking for," Penelope said as she spread the guest lists across the table. "But whatever it is, we'll know it when we find it."

"That doesn't sound particularly helpful." Jane sat at the opposite end of the library table they had commandeered for their purpose.

The guest lists were many and long. Very, very long.

"How did Samuel come by so many?" Jane asked, picking up one of them.

Penelope shrugged. "You know Samuel."

"I do indeed." Jane shot her sister-in-law a knowing glance. "Where do we begin?"

Before Penelope could answer, the door opened, and Nora entered, with Jane's grandmother, the dowager duchess for whom Jane was named.

"My darling Jane, whatever have you done!" the woman called across the library with a sweep of the hand that wasn't using her cane to haul herself across the floor.

Jane stood and went immediately to the old woman, pulling her into a tight embrace.

"I am fine, Grandmother," she said. "You mustn't worry."

Lady Jane Black, the Dowager Duchess of Lofton, was not worried in the least, and Jane knew that. But she enjoyed a little tête-à-tête with her grandmother, and she was rewarded with a smirk.

"It's not the attempted kidnapping that draws my concern, dear child, but rather the amorous intentions of your rescuer." Lady Jane pulsed her eyebrows suggestively, and Jane's face burned with sudden heat.

She looked down at the floor. "I'm not certain I know what you mean."

Lady Jane laughed a great walloping laugh. "Oh child, you undo me sometimes." Her grandmother pulled her arm through hers as they made their way back to Penelope and the pile of guest lists. "I must start picking out what hat I shall wear to your nuptials."

"Grandmother." Jane knew scolding the woman was futile, but felt she must. "I am only in my second season and far too young to think of such things."

Lady Jane only smiled. "You are not too young in the least."

They had reached the table to find Nora combing through a box she had brought in with her.

"Some of Richard's things," Lady Jane said as Nora pulled a ream of paper from the box.

Jane felt a stab of sadness at her grandfather's name, his death still so recent, and held onto her grandmother's arm a little tighter.

"I thought it may come of use." Lady Jane settled into a chair at the table. "I know we're searching for a name that comes up in more than one place, and I thought it may be useful to have another cross reference."

"These look like lists of names," Nora said as she pulled another stack from the box.

Lady Jane nodded even as she pulled some of the guest lists toward her. "Richard always kept lists of those he corresponded with and checked them off as he wrote off replies and such. It was his own system of keeping track of necessary correspondence." Lady Jane reeled back in her seat as she took in the guest list she had picked up. "All of these names?"

Penelope made a noise in the affirmative. "I'm afraid so." She settled into a chair then as well, her hand absently massaging her belly. "If only I could remember who it was."

"You must have a remarkable memory to recall having danced with the man." Nora finished pulling stacks from the box Lady Jane had brought and settled in as well.

Penelope shook her head. "It's a writer's curse. Everything seems to stick because you might use it one day in a story."

"Remind me to behave myself when I'm around you then." Lady Jane winked at the young woman.

Penelope shot a smirk right back. "Too late."

They fell into a silence then as each took up a list of names, searching for a pattern they didn't know or could fathom. Having spent so much time at her father's ledgers, Jane easily settled into the task, her eyes scanning each neat line of names, searching her mind for a connection, a flicker of memory, anything.

"How many gentlemen did you dance with last season?" This was from Nora.

Penelope shrugged again. "I'm afraid I can't really say. It was my first foray into the heart of the season, and it was rather overwhelming."

Lady Jane gave a snort. "That's a word for it."

Jane would have used a very similar word, especially when an image of the Marquess of Evanshire floated into her mind. She squashed it down and concentrated on the lists in front of her.

"You danced with the Earl of Wessex, didn't you?" Jane asked when her finger slid along the earl's name.

"The Earl of Wessex?" Penelope asked.

"Short chap with a bristly mustache," Lady Jane supplied.

Penelope grimaced. "Smells like garlic?"

Nora nodded as she tried to stifle a laugh. "That's the one."

"Yes, unfortunately," Penelope answered. "But it most certainly wasn't him."

"Lady Jane." Nora's voice had gone soft suddenly. "I keep seeing the name Seymour on Richard's lists. It's repeated quite often in 1814 and 1815."

Jane looked to her grandmother in time to see her expression close up.

"Seymour." She shuffled the lists absently in her hands. "That would be Dr. Milton Seymour. He joined the War Office during that incident with Napoleon. He—" Lady Jane paused and licked at her lips, a gesture so unlike her, Jane straightened. "He's a good man. Dr. Seymour. I'd nearly forgotten about him."

"Was he ever a social acquaintance?" Nora asked.

Lady Jane hesitated. "He might have been except…well, except that his wife was rather odd. She became overwhelmed quite easily and very rarely did the Seymours accept invitations." Lady Jane shook her head as her gaze drifted away as if searching for a past that was no longer there. "But I know Richard was quite close with the doctor. Relied on him for certain intelligence. As a doctor, the man was able to get very close to certain parties without drawing suspicion. He was quite valuable during the war." Her gaze dropped immediately back to the guest lists in her hands.

"Grandmother," Jane prodded, knowing very well there was more to the story. "What happened to Dr. Seymour?"

Lady Jane drew a deep breath. "There was an incident. It's still unclear what really happened, but whatever it was, Dr. Seymour left the office."

"He resigned from the War Office?" Nora asked.

Lady Jane nodded. "Rather abruptly. Richard tried talking to the man but he refused to speak on the matter. He only said something about it was in the best interest of he and his family that he should retire from his work with the government." She shrugged then. "I can't imagine what it was that happened. The man had been carrying out rather routine assignments for the latter part of the war."

"Did you ever speak to him again? Or did Richard ever correspond with him again?" Nora looked back down at the papers in her hand as if searching for a later date of correspondence.

But Lady Jane shook her head. "That was the oddest part of it. Not only did Seymour resign so abruptly, he also withdrew from society. Some rumored he had taken on his wife's frailties when it came to interacting with society. Suggested he may have just succumbed to the inevitable."

"Do you think that?" Jane asked.

"God, no," Lady Jane was quick to answer. "Dr. Seymour was a stalwart agent with a sound head on his shoulders. That's what made it all so odd. That he should just leave off like that." Another shake of her head. "He just handed in his resignation, and Crawley simply accepted it. No questions asked."

"Crawley?" Penelope interjected. "Isn't there a Lord Crawley at the War Office now?"

"That's his son. There's always been a Crawley at the War Office since time immemorial." Penelope raised an eyebrow to which Lady Jane responded with, "And yes, they've all been just as watery."

Penelope let out a soft laugh. "It must run in the family then."

They lapsed back into silence, the air filled only with the sound of shuffling papers.

It was some time later that Penelope gave a cry from the end of the table. "Seymour!" and thrust her finger at the page in her hand. "Mrs. Bethany Seymour. It's on the list of those who attended Richard's funeral."

"Really?" Lady Jane extended a hand for the list. "I don't recall seeing her there."

Penelope handed her the list, and Lady Jane quickly scanned it. "Well, that's certainly her. That's Dr. Seymour's wife."

"But I thought you said she didn't go out in society?" Nora asked.

"She didn't." Lady Jane looked up from the list. "I suppose she likely didn't want to draw attention to herself. That's why I don't recall seeing her there."

"I hardly think a woman such as Mrs. Seymour would be the culprit behind this. I thought we were after all looking for a man," Jane added even though her fingers worried the guest list in her hand.

"No, I think you're right, Jane." This was from her mother. "We are looking for a gentleman, but isn't it odd that the only names of significance that we've come across on two lists should be that of Seymour?"

"There must be other names surely," Penelope put in. "Richard lived a long and accomplished life from what I've gathered. There must be more intersections."

Lady Jane sat back in her seat and put a hand to her chin. "No, you're right, Pen dear, but there's something here that bothers me. Why was Mrs. Seymour there and not her husband?" She leaned forward. "Check the list again, dear. There's no Dr. Seymour listed?"

Penelope shook her head. "No, I'm sure of it."

Jane pushed to her feet. "Why would a woman known for her reclusive tendencies appear in society nearly twenty years after she and her husband disappear from social engagements?"

Penelope leaned back in her chair with an exaggerated sigh. "Oh, there's a story here, most definitely. I think you're right, Jane." She paused and looked between Jane and her grandmother. "Both Janes, as it were. I think this is rather suspicious."

"Does Mrs. Seymour still live in town?" Nora asked.

Lady Jane sat up. "At last I heard, yes. She and the doctor have a place in Bloomsbury, but that was more than ten years ago that I heard any such thing about them."

"Is the doctor..." Jane hesitated and gripped her hands together. "Would the doctor still be alive?"

Lady Jane's smile was soft as she likely understood the pain of Richard's death was still sharp for Jane.

"Oh yes, it's quite likely he is. He'd only be a little older than your father." Lady Jane looked to Nora. "We could pay a social call on her." Lady Jane got to her feet, her cane forgotten against the table. "I would be calling to introduce my new family members." She gestured to include all of them in this, and Jane swallowed a hiccup.

While she had been quick to offer to help in the investigation, she hadn't realized quite how involved she would be getting. She had a vow to uphold, so there was no sense in allowing it to get the best of her sensibilities. Once this was over she could go back to the life she had planned.

Only...

Austin.

She squared her shoulders. "Yes, I think a social call would be perfect. Let's go."

But before anything else could be said, the library doors opened, and her brother and Austin swept in.

Samuel stopped feet from their table and put his fisted hands to his hips. "No one is going anywhere. This house must be secured."

CHAPTER 4

"You're an annoying little boy, Samuel Black," Lady Jane said.

Austin hid his smirk behind a cough.

"We received a tip at The Bent Broom, and it seems our friend, Jencks, has resurfaced."

"Jencks?" Penelope sat up in her seat. "The solicitor who tried to buy Professor Mesmer's technology before Bobby was murdered?"

"The same." Samuel's frown intensified. "We need to exercise greater caution, and in order to do so, the vulnerable members of this family need to be under greater security." Samuel looked about the room. "Where is the professor?"

As if on cue, the library doors opened, and the professor appeared. Along with Lady Emily.

Austin stepped to the side as all attention shifted to the doors, and he took the opportunity to touch Jane's elbow. She, too, had been watching the doors and started at his touch. Her gaze flew to his then, and he smiled softly to calm her. While her countenance settled, her expression did not.

Her eyes remained huge and unfocused, and a small part of him thrilled that he had such an effect on her.

Until he recalled his conversation with Samuel at The Broom. Did he really hold the reputation of being a rogue? And if so, what was he doing with Jane?

"I just wanted to ask how you are." He kept his voice low, but it needn't matter. Lady Emily was tearing a streak about the room, regaling the audience with her mistreatment at the hands of the professor and how England had already expunged its rubbish to America and how the professor should go back.

Jane's eyes finally focused on him, and a smile played at her lips. "I'm quite fine. Thank you." She gestured behind her. "We think we found a lead in the guest lists."

He stepped forward at this. "What is it?"

"The name Seymour. It seems to be an old War Office acquaintance of my grandfather's. Seymour terminated his services with the War Office under suspicious circumstances during the conflict with Napoleon."

"What sort of suspicious circumstances?"

Jane shrugged. "Don't know. My grandmother only said that one day during the conflict he reported in to Lord Crawley and resigned."

A crash across the room drew their attention. Lady Emily had apparently hurtled a globe at the professor with encouragement to figure out where it was he belonged on it. Samuel took the opportunity to jump between the pair.

"Stop it, both of you. And you!" Here Samuel pointed across the room directly at Austin. "Get your hands off my sister. I don't care if you are a marquess."

Austin looked down to find that the hand he had used to touch Jane's elbow had, in fact, come to circle her arm in a rather possessive way. Jane stepped away with a soft exclamation as he snatched his hand back. He looked up quickly enough to see the blush stain her cheeks.

"If everyone is finished with the inappropriate behavior —" Samuel started but was again quickly interrupted.

This time by the brothers Black, Nathan and Alec, as they stampeded into the room.

"We are not allowing Sarah to conduct herself as bait, and that is the final—" Alec began and then—

"So we are going to use my daughter to ensnare the traitorous bastard!" Nathan finished.

"Boys!" Lady Jane yelled over all of them with a snap of her cane against the floor. "Behave yourselves. What is this about?"

"I'm perfectly capable of acting as bait." Sarah came into the room to stand between the brothers. "We'll have our man in no time."

"No," Alec said at the exact moment Nathan said, "Precisely."

The brothers glared at each other, and now Samuel came to stand between them.

"No one is acting as bait," he declared.

"I beg your pardon?" Sarah questioned with just a note of hurt in her voice.

Austin wouldn't doubt the woman's desire to play such a dangerous role nor would he doubt the equally strong objections of her husband.

"This situation is far too perilous, and we must act in concert if we are to catch this man." Samuel dropped his arms from where he had been holding the Black brothers at bay. "Now, can we all agree to behave civilly in order to proceed with the investigation?"

"As long as I don't have to stand next to *him*." Lady Emily gestured with an elbow at the professor.

"Afraid I might get my American soil on you, your highness?" the professor returned.

Lady Emily scoffed with wide eyes. "You don't even know proper titles, do you, you heathen!"

The professor rolled his eyes but turned away to take up a post across the room from her.

"Thank you." Samuel heaved an exaggerated sigh. "Now we can begin."

"You mean we're going to discuss your carelessness in referring to your grandmother as vulnerable?" Lady Jane asked as she folded both of her hands over the top of her cane, her gaze pointed and direct.

Austin shuffled back a step only to be stopped with a touch on his arm. He looked down to see Jane's hand there, the sight of it arresting him in mid-step.

"Don't back up," she whispered. "She'll see it as a sign of weakness."

He set his foot down and leaned closer to her. "Noted. Thank you."

He thought she cast him a small smile, but she hid her face so quickly he couldn't be sure.

"I retract the word," Samuel said. "How would coveted sound?"

"Coveted? What do you mean?" This was from the duke.

"The man calling himself Jencks did indeed offer a sum for the delivery of Jane," Samuel said.

"But why is it Jane now when it was Emily last spring?" Alec stepped forward. "Why would he change directive like that?"

"Does he think Jane is really the one that will get him what he wants?" This was from Lady Jane. "Considering she is the eldest daughter of the elder son."

Nathan Black was not the duke but he was, in fact, the older brother. Austin only vaguely understood how it was that Nathan had risen so high in the echelons of society from a bastard son to an esteemed genteel farmer.

"You think he's playing on sentimentality?" Austin asked.

Samuel nodded. "Something like that. He's already tried once to abduct both of them and found both to be more adversarial than I believe he reckoned. But then there was the Brownlow affair." Here Samuel's gaze drifted to his wife, and as if feeling his gaze upon her, she cupped her growing stomach and looked up, a smile coming to her lips.

"But he wasn't successful there," Nora said. "You don't believe he's getting desperate, do you, Samuel?"

Samuel shrugged but his gaze remained on his wife. "I can't tell."

Jane shifted beside him, and Austin felt her touch on his arm as if her hand still rested there.

"I think Samuel's right," he said, straightening his shoulders. "I think the house should be secured with those who are most likely being sought kept safely inside while the m—"

"Don't finish that sentence!" Jane hissed the words so loudly, so sharply, so *unexpectedly* the entire room focused on her. He watched her swallow and take a step to the side.

"My grandmother will run you through with her cane," she said with a small gesture to Lady Jane.

"Her cane?" Austin felt every eye in the room on them, and he didn't care. In the year or more that he'd known Jane Black he had never heard her speak out of turn. That she should interrupt an entire room for his sake was rather...appealing.

Jane's eyes darted back and forth beneath her fringe. "An object's dullness has never stopped her from attempting such a feat."

"She's quite right, you know," Lady Jane said.

Austin backed down, and he swore he could hear a measure of relief in Jane's exhale.

"I still agree with Samuel. The culprit's actions are bordering on unpredictable. While he may not yet be desperate, he is operating erratically."

"I agree," Nathan said. "We exercise greater caution." He looked to his wife. "Have you accepted any invitations for the coming weeks? Perhaps we should curtail our social outings to reduce our exposure."

"Yes, I think that's a good idea. Sarah?" Alec asked of his wife in turn.

"But my season!" Lady Emily cried and fisted her hands into her skirts. "You're ruining my season!"

Alec looked to the ceiling as if wishing for patience. "This is a matter of life and death, Emily. The season can wait."

Emily's fist tightened until Austin was sure she would rip her skirts to shreds before she pounded across the floor to mere inches in front of Jane.

"This is your fault!" she screamed at her cousin. "You always ruin everything!"

"Emily." Alec's voice was like steel, but he didn't take a step forward.

Austin watched Emily as well. Watched Jane. Waited. But Jane never raised her chin. Her eyes remained hidden behind the curtain of fringe.

"Just because you're plain and smart and boring and no one likes you, doesn't mean you can—"

The crack of an open palm against skin reverberated through the room. The strike happened so fast Austin wasn't sure when Jane had moved. Both of Emily's hands flew to her face as she let out a squeal of pain, and real tears sprang to her eyes.

But she ceased her rampage.

He watched Jane swallow. Finally raise her chin. "By calling me such things, you not only disparage me, you disparage my mother and my grandmother for I descended from them and was raised to be the person I am by them. Grandfather said nothing comes before family, and by speaking such things, you dishonor his memory." She stepped forward and around Emily before the woman could make a sound in response. Jane walked up to her brother, her shoulders square. "I will not be a captive in my own home while this villain runs free. We have a lead, and I intend to follow it."

She turned neatly on her foot and strode to the door. She stopped. Turned to look back at Emily. "If you don't know what disparage means, there's a lexicon on Grandfather's desk. Someone can show you how to use it."

And then she left.

Emily erupted into shrieks of despair while the professor burst into a peel of laughter. Penelope lurched out of her seat and began a mad search for paper and quill while her husband made noises about not putting this scene in a book.

Austin slipped away amidst the chaos. He made it to the hallway just as Jane reached the stairs.

"Jane," he called, eclipsing the few steps between them.

"Do not try to stop me." She spoke the words toward the stairwell and did not turn her head to meet his gaze.

He touched her elbow as he had done in the library and finally she turned, her wide, brown eyes watchful.

"I'm not going to stop you," he said. "I only hope you'll allow me the honor of watching your back while you embark on your mission."

* * *

Mission.

That was what her grandfather had called his assignments for the War Office. Things Jane knew she never had the courage to attempt.

But Austin had just called what she was about to do that very thing.

She met his gaze and although she still felt a ripple of apprehension at his nearness, it no longer spilled into the ridiculous flutters of an unschooled young woman.

"I shouldn't have slapped her." She shouldn't have done it, but she could admit at least to herself that it had felt good.

"She deserved it." His gaze never wavered as he answered.

"While I agree with you, whether or not she deserved it holds little regard in the matter of whether or not I should have done it. Emily has a tendency to rankle nerves, but it is a sign of a more mature person who holds her tongue." She looked about her. "Or her hand, as it were."

He reached out then and took said hand. Her toes clenched in her boots, and for one horrible moment, she thought she might be sick. He turned her hand over and traced a line along her palm.

She wore no gloves and neither did he. The gesture was erotic, his touch molten. She pressed her free hand to her stomach as a low pain began to burn there.

Just when she thought she could take no more, he stopped, retracting his hand until it hung harmless at his side. The hand that had been caressing her that was. The other still firmly gripped hers, and he carried it to his mouth, pressed a kiss to that delicate skin at her wrist.

She made a noise that sounded suspiciously like a moan, but she'd never before made such a base noise. Never before knew she was capable of it. And yet.

His lips were warm. So very warm. With just a hint of wetness.

But his eyes.

His eyes stayed focused on her. Direct. Cutting. Knowing.

He knew what he did to her. What the touch of his lips

ignited inside of her. The burning in her stomach flared, and a new keening began to hum lower. Much lower.

She snatched her hand away, pressed the tortured wrist to her chest, opened her mouth to admonish him.

Nothing came out.

She stared at him, her mouth agape. He stared right back. Until…

He blinked. But just before he blinked something passed over his eyes. A darkening. A shadow. A wariness.

No, that wasn't it.

Uncertainty.

He took a step back. Away. The burning in her stomach turned into a wrenching torment, and she held the wrist he had kissed harder to her chest.

"I'm s—" He didn't finish the word. He licked his lips. Looked anywhere but at her. "I shouldn't have done that." His eyes were finally back on her, but they no longer held the intensity they had when he'd pressed his lips to her flesh. He smiled, but it was more a movement of lips than an honest expression. "I guess we're both committing acts we rather regret today."

Regret.

If he had used any other word. Any. Other. Word. Not that one. Not that when it came to plain, boring Jane.

"I hope you will still allow me the honor of assisting you in following this development." He stood so far away now he was nearly to the other side of the hall. The keening deep within her had evaporated, and she wondered if she had truly felt it at all.

For now all she felt was the familiar pain. The ache in her chest that came whenever she was reminded of the things she lacked.

He expected an answer from her, and she nodded. "Of course."

No, she hadn't meant to say that. She didn't want his assistance. Not now. Not ever. She wanted to flee to her room. Hide under her covers in the smallest of balls.

She wanted to escape to her father's study, feel the smooth pages of a ledger beneath her fingers, lock the door, and allow no one to enter, only to emerge once the pain was erased.

But her father's study was in Kent.

She squared her shoulders much as she had done earlier. Pushed the pain down until it was a hard ball of resolve.

"My grandmother plans to call on Mrs. Seymour. She thought it would be appropriate to introduce the woman to her daughter-in-law and granddaughter. No matter how late an occurrence it should seem." The words came out more matter-of-factly than even she could have supposed, and she took a measure of pride in that.

"Then I should be pleased to offer my companionship in the endeavor." He made a neat bow. "Until then, Miss Black."

He didn't so much as accidentally brush her arm as he passed her on his way to the stairs.

CHAPTER 5

Jane had developed an unusual skill at quite a young age. A rather abnormal skill. One which most young ladies would not, or rather, *should not* have acquired.

Jane was unusually good at ignoring people.

It was more than that though.

Ignoring someone was rather routine. Jane, on the other hand, could make them disappear from her mind entirely.

She employed this skill with cunning dexterity the next day in the carriage when the Marquess of Evanshire took the seat opposite her. She had already spent far too much time analyzing the disaster, which had occurred at the top of the stairs the previous afternoon and with the amount of sleep lost on the subject, she felt no further mental faculties were due.

Until his knee brushed hers.

Her eyes sprang to his involuntarily, and for a moment, their gazes locked. She pivoted her head to the window before he could make an unwanted overture.

"It could have at least refrained from raining whilst I was

forced to make such a foray into society." Lady Jane settled on the opposite bench next to the marquess. "The good Lord knows how I hate bouncing about in these contraptions day in and day out."

Nora rested her reticule in her lap as she took the seat next to Jane. "You do not."

Lady Jane raised an eyebrow. "I had rather hoped Samuel would have allowed Pen to join us. Everything seems so much more exciting when she's with us.

Jane's gaze flicked to the marquess again, and a stab of longing so fierce cut through her, she had to look away to hide the sudden tears.

Nora smiled. "It certainly does, but he's right to worry over her and the baby." She moved her attention to the marquess. "Evanshire, it is rather good of you to accompany us today. It was a great deal easier to convince Samuel to allow us this expedition knowing you would be in attendance."

They passed the park, and Jane kept her eyes fixated on the passing scenery. A lovely tree there. A nice piece of shrubbery there. A decided lack of anything else on which to rest her attention because the blasted rain had forced everyone indoors.

And Austin's knee continued to bump hers.

"I have just as much interest in seeing this man in custody as you do, Mrs. Black." Jane felt his gaze on her even as she tried to ignore him.

Regret.

The word played over and over in her head until she thought her ears would ring with it. He wasn't concerned for her safety. Surely not.

Regret.

The ghost of pain flashed in her chest, and she swallowed.

Hard. Forcing her thoughts back to safer ground just as the carriage came to a stop.

"We shall send up the battle cry should anything untoward happen." Grandmother waggled her eyebrows as the tiger appeared in the door to offer her a hand.

Nora went next, and for a terrifying moment, Jane was alone in the carriage with Austin.

"Jane." He stopped her with a touch at her elbow much as he'd done the day before.

The touch was chaste. His tone neutral. And yet her insides reeled as though the entire carriage had overturned. Before she knew what she was about she swung her gaze to him, her expression stony.

Never before in her life had she behaved thus. But she was so tired. So spent. So done with all of this. There were no more words for her to summon. An entire season she had played her part. Held her back straight no matter the cost to her nerves. To her countenance. To her happiness.

For she didn't want this.

She didn't want this attention. She didn't want this danger. She didn't want any of this. She had only to endure, and then she could marry Mr. Smith. She had it all planned.

Until then, she simply wanted to be left alone.

Austin retracted his hand, and she descended the step to take her mother's arm. A servant opened the front door before they reached the top of the stoop and ushered them inside out of the rain.

"Your Grace." An older woman with steely gray hair peeping from beneath a white cap sprang forward from the recesses of the house and rushed to Lady Jane as if to take her things except she didn't. "I shall tell Mrs. Seymour you have come calling. Won't you please wait in the drawing room?"

The woman herded them into a drawing room off the

front foyer and vanished before saying anything else. They dripped water on the carpets as they were still cloaked in their outer garments.

The home was small when compared to Lofton House, but Jane thought that an unfavorable comparison. The drawing room was nicely appointed while the furnishings were rather worn as if the occupants' wealth had declined steadily over time.

Lady Jane cast a speculative glance at them before another woman appeared, far more flustered than the first. She rushed into the room, her arms thrown wide as if encompassing their entire party.

"Bethany," Lady Jane said stepping forward, but her outstretched hand was rebuffed with a none too gentle slap.

"You mustn't be here!" It was then Jane noticed the wildness in the woman's eyes. The pallor of her too-thin face. Her hair that had slipped from the confines of its chignon. "You mustn't be here, Jane. He'll know. You must leave at once."

The woman seized Lady Jane's arm before either Jane or her mother could intervene. She began pulling.

"Please, Jane, you must go. Now. Immediately. There isn't a moment to lose. He'll know you're here!" She was frantic now. This woman who was likely Mrs. Seymour, the doctor's wife.

Jane tried to remember if she had seen the woman at her grandfather's funeral, but Jane was rather overcome herself at the time and could recall very little of the day.

Mrs. Seymour had managed to pull Lady Jane from the drawing room, and they were once more standing in the foyer. Nora had Lady Jane's other arm, attempting to still Mrs. Seymour's rash movements.

"Bethany, calm yourself." Lady Jane tugged on her arm to draw Mrs. Seymour's attention. "Whatever are you babbling on about? Who is going to know we're here?"

But Mrs. Seymour had already opened the front door and with no ceremony whatsoever, she tossed a dowager duchess out of her home. Jane and Nora sprang after her, catching Lady Jane as she reeled unsteadily on the slick stoop, her cane slipping in her grip.

"Bethany!" Lady Jane righted herself with the help of Jane and her mother on either side of her. "What is going on? Where's Milton?"

Mrs. Seymour had both hands on the door, her knuckles white. Her eyes so, so wild. "He's not here, Jane. He hasn't been here for six years now. It's safer that way." She used both hands to close the door, but Lady Jane swung her cane against it, stopping its progress.

Mrs. Seymour cried wildly and fought against the pressure of the cane as Jane struggled to keep her grandmother upright.

"Where is Milton, Bethany?"

Mrs. Seymour's mouth opened and for a moment, Jane thought she could no longer speak. But then she said, "He's in Bedlam, Jane."

And then she slammed the door in their faces.

* * *

"I DO BELIEVE that is the first time I've ever been thrown out of someone's home." Lady Jane wrapped both of her hands around her cane as she peered out the window at the Seymours' receding townhouse.

"What happened?" Austin leaned forward to catch the dowager's gaze, but she fluttered a hand at him.

"Bethany acted most oddly to our arrival and threw us out." She looked across the bench to her daughter-in-law. "What was she going on about? I only caught perhaps two thirds of it."

"She said he'll know we're there." The sound of Jane's voice in the small confines of the carriage had an unusual effect on him.

She had ignored him since he'd arrived at Lofton House that morning to embark on their endeavor, and while it had cut him, he couldn't say it was undeserved. His behavior on the stairs the previous day had been appalling. Treating her as if she were some harlot. Some...

God, she tasted good.

He stared at her, recalling the taste of her skin. The saltiness of it. How soft her pale flesh was against his lips. Imagined what her skin was like in other places on her body. Hidden places.

The sound of Samuel's voice rang in his head, and he tried to rid his memory of it. Was Samuel right? Had Austin never before shown an interest in a woman that went beyond temporary pleasure?

It was terrifyingly likely. Thoughts of marriage often brought thoughts of Peregrine Hall, and he resolutely shoved both away.

Until Jane.

"Who will know?" he asked.

Jane looked at him for the first time that day. "She didn't say. She was almost—"

"Wild." Mrs. Black said this with a nearly neutral expression as if she were still trying to decipher the woman's outburst.

"Yes, that's exactly what I thought." Jane reached over and squeezed her mother's hand. "She was just so scared." These last words were spoken with a great deal more solemnity, and a look passed between mother and daughter.

"What would cause her to behave thusly?" he asked.

Lady Jane shook her head. "I haven't the faintest idea. The Seymours were always quite lovely people. Good people.

Milton did so much for the orphaned children, you know. I can't imagine..." Her voice trailed off as her gaze returned to the window.

"And she never said who it was she was afraid of?"

Jane peered at him again. "That's just it. She never said a name. She only kept repeating that he would find out, and that we shouldn't be there."

"Was she speaking of her husband?" He turned to Lady Jane. "You had indicated he had left the War Office rather abruptly. Did something happen that would cause him to resent your presence?"

Lady Jane turned her attention back to Nora and Jane. "Oh, it's not that, my boy."

"How can you be sure?"

Lady Jane looked fully at him. "Because she said Milton has been in Bedlam for the past six years."

He sat back against the bench. "Bedlam?" His eyes involuntarily moved to Jane, but he knew only too well why he should think to look at her at such a revelation.

He hadn't realized how accustomed he had grown to seeing her face, hearing her voice, until she had retreated to Kent the previous season after the Brownlow affair. The winter had been long and cold and lonely without her, and now he was making a mess of things.

Jane nodded. "She said he was gone. Nearly six years. In Bedlam." The last two words came out with a certain reluctance.

He couldn't blame her. The word carried with it an unpalatable quality. The rumors out of the institution were unsavory at best, heinous and deplorable at worst. He sat back against the bench once more.

"So if the doctor is in Bedlam, what do you believe this suggests?"

"He's hiding something." Lady Jane said this so quickly he was taken aback.

"Hiding something?"

Lady Jane thumped her cane against the floor of the carriage then. "I should have known. Gah!" She thumped it again, wrapping and re-wrapping her hands around its head. "I should have known something was wrong when Milton began acting so strangely. I should have known."

Jane leaned across the space and rested a hand on her grandmother's knee. "There's no way you could have known, Grandmother. From all appearances, the Seymours could have simply been going through difficult circumstances. Private circumstances in which it would have been inappropriate for you to intervene."

Lady Jane seemed to settle at her granddaughter's touch, but her mouth remained pinched. "I should have questioned it more."

"You already question things far too thoroughly," Jane said, sitting back against the bench. "And it would be more expeditious if we were to figure out what we're going to do now that we know the circumstances rather than fret over what we should have done."

Austin asked, "How can we even be sure he's hiding something?"

Lady Jane sat forward with energy. "Because Milton Seymour is not mad, and so what would be the only reason for a person to do such a thing?"

"So what is it we're going to do now that we know Milton Seymour is in Bedlam?" Nora's tone strove for calm.

"We're going to pay him a visit." Lady Jane's expression dared anyone to contradict her.

"And how do you plan to achieve such a feat? They no longer allow the general public to view the inhabitants of Bedlam as if they are animals on parade," Austin said.

"Do you really think rules have ever stopped me, boy?" Lady Jane thumped her cane. "We'll get in to see him, and we'll find out what's really going on."

"I'll do it," Jane said.

Three words had never had the power to rip through him with such startling pain.

"You will not." The reply erupted from him before he could stop it.

Jane glared. "You promised not to stop me."

"That was when you were merely paying a social call. You will not be going into Bedlam."

"You are not my brother."

"And if your brother were here he would agree with me." He leaned forward now, elbows on his knees to bring his face closer to hers.

"You would both agree to be tyrants?" She leaned in as well, and he could see the gold flecks in the irises of her eyes.

"I am hardly being tyrannical for forbidding you to enter England's most dangerous—"

"Forbidding?" Her voice had gone up an octave as she leaned even closer. "You're forbidding me now? I do beg your pardon, *my lord*. I wasn't aware that I had given you permission to forbid me to do things."

He closed his eyes. "Perhaps that wasn't the right word."

"Oh, it most certainly was not the right word. I'm going to Bedlam, and I will speak with Dr. Seymour."

"Perhaps we should send Nathan and Alec to do it." Nora spoke so softly her words hardly registered between them.

"And how do you plan to get in?" He sat back with a flip of his hand as if to invite her to relay her nefarious plan.

Her mouth opened but no words came out. Her eyes traveled to the ceiling of the carriage as if looking for a solution, and he laughed.

"Precisely. You don't know how. So it matters not if I forbid you to go."

Her eyes snapped back to him, the fire in them burning hotter. "Your permission has no regard in the matter. I thought I had already made that clear."

"Jane dear, perhaps they're right. Bedlam is a rather dangerous place for a young lady to conduct herself." Lady Jane extended a single hand, palm up as if in a peace offering.

Jane's gaze moved with such speed he almost missed her words. "But I made a promise."

The silence that fell then was weighty enough to suffocate every occupant in the carriage. Lady Jane's hand hung in the space between them, her lips formed into whatever word she had been about to speak, but which she'd allowed to slip away at Jane's outburst.

"What promise?" Nora asked, looking between granddaughter and grandmother.

But neither of them answered.

Instead, Jane pleaded. "Please, Grandmother."

Her voice held an edge of earnestness he had not heard before. The skin along the back of his neck prickled, and he sat up.

"Yes, what promise?" he asked, echoing Nora's words but his eyes never strayed from Jane.

Finally, Lady Jane allowed her hand to drop. "You're right," she said.

"Why is she right? What's going on?" Nora sat up, her hands fisting against her reticule. "Jane, what did you promise?"

But the spell had been broken, and Jane hid her gaze behind that blasted fringe.

"I must go to Bedlam, Mum. I'm sorry I cannot explain further."

"I don't understand. Lady Jane, would you care to elaborate?" Nora pinned her mother-in-law with a glare.

But Lady Jane only shook her head and settled into the corner of the bench as if in resignation. "It's not my secret to tell, my dear."

Frustration threatened to swamp him. "Regardless of whose secret it is, it's pertinent to the safety of your person that I understand exactly what you're about."

Jane lifted her gaze but kept her chin down so she peered at him through that dull blasted fringe. "I'm going to Bedlam. I must speak with Dr. Seymour. That is what you must know."

When she would have looked away, he sat forward and gripped her chin in his hand. She gave a startled squeak but didn't try to free herself.

"Then you must understand, Miss Black, that I shall be going with you."

CHAPTER 6

Jane twisted the gold band around the third finger of her left hand.

"I think this is rather overdone."

Her grandmother swatted away her hand. "It's the first thing any spy is taught. Every detail, no matter how small, can devastate a mission before it's begun."

Jane held out her hand. "So the wedding band is necessary?"

"If the occasion should arise that you remove your glove, it is most necessary. It would be the first thing to have the guard suspect that you are not who you say you are."

She gritted her teeth. "But must I wear *your* wedding band? It's so..."

Lady Jane wrapped both of her hands around the one Jane held aloft. "I know, child," she said when Jane finally met her gaze. "I know. But this will lend the authenticity we need to accomplish the mission."

There was that word again. Jane swallowed. "Very well."

She would never say she regretted the promise she had

sworn to her grandfather. The promise to protect Lady Jane and thus, the family Black. And she truly believed she had overcome her initial difficulties in handling the promise after her grandfather had died. It wasn't as if she could have kept the vow a secret from her grandmother. The woman was much too sharp for that. But it didn't make the burden any lighter.

It weighed heavier on her now. She had never considered the possibility of not being physically able to carry out her promise. In that, she would be dead.

She swallowed at the thought, pushing the memory of a sewing needle sinking into flesh from her mind. Madame LeFevre's eyes had been wild with her intent to harm Jane. To drug her. If Jane hadn't been cunning enough, aware enough, if she hadn't thought so quickly…

What, if, then, but…she could keep going forever. She squared her shoulders and shoved the hand with the heavy gold band into her glove as if not seeing the thing would make it any less lethal. The only way to end this was to find the culprit and stop him.

Then she could return to Kent. To her father's farm. To Mr. Smith.

She waited for the sense of ease to settle over her at the thought of her carefully laid plan. Of marrying Mr. Smith.

But instead of feeling at ease, she saw the Marquess of Evanshire's face quite literally.

She had just rounded the landing to the ground floor, Grandmother at her elbow, when she spotted him in quiet conversation with Samuel. Instead of ease, embarrassment's dull edge scraped her heart, and she stumbled. She gripped the bannister as if she'd merely taken a slip against the carpet, but her grandmother's grip tightened on her arm.

Jane looked at her, but her grandmother only smiled softly and returned her attention to the floor below.

"I do not like this," Samuel said as soon as they approached. "I should be going instead."

Jane released her grandmother's arm to face her brother directly. There wasn't a moment that passed that she didn't wonder why her grandfather had made her swear the oath instead of her police inspector brother. It was another one of those questions that would never receive an answer.

"Then you should have been less vocal in your support of the police force, Inspector Black. Everyone knows who you are from those remarkable sketches of you in *The Times*."

"That is a choice I do not regret in the least." He stood with his hands behind his back much in the way Mum did when she was displeased with something.

She shook her head. "Then there is nothing more to be discussed." Finally she turned her gaze to Evanshire. Somewhere deep within her, she heard the metal clang of the lock she placed over her heart. "Shall we?"

Evanshire gave one last glance to her brother before extending his arm to her. "Shall we, Mrs. Blevenstock?"

She couldn't stop the grimace. "Are we really using that name?"

Evanshire shrugged as she placed her hand on his arm, and they turned toward the back of the house. "It's the only name available for us to use. While a great many names appear alongside Dr. Seymour's in his work with the War Office and in medicine, Blevenstock is the only one to disappear into obscurity shortly after the conflict with Napoleon. We can only assume that name will have enough of a connection to get us inside whilst not drawing too much attention."

Evanshire's arm was far too solid beneath her hand. "I suppose you're right."

They descended the stairs and passed through the kitchens. She had hoped they would escape the house without incident, but the old cook caught sight of them. She turned a teary eye to them and mumbled, "So proud of ye, girl. Your granddad would be so proud of ye, too."

Jane cast her gaze about to see most of the kitchen staff had arrested their activities to watch their departure through the rear entrance of Lofton House. She smiled, but even she could feel the expression's unsteadiness.

A carriage waited by the mews. A nondescript vehicle Uncle Alec had procured by questionable means as it was imperative the vehicle carry no recognizable colors.

It wasn't until Evanshire handed her up into the carriage that the reality of the situation slammed into her. Especially when Evanshire took the seat next to her and shut the door, closing them into the quiet, dark space.

Entirely alone.

For a moment, she tested the lock around her heart and drew a fortifying breath when she knew it to be secure. She had allowed herself the fanciful notion that Evanshire may have any interest in her beyond the practical for long enough, but she knew better now. She had a vow to fulfill, and that was all. She had only to endure his company for a little while longer.

"Jane," he said straightaway, startling her in the semi-darkness. "I would have you know you have nothing to fear from me."

She swallowed. "You mustn't say anything further, Evanshire. I hold no unsound conclusions as to our acquaintance."

He stared out the window as the carriage made its way through the alley to the main thoroughfare beyond, so it was rather startling when he said, "I promise I shall act the perfect gentleman despite my growing attraction to you."

"I'm sorry?" Her voice came out stronger than she had expected but also with quite a piercing quality to it.

He drew his gaze away from the window, and his warm eyes settled on her. Even in the dimness of the carriage, she could see the kaleidoscope of browns in them. It unsettled her, but worse, she rather enjoyed how her stomach fluttered, and her toes clenched in her shoes.

"I acted untoward with you the other day. I know I have apologized for it, but I also know that you are rather unschooled in relations between a man and a woman, and I did not want my ungentlemanly behavior to cause you undue stress during the course of our investigation."

There were several things in his statement, which could have caused her quite a deal of undue stress, but she, of course, settled on the one that induced the greatest degree of embarrassment.

"I am not unschooled in the relations between a man and a woman."

The fact that he did not immediately burst into laughter at her expense was a credit to his gentlemanly upbringing. But her face flamed at the smirk he tried to hide, and she looked away, employing the thinking of a child in believing that if she didn't see him, he wasn't there.

"Is that so?" he asked, and there was nothing mocking in his tone.

She still wouldn't look at him. "Yes, as a matter of fact, I am."

"Are the primal relations a topic of conversation in the upbringing of most young ladies of the peerage? For I have never before seen evidence of such."

She did look at him then even though her face flamed hotter to do so. "You might remember I am not of the peerage. I studied animal husbandry to aid my father when a rash of calves were born dead."

Evanshire's face sobered immediately. "Oh, well, that's quite sad actually."

"It is." She toyed with her glove only to have her fingertips find the bulge of her grandmother's wedding band. She twisted the band on her finger, ruining the fine crisp texture of the gloves. "But I assume the matter of animal procreation is not unlike that of the relations between a man and a woman."

He raised both of his eyebrows, but his tone was casual as he said, "Yes, one could say that."

She suddenly wanted very much to rip her gloves off, remove the band from her finger, and tell the coachman to turn the carriage around. She couldn't do this. She simply couldn't do this.

But even as the thought surfaced, she saw her grandfather's face. Heard his voice. Heard her own swear to his promise. She pressed her hands together and faced the marquess.

"Why on are earth are we speaking of animal husbandry? We should discuss how we are going to approach the guardsmen at Bedlam. They are not likely to simply let us in, no matter the ruse we are playing."

Evanshire pulled at the lapels of his jacket. "We shall use the cover that I am the son of Major Blevenstock. My father is on his deathbed, and he asked that I carry word to Dr. Seymour. It is a dying man's wish that Dr. Seymour know how much his companionship during the war was appreciated even if the good doctor may be incapable of understanding."

"Do you truly believe that will be enough to get us through?"

"The guards at Bedlam will likely have drawn from military service themselves and will be inclined to aid a fellow soldier in his dying request." Evanshire had moved his gaze to the window once more. "Or so they should."

His voice had changed with those last words, and Jane suddenly remembered their first encounter when he had rescued her from near abduction. She had been unduly transfixed by the long, thin, pale scar that ran from his eye to his jawline. There were times when Evanshire was the utter gentleman. The born marquess.

She sometimes forgot he'd been a soldier.

That he'd seen war. Bloodshed. Loss.

She swallowed, realizing the pieces didn't fit together, and she should have realized much earlier than she had. He was a marquess. The first born son. He need not go to war at all. And yet…he had.

For the first time since she had made his acquaintance, she felt her stomach settle in his presence. Her nerves calm. She reached out a hand and laid it on his arm. He jumped but only slightly as if the touch of her hand was the last thing he'd expected, as well it should have been. He met her gaze with a questioning expression.

"Why did you join up?" The question was impertinent, and she had not known him long enough to pry as such. But his voice. It seemed almost as if it were longing for a time gone. But who would long for war? How bad must his peace have been to crave such a thing?

His gaze darkened, but she wasn't afraid nor surprised.

He shook his head. "That is a very long story."

"I'm happy to listen." There was something dangerous lurking in his expression. A long story, maybe, but certainly one filled with heartbreak.

He looked away from her, and her heart fell, wondering why he wouldn't entrust his story with her.

But then he said, "We've arrived."

Her stomach turned as she peered out the window at the looming stone edifice that was Bethlehem Hospital.

It was a massive complex with wings that fanned out on either side and stories and stories of shuttered windows begging the onlookers on the outside to only imagine what might be happening within.

"Are you ready for your first mission, Miss Black?" Evanshire asked from beside her.

She really did hate that word.

* * *

THE FIRST GUARD gave little resistance, but as he was half asleep, Austin expected nothing less. He held Jane's hand firmly to his arm as they passed the first gatekeeper to enter the receiving hall of Bedlam.

The screams could be heard from here. Screams of innocence. Screams of outrage. But worst of all, screams of fear. He tucked Jane's arm more firmly to his side and approached the desk where another guard sat. Their footsteps were muted in the vast cavernous space of the entrance, but he kept his eyes on the guard, his pace subdued.

"Name," the guard barked before they had even reached his station.

"Mr. Nigel Blevenstock," Austin said as he gripped the lapel of his coat for added pomp. "My father is the decorated major in His Majesty's service, Cornwallis Blevenstock. We are here to see Dr. Milton Seymour on an urgent request from the deathbed of my father."

The guard did not so much as blink under eyebrows the size of caterpillars. "Family only to see the patients then. Move along."

The blatant disregard for the mention of the military had him pausing. One's allegiance to one's fellow soldiers was strong. Unbreakable. The roar of emotion that swept through him at this had him regretting not telling Jane exactly why it was he'd joined up.

"Please, sir." Jane stepped forward and even put a hand on the guard's station. "It is a most heartfelt request from a dying soldier. He served with Dr. Seymour, you see, and he

—" Jane's words were caught in a muffled cry as she pressed a handkerchief to her face and ducked her head.

Austin reached for her and drew her back into his embrace. She may have come to spying reluctantly, but she was proving rather good at it.

The guard hesitated, and Austin pressed on. "There dear Caroline, you needn't worry. I am sure Father will understand. Dr. Seymour is so very—" He let his own voice catch and cleared his throat demonstrably.

The guard rose from his seat. "Blevenstock, you said?"

Austin peered over the top of Jane's bonnet as her head remained tucked into his shoulder. "Yes, good sir. Major Cornwallis Blevenstock served with Dr. Seymour. It is an old camaraderie between soldiers we seek to address as my father lays dying."

"I'll need to ask my superiors like for an exception. You know there's rules for a reason." He hitched up his pants and straightened the lapels of his uniform.

Jane turned her head toward the guard with an extra sniffle. "Oh, good man, you would?" She backed up to lift her face to him, and he had to catch his smile at the stain of tears on her cheeks before he gave away their ruse. "Do you hear that, Nigel love? He's a good man, isn't he?"

When his heart tripped over the word *love,* the urge to smile quickly vanished, and he faced the guard more soberly. "It would be much appreciated, my good man."

He wanted to shake his head to clear it of the sudden fog that sprang up at Jane's use of an endearment toward him even if it were all a part of the charade. He needed to stay alert no matter the turmoil his stalwart bachelor existence found itself in. Jane eased out of his arms to assume the more polite stance of simply holding her arm through his. The loss of her heat helped to clear his mind, but an echo still lingered. An echo of Samuel's words and his own traitorous response to Jane's nearness.

The guard had gone to speak to a man in a worn suit some distance behind his station. The man looked up as the guard spoke and then immediately returned to address the files in his arms with a quick nod of his head and a flippant wave of a hand. The man disappeared behind the gates at the end of the entrance.

The guard ambled back to them and hitched up his pants before resuming his seat. "I'll need you to sign in here. You've been cleared to see the doctor. I'll send for a nurse to take you down."

Austin pulled his arm free of Jane's to step forward and sign the ledger the guard offered. He dashed off a signature that looked nothing like a legible name and drew Jane's arm back through his.

The guard gestured behind him. "You can wait over there until the nurse comes to fetch ye."

The gesture did not include anything in particular, so Austin bowed and stepped beyond the station, drawing Jane alongside him. The screams were louder and more distinct when they reached the gates at the end of the hall, and he pulled Jane a little closer to his side. She came willingly, and he tried not to think about her softness, the way she seemed to fit perfectly beside him. The way she smelled like…was that honey?

"You don't have to do this." He whispered the words as he leaned down closer to her ear to avoid being overheard.

She looked sharply at him. "But I must." The words were spoken with enough feeling that he could brook no argument, but he wondered once again just what it was that drove quiet Jane to engage in espionage.

"I know it isn't my secret to know, but I hope you realize you can confide in me." He paused and peered at her face, shadowed by the brim of her bonnet. "Whatever it is that compels you to do this."

Her expression clouded, but he couldn't be sure exactly what it was she felt. She watched him as if assessing, and for an absurd moment, he thought he should straighten his jacket or fix his hair beneath his hat. But then her expression cleared, and she merely shook her head.

"It's nothing," she said.

And he hated how it made him feel let down.

"Blevenstock." The bark was louder than the guard's, and he turned toward the gate to see a stout woman through the bars. Her gray hair was pulled so tautly to the nape of her neck, her cheekbones extruded until she almost appeared a skeleton.

"Yes," he replied as the woman appeared to expect an answer.

"Come with me then." There was a different scream then as metal protested against metal, and the gate swung wide to allow them entrance. "The doctor is just this way."

Austin held them several paces behind the nurse, and he squeezed Jane's arm to get her attention. "Are you certain?"

She didn't speak, but her eyes gave away her answer.

"All right then. Let's go."

The floor here was stone, and their footsteps echoed with the cries of the patients lurking somewhere in the depths of the corridors that sprang off of the main one through which they passed. He kept Jane's arm pressed tightly to his side, but she gave no sign the growing cries upset her. After her performance in the entrance with the guard, he knew he would never again doubt her ability to put on a front.

The nurse stopped at a door at the end of the hall and drew out a rattling chain of keys. She riffled through them until she found the one she desired and inserted it into the door. It gave a mighty screech as she pulled it open and stepped to the side to allow them to pass her into the darkened space beyond.

He stopped short, pulling Jane beside him as he realized they had entered a stairwell. The nurse ambled inside the small space and banged the door shut behind them all. She went through the same process with the keys before turning up the stairs. There was only a single sconce lit on the landing above, and Austin pulled Jane completely under his arm to guide her up the stairs.

Her shoulders were stiff against him, and they pressed on to the next landing where the nurse once more performed her ritual with the keys before opening another metal door.

This floor was much quieter. The space filled with an unceasing mumble of voices like the trickle of a stream of confusion. Cells opened on either side of the main hall here, and Austin kept Jane tucked under his arm. He couldn't prevent his gaze from wandering into one cell and then the other as he passed along the corridor.

Here the patients appeared more subdued or perhaps deeply overcome by their illness, so much so, that their cries had long since vanished. He swallowed at the thought and returned his gaze to the nurse before them. She stopped a quarter of the way down the passage and turned.

"Here he is. Ye've got five minutes." She turned away and disappeared down the passage before they could utter a word.

At the sound of Jane's gasp, Austin swung his gaze from the nurse to the cell beside them. It was a small structure of stone and metal with a single bunk, a table, and a chair. A small lantern sat on the table and gave off enough glow to see what had been done to the room.

Drawings. Drawings everywhere. All over the walls and the floor. The hazy quality of them suggested the artist had only the use of chalk, and then only a select handful of colors at best. One wall was an entire scene of trees and rolling hills, and this melted into another scene of babbling brook and centaurs. Three of them standing around the brook as if conversing. And then on the other wall a great castle rose up from a mountainside.

But the floor. The floor was covered in only one drawing done over and over again. A depiction of a five pointed star. Some were drawn with great detail while others were scratched off in haste either from the artist's panic or the scrambling shoes of the occupant.

The occupant who now sat at the table in the corner hunched over a text. He rocked, his hands held tightly in his lap, as he murmured indistinguishable words.

"Dr. Seymour?" Jane's voice was clear and strong but soft enough to be cajoling.

The doctor stopped his rocking but did not turn.

"Dr. Seymour, we come as friends." Jane took a step closer to the cell, but Austin kept a hand out to stop her from getting too close.

The doctor looked up now, and the soft light of the lantern shone off the lenses of round spectacles sunk low on his nose. What little was left of his hair was white and sprang away from the crown of his head like an absurd hat. He was round but not in the sense of overeating, but rather, swollen. Austin wondered what drugs they gave him to keep him quiet as the pale, swollen girth of his skin suggested such. His clothes were worn but not tattered. Shirtsleeves, waistcoat, and old fashioned breeches. He stared directly at Jane as if Austin were not even there.

"Friends." This word was clear now. Stark against the unending murmurs of the other patients along the corridor.

"Yes, friends. My grandfather—" She looked up and down the passage as if to ensure they were alone. "My grandfather was Richard Black, the Duke of Lofton."

If Austin had not been a trained soldier, he would have missed the twitch along the doctor's brow at the sound of his old friend's name. The muscles at the back of Austin's neck tightened, and he stepped forward now as well.

"Richard." This word, too, was clear. "Was."

Jane nodded solemnly. "He passed away a year ago." The doctor frowned, his mouth trembling, and Jane rushed on. "Peaceably. He died an old man."

The doctor's face cleared, but his eyes remained hidden behind the glare from his spectacles. And then he stood with two hands against his knees as if he wasn't used to standing upright. His walk was more of a saunter as he made his way to the bars of his cell. Austin reached a hand to Jane, but she remained where she was as the doctor approached and leaned closer to them, his hands on either side of his head at the bars.

"I will tell you a secret then," the doctor whispered.

Austin leaned in. He couldn't have stopped himself. The murmurings and the soft glow of lantern light, and the darkness that surrounded them. He did not want to miss a single word.

The doctor whispered again. "I'm a unicorn." As soon as the words were out, he erupted into a peel of uncontrollable laughter and twirled about in his cell.

The riotous laughter mixed with the sound of a metal cup falling over as the doctor pranced over to his desk and seemed to extract a piece of chalk from the cup. He swung it into the air.

"I'm a pretty white unicorn that tells little girls fairy tales!" He sang the words as he pranced about and suddenly dropped to the floor. His hand began to fly across the stones of his prison and more stars erupted under the chalk.

"Oy there! You settle down or we'll make ye settle!" The nurse had returned, hand raised at the doctor through the cell, but the doctor had already quieted, his full attention on the stars he drew across the floor of his cell.

He'd gone back to muttering but now Austin heard the words.

"I'm a pretty unicorn. I'm a pretty unicorn." Over and over again.

"Ye's time is up. Let's go."

The nurse was much quicker about expelling them from the hospital than she'd been about leading them up to the doctor's cell, and before long they were once more in the rented carriage headed to Mayfair.

"Well, I suppose it could have been worse," he said as he settled into the bench, but Jane suddenly sprang up and took the bench opposite him.

He thought for a moment she might be unsettled from their excursion into Bedlam and their obvious failure at questioning the doctor, but then he realized she was smiling. Brilliantly, infectiously smiling.

"That couldn't have gone any better!" Her voice rang with joy, and her hands clenched in her lap as if she couldn't contain herself.

"Better?"

"Don't you see?" She leaned in much as the doctor had done earlier, and he couldn't help but be swept into her excitement. "I recognized the good doctor's drawings."

CHAPTER 7

"They're on the endpapers of a book," Jane called behind her as she all but ran up the stairs of Lofton House.

She heard Austin's footsteps behind her, so she propelled onward, heedless of her unladylike behavior.

She threw herself through the library doors, startling the occupants inside enough to illicit small gasps of surprise.

"Jane, what's happened?" This was from her grandmother who appeared to have fallen asleep by the fire and was only roused at Jane's entrance. "Did you see Seymour?"

Jane didn't answer. She couldn't. She had to find the book. She knew it was there. Somewhere on the shelves. Footsteps rushed into the library, and she heard her mother greet Austin with a question about their outing to Bedlam.

"The doctor had drawn a rather elaborate scene across the walls of his cell. Jane thinks she's seen it before," Austin replied just as Jane's hand closed around the book in question, and she spun around, the book held aloft triumphantly.

"I know I've seen it!" she cried. She couldn't help it. All her life she had believed herself incapable of spying like the rest of her family, but really, it wasn't that bad at all.

"My God," Austin muttered, and Jane pulled the book down to look at the cover.

Emblazoned across the front of it was a five-pointed star. Her gaze met Austin's.

"The doctor isn't mad," she whispered.

"He's hiding." Austin's jaw tightened, and he turned just as the door of the library flew open, admitting her brother in a striding stomp while her poor sister-in-law waddled up behind him.

"What is it?" Samuel asked without greeting. "What happened with Dr. Seymour?"

Jane clutched the book to her chest and looked expectantly at Austin. But he did the oddest thing just then. He took a step back, almost as if he were bowing out of a dance and gestured behind him at Jane.

Every pair of expectant eyes fell on her, and she nearly swallowed her tongue.

"Dr. Seymour appears to be quite well of mind," Jane said.

Samuel's brow furrowed. "Whatever do you mean? He's been in Bedlam for six years."

Jane swallowed against her suddenly swollen tongue. "Yes, that would be true according to appearances, but we have evidence to support the contrary."

She didn't miss the squelch of a smirk on Samuel's face as he said, "Please continue."

She felt a rush of lightheadedness and stepped closer to the group. "Dr. Seymour has created a rather elaborate drawing across the three walls of his cell. One panel depicted a forest, a second centaurs, and the third a castle." She passed Samuel and pushed aside the guest lists still strewn upon the large table in the center of the library. She carefully laid down the book and flipped it open to expose the endpapers. The scene from Dr. Seymour's cell shone up at her.

"Dear God," Austin whispered from somewhere over her shoulder.

"It was this scene," Jane said with a pointed finger as she looked back at her brother.

Everyone joined her at the table, peering down at the intricate drawing of muted watercolors spread across the endpapers of the book. A forest scene spilled from left to right with three centaurs and a castle springing forth from a mountainside. It was all very much as the doctor had drawn it. And the star.

She flipped the lid closed and ran her finger over the five-pointed star. "He had drawn several of these across the floor of his cell. Over and over." She let her words fade as she recalled the almost manic illustration of the stars over the stones of Dr. Seymour's cell.

"It's a copy of Grimm's fairy tales," Samuel said finally. "How did you know of this?"

"Oh no." Everyone looked at Lady Jane just as her face went white. Samuel was the first to reach her and caught her before she sank to the floor.

"Mum!"

Jane looked up startled as her father ran into the room followed by Uncle Alec, both taking the burden of Lady Jane from Samuel as together they eased her into a chair. When it was determined she was all right, Jane suddenly became aware of a hand pressed to the small of her back. The weight and heat of it radiated comfort through her like she never would have guessed, and she settled back against it as she smelled Austin's familiar aroma of vanilla.

"Grandmother?" Jane prompted when the woman looked as if she would be all right.

"Your grandfather," Lady Jane said, her voice unlike Jane

had ever heard it. Strangled and raw as if the past eighty years had finally caught up to her all at once.

Jane stepped toward her, relinquishing the comfort of Austin's touch to sink to her knees in front of her grandmother. "Grandfather read to me from that book when I was a child."

Lady Jane nodded and took Jane's hand into hers. "Seymour gave your grandfather that book upon the occasion of your birth." Moisture glistened in the old woman's eyes now. "Your grandfather loved you so much."

Jane felt the squeeze of her vow to her grandfather as if it were the very day she had made it. "We will find out who the villain is, Grandmother. I swear it just as I swore to protect you." She didn't miss the curious glances from her family, but she needn't respond because just then Austin made a noise from behind them.

"Jane." His voice was sterner than she'd heard it before, and she turned on her knees to peer over her shoulder at him.

Austin held the book aloft for her to see, but instead of the front endpapers as she'd left it, she now saw the back ones.

It was a unicorn.

A beautiful unicorn done in every color of the rainbow.

Slowly she gained her feet and let her hands slip from her grandmother's as she made her way back to Austin. Carefully she took the book from him and studied the pages.

"I'm a pretty unicorn," she whispered. She had to let the book drop to the table as she no longer had the strength to hold it. "I'm a pretty unicorn that tells little girls fairy tales." She met his gaze. "Oh God, Austin, Seymour isn't mad. He's —" She couldn't bring herself to say the word. She only stared at him.

It was Lady Jane who said, "He's a prisoner."

Silence descended on the room until she thought she would suffocate in it.

"But why this book?" Jane stared down at it. "Why lead us to this book?" She reached out a single finger and traced the outline of the unicorn, her mind seeing the moment Seymour's face had given away the farce. The moment she had told him her grandfather was dead.

That was when her finger encountered a bump. A ridge in the seemingly flat plane of the endpapers. She must have made a noise, because Austin touched her elbow.

"What is it?"

She ran her finger around the outline of the unicorn again just to be sure. "There's something under here." She reached behind her and grabbed Austin's hand to pull it toward the unicorn.

He traced the edge of the mythical animal. "There is something under there. We need a letter opener, a knife, anything we can use to pry the glue from the endpapers."

The occupants of the room swarmed the table now, each studying the unicorn drawing as Samuel and Austin searched the desk for a letter opener or a penknife.

"Well I'll be," Penelope sighed, and Jane knew exactly what such a curious sigh meant.

"You cannot think to put this in a book." Jane watched her sister-in-law.

"How can I resist it?" The smile Penelope gave her was nothing short of mischievous.

Austin came up behind her then with a letter opener and began to wedge the implement between the binding and the endpaper. There was a pop as the aged glue gave way at the corner and from there, he was able to slip the metal prod through to the corner of the cover. The endpaper sprang free, and Jane swore she heard a resounding intake of breath as Austin slipped his fingers under the drawing of the unicorn and produced a small, square piece of paper. Perfectly crisp. Perfectly pristine. Perfectly preserved beneath the protection of the unicorn.

It contained only four words. Words Jane read as she balanced precariously over Austin's shoulder. "Beware the Frog King."

"Beware the Frog King?" Samuel's dubious expression matched the incredulity in his voice. "What does that mean?"

Penelope leaned on the table. "Isn't the Frog King the one who turned into a human prince? Why would we need to be wary of him?"

Austin handed the slip of paper to Jane as he picked up the book, running his hands over the endpapers. "These aren't original to the binding," he said after some scrutiny of the book. "These endpapers were glued on later. After the book was bound." He held the book out to the rest of them. "You can see here where the pages don't just quite match up to the cover."

Jane cradled the paper with the mysterious words in her hand. "The doctor wanted to be able to send a message if he had the chance." She looked up at the faces surrounding her. "That's why he must have changed the pages." She laid down the piece of paper and picked up the book, turning it to face everyone else. "There are no unicorns in Grimm's fairy tales."

"But a unicorn would be easily discovered," Samuel muttered.

"It would stick out. Be memorable. Anyone could find it if given the clue." Uncle Alec perched on the end of the table. "So why this clue?"

"You're forgetting about the time as well," Lady Jane said from where she was still seated beside them. "Seymour gave Richard that book in 1815."

"What happened in 1815?" Penelope asked.

Lady Jane shrugged. "That's just it. We still don't know.

But I have a terrible feeling the Frog King did it. Whoever that is."

"Mum, was Father keen on giving his comrades at the War Office pet names?" Nathan reached down and picked up the paper from where she had set it on the table. "Perhaps the Frog King was an agent gone rogue."

Lady Jane straightened even as Nora let out a soft gasp.

"Do you think that's it?" Nora asked mostly to Lady Jane. "Do you think that's why Seymour left the Office so quickly?"

Lady Jane pressed a hand to her brow. It was a gesture so unlike her it was as if the entire assembled crowd leaned toward her in concern. Jane's heart thumped in her chest, and for the briefest of moments, her grandmother seemed old.

"Dear God, what if it was?" Lady Jane gestured to the scrap of paper. "What if the Frog King is our villain?"

"Who in God's name is the Frog King?"

The lot of them looked to the door just as Professor Mesmer came through it.

Nathan extended the piece of paper. "Jane and Evanshire have found a clue from their visit with Dr. Seymour."

"Beware the Frog King?" Mesmer read from the paper. "What does that mean?"

"That's what we're trying to figure out," Uncle Alec muttered, running a hand along the back of his neck. "If it really is a rogue agent and if Dr. Seymour found out, why wouldn't he tell Father outright?"

"Unless the man is too dangerous." Jane hadn't realize she'd spoken the words until the rest of the room fell silent around her.

Lady Jane gave out a noise then. One that didn't quite match frustration nor despair, but perhaps landed somewhere in the middle. "Oh, Richard, why did you have to leave us?"

Jane felt a flash of pain pierce directly through her heart, and it was as if her grandfather was there. Imploring. Beseeching her to protect her grandmother. She squared her shoulders. "It needn't matter if he is too dangerous. We will find out who he is and watch him squirm."

She was saved from having to answer to the overtly suspicious gazes of her family members when Aunt Sarah came into the room, asking, "Who is too dangerous?"

Mesmer straightened immediately. "Aren't you watching that wretched creature you call a daughter?"

Aunt Sarah nearly tripped over her own feet, which was as out of character as Lady Jane appearing old. "I thought you were watching her."

Mesmer's face hardened, but it was Uncle Alec who spoke. "God save us from Emily's confidence." He looked about the room. "I suppose it's my turn to go find her, isn't it?"

Mesmer pulled on the sleeves of his coat. "I've been charged with her person. I will see to it." He left without so much as another word.

Aunt Sarah stared after him. "Do you think we can offer him a large enough dowry to marry her?"

"We're not that wealthy," Uncle Alec replied.

"Pity," Aunt Sarah muttered. "Now then. Who is the Frog King, and when do I get to watch him squirm?"

* * *

"OH, Harlow, it is simply too awful." Emily pressed the back of one hand to her forehead. She knew Harlow enjoyed nothing more than to act the hero to a damsel in distress, and she was happy to oblige him. "The nerve of them." She spit the last word and was rewarded with a frown from her companion.

"My dear, dear Emily." He peeled the hand from her forehead to press it between both of his. Her stomach rolled a little at the contact, but she fortified herself when she recalled his title. His beautiful, weighty title. It needn't matter that he was old and hunched over. It made no difference if his hair was sparse on his head or his nose ran continuously. All that mattered was that Lady Emily would stay Lady Emily upon marriage. Only better. She would be the Duchess of Merritt.

She forced a smile. "Oh Harlow, you do so understand what they put me through."

He smiled, which always seemed like a mere spreading of his overly thin lips. "I do understand, pet, and I swear to you, one day I will make everything better. I swear it, my darling."

The sounds of ladies taking their afternoon strolls through the park were muted here in their secluded grove, and the hushed noise brought her comfort.

He would make everything better. He would make her a duchess. And that would be better than her dratted cousins. Even better than her own sister. She would have everything and the title to prove it.

"Of course, I do, my darling," he said and drew her gloved hand to his lips for a kiss.

She steeled herself against it. It was something she was getting quite good at. Concealing her true reactions. Play-acting a charade that got her exactly what she wanted without intruding on anything messy like emotions.

"But, Emily, my love, surely your mother wouldn't have been so cruel as to have you dragged back to Lofton House? She knows how important your constitutionals are." He grinned at her, which wasn't really at all like a grin. His face just sort of propped up his thin lips on one side and created an accordion of fleshy wrinkles under his eye.

She giggled at the expression anyway. He liked when she

giggled. "Oh, it wasn't my mother that did it. Although she would have been capable of such a thing."

The grin faltered, and for a moment, panic squeezed her chest. She giggled harder and peered up at Harlow from beneath her lashes. "Oh, you know how she is. Mother is rather domineering when it comes to raising just the right kind of young woman." She couldn't have Harlow thinking her mother was uncouth. Emily's reputation was entirely pristine, and she planned to keep it that way until the marriage agreements were signed.

"She is at that," Harlow muttered.

There was something strange about his words, and she dipped her head to display a lack of understanding rather than curiosity. Harlow liked to flaunt his intelligence over her, and she let him. Curiosity was never favored in a young woman worthy of being a duchess.

"How is that, my lord?"

His face propped up the grin once more. "Oh, it's nothing as grand as all that. Just what society has rumored about. Your mother has been known to be quite the matriarch in certain circles."

Emily cooed, ducking her head against her shoulder. "That is mother, I should say. And she's taught me exactly the qualities a good matriarch and wife should have." She flashed a smile at him, her gaze demure. "Like the wife of a duchess is expected to have."

He touched the tip of his finger condescendingly to her nose, and she bit the inside of her cheek. It was one of his gestures that always seemed to go a bit too far, but she played the same words over and over again in her mind to quell her rising anger.

Lady Emily, the Duchess of Merritt.

Lady Emily, the Duchess—

"That's all well and good, my darling, but if it was not

your mother who summoned you home and maliciously ruined our precious few moments together then who was it?"

The question was prodding, but if she were to get this man to marry her, she supposed he would know a great deal more than that.

She waved a hand in the air as if to dismiss the whole thing as though she did not wish to remember exactly whom it was that had so mistreated her. "A friend of the family is all."

Harlow's gaze darkened, and she realized how terrible it would look—had looked—for her to be seen so in the embrace of a man not of her family.

She rushed on. "His name is Professor Mesmer. He's simply staying with our family while he is town."

Harlow's expression cleared almost immediately, and she drew a measured breath of relief.

"Mesmer, you say?"

She smiled, allowing even her eyes to crinkle with the expression. "Yes, but enough of him. When is it I shall see you again? Our time is drawing short, and I simply cannot bear to go without your touch for too long."

She could go entirely forever without his touch, but she feared letting him out of her clutches for too long. A duke was quite a boon, and she couldn't let another one of the debutantes of the season have him. After all, this was her second season.

Second.

Gah, the shame of it!

And it was all stupid Jane's fault. She could still recall the sting of Jane's slap, and she gritted her teeth. She'd show all of them. She was going to be a duchess.

"In a moment, dear. This Professor Mesmer, how did your family happen to make his acquaintance?" Harlow's voice had gained an edge to it. One she'd only seen him use rarely and mostly when speaking of other members of the ton with whom he'd taken a dislike.

She shrugged softly. "It's probably something to do with Father's business and such. I don't really know. Now Harlow, my dear, when shall I see you again? You know how I fret." She stuck out her lower lip in far too much exaggeration, but it nearly always worked to make men do what she wished.

"Your father's work? What sort of work is the duke involved in?" The edge of his voice deepened.

For a silly moment, Emily almost thought she was worried, but that was ridiculous. Harlow was a mere echo of a man. Nothing she couldn't handle. And yet. There was something about his voice.

But really, what did it matter?

Lady Emily, the Duchess of Merritt.

She laughed more jubilantly and squeezed both of his hands in hers. "You ask the silliest questions sometimes, Harlow. As if I would dirty myself with men's work." She stood and released his hands with the presumption that her bonnet required attention.

She had a very keen sense that sometimes these old dodders got drunk on her affections and a quick escape was necessary to bring them back to their senses.

"Emily, my darling." He grabbed her arm before she could get out of reach. "Is this professor an American, by chance?"

She wanted to pull her arm away. Instinct drove her to turn and run, but she knew from watching her mother that was exactly what one shouldn't do in this situation. So she turned toward him, leaning against his thin chest.

"Oh, Harlow, you are just splendid." She stood up on tiptoe and pressed a kiss to his cheek.

Startled, he released her, and she was gone before he could say another word.

CHAPTER 8

"You want to save the good doctor."

Austin took some measure of comfort in the fact that she didn't start at the sound of his voice. She merely looked up from where she was hunched over a pile of ledgers on the desk. She blinked at him, and her lashes toyed with the edge of fringe that she so skillfully used to hide her face at times.

He had returned to Lofton House on the presumption of seeing Lady Jane and asking after her health because of how shaken she'd been when he'd finally departed the previously afternoon. When the butler had offered to fetch her, Austin had simply said he'd find his way to the library as that seemed to be where the family gathered.

But it wasn't Lady Jane's health that concerned him.

The library was empty today except for Jane. Quite unlike the spectacle of the day before when he'd witnessed a display like he had never seen. Agents from the War Office debating with an inspector from the Metropolitan Police Force who were all outnumbered by the headstrong women of the family over conjectures in a case where facts were scarce. He had wondered how often such debates ensued at Lofton House and could too well remember the silences of Peregrine Hall.

Austin had bowed out quietly when evening approached and propriety dedicated he should leave the family to their own audience. He had respectfully claimed estate affairs required his attention, and the lie had caused an unusual twinge somewhere inside of him. The fact that he had neglected any estate matters tied to the title of Evanshire for years now had never before bothered him, and there was no reason it should now.

Except…

The ledgers Jane so protectively hunched over were the one's for her father's estate. Austin knew this as it was something the family often mentioned in passing.

She bent over the books now almost as if she somehow drew comfort from them. The idea was so startlingly in opposition to his own feelings on estate management, he pulled at the sleeves of his coat before taking a chair across from her.

"Good day, my lord." Jane laid down her quill. "What brings you to Lofton House today?"

He smiled at her avoidance of the topic. "A quest for truth."

She raised an eyebrow. "Truth? Might I suggest a philosophy text then?" She gestured around her at the shelves of books ringing the room.

"Perhaps I misspoke. I'm after whatever it is you plan to do about the doctor."

Something passed over her features then, but she was quick to push it away. "First we would need to know if there is anything which requires doing." Jane rested a hand on her quill. "If one were to deal in specifics, we would be appallingly short of facts."

"Facts? Not truth then?"

She gestured at the ledgers in front of her. "Numbers are comfortingly reliable, my lord. They tell a story free of subjective adjectives, and yet very few can see it."

"And when it comes to the doctor, we have no numbers. Is that what you're saying?"

Her eyes did not match the rest of her neutral expression. No, they were warm, curious...wary. "We have only what we know to be facts. Which are that Dr. Seymour resigned from his position with the War Office some time in 1815. He gave my grandfather an edition of Grimm's fairy tales in which he concealed a note using augmented endpapers. We know Dr. Seymour has been in Bedlam for the past six years. Those are the facts. The rest is conjecture."

"You're forgetting about Mrs. Seymour." Her eyes flicked unguardedly, and he knew he had hit on something. "Mrs. Seymour is convinced someone is watching her. Someone who can bring her and anyone near her great harm. Perhaps it's the Frog King?"

Jane sat back in her chair but not enough to relax against it. She appeared incredibly small just then. Vulnerable. In need of protection. His protection. The thought was ludicrous, and he shook it from his mind.

"Yes, Mrs. Seymour did react unusually to our presence in her home, but as a woman living alone with a husband in a mental hospital, it would not be strange for her to react with a measure of concern."

He raised an eyebrow. "Measure of concern?"

"I can only imagine how difficult living without her husband must be for her." Her expression remained unchanged, but her eyes continued to belie her underlying curiosity.

He leaned forward and put his elbows on his knees. "Do you plan to wed, Jane?"

Her eyes widened at his question, and her mouth tightened. Her relaxed if yet still polite posture of seconds before vanished, and in its place was the skittish young woman he had first discovered that day on the pavement.

"Yes, I do plan to wed, my lord, but I hardly see why that would be of interest to you." Her tone was not impolite, but it held a degree of steel that warned him not to proceed.

He did anyway. "And how do you plan to accomplish such a goal when you do not enjoy engaging in the activities of the season? Activities specifically designed for just such matters as matrimony?"

Her chin went up at this. "I've already selected a suitable husband actually. I have no need for a season and have only agreed to engage in such an endeavor for the sake of my cousin, Emily." Her expression soured slightly, but she hid it quickly with a tight smile. "However ungrateful she might be."

"And just who is this person you have selected?" The churning in his gut caused by the determination in her voice had him asking questions he would normally have no interest in. Why should he care who she planned to marry? It wasn't as if he planned to wed her.

Did he?

"I most definitely do not see how that is of any interest to you." Her gaze zeroed in on him with cunning defiance.

He sat back and folded his arms over his chest. "Is he not deemed acceptable by your family then?"

Her mouth opened without sound emerging, but she recovered herself quickly. "If you must know, he is the son of a local farmer near my father's estate in Kent. He has excellent morals, a pleasing degree of intelligence, and wonderful prospects. He is most suitable for a husband."

Her list of attributes ran like an advertisement for a governess. "Do you love him?" He didn't know why he asked it, but for unknown reasons, her answer suddenly meant a great deal to him.

Her gaze didn't waver, but he knew she weighed her words. Finally she said, "I hardly see how that's important in such a decision."

He realized he hadn't expected a different answer. It left him feeling hollow and sad. Sad for her, yes, but he suspected sad for himself as well, because he could empathize with the notion.

"I see then," he said. "And what is this good gentleman's name?"

"Mr. John Smith." She straightened the ledgers on the desk before her, but it was not a nervous gesture. Every movement was precise and controlled. "His father's estate borders my own father's land, and we practically grew up together."

"He's a mister then?" Austin had never been one to play favor to those lucky enough to be born with titles. The fact that his first true and dear friend since his childhood should be a mere mister bolstered that fact. But for some odd reason, hearing that she might marry such a man left him feeling…hollow again. He pushed against the feeling, but it refused to dissipate.

"Yes, he comes from a quiet family of certain means and respectability. It's a perfectly suitable match." She finished straightening the ledgers and stood. "I'm certain you did not come here today to inquire after my future plans, Evanshire. If that is all…" She didn't finish the sentence as she moved around the desk toward the door.

He stood, following her. "Actually, I did come here today to see you, but it was not to inquire after personal matters." He stepped carefully beside her, not blocking her escape but applying the slightest pressure. "I do earnestly seek your thoughts on Dr. Seymour."

She folded her arms across her middle and regarded him. "My brother has gone looking for any old Bow Street Runner reports that may have been filed at the time Dr. Seymour suddenly resigned from the War Office. He's hoping something will turn up that may shed light on the identity of the Frog King."

He was aware of this as Samuel had asked him to come along, but Austin had refused. He had other matters to attend to, although he wasn't entirely clear on what they were until his stomach had tightened at the sight of Jane hunched over those ledgers.

"And that is all? You're going to let matters be until Samuel returns?"

"Of course," she said. "I wouldn't want to confuse the situation."

"You're going to quiz Lady Jane on anything she remembers around the time Dr. Seymour resigned."

She let her arms drop. "I don't know what you mean."

He smiled. "You do, in fact, and I would be honored if I may accompany you."

"I cannot invite you to attend a matter which I am not attending to myself." Her gaze didn't waver although her lashes flicked nervously along the line of fringe at her brow.

"Is that so?"

Her lips pursed. "Oh very well. You may come with me, but I will be asking the questions."

He raised an eyebrow. "Why is that?"

She hesitated. Her eyes went back and forth across his face until she finally said, "She finds you utterly charming, and I think it distracts her."

He couldn't help smiling again. "Utterly charming?" He should stop the conversation there. Allow her to leave the room and find her grandmother. A gentleman would have done so. Austin was not that kind of gentleman. He leaned in.

"Tell me, Jane. Do you find me utterly charming as well?" He was so close to her now he could see the variations in the browns of her eyes. Her tongue came out against her lower lip, and it was all he could do not to lean in and capture her mouth in a smoldering kiss.

But she leaned away from him. No, that wasn't it. She'd tilted somehow, and he realized she'd taken hold of the back of a nearby chair. Her knuckles turned white. He backed away.

"I hear most of the ladies of the ton think so." He defused the tension between them as though he had snuffed out a candle and made himself appear like a total ass.

Her face hardened, and she opened her mouth as if to relay a massive admonishment, but she stopped. "You did that on purpose." Her voice was soft, and her fierce expression melted at her words. "Why?"

He swallowed, unable to explain how the beckoning look she gave him pulled at his heart. "I told you, Miss Black. I have no wish to make you uncomfortable because of my own shortcomings."

Her eyes turned from curiosity to wariness, and he couldn't stop himself. He stepped forward, closing the distance between them. He wanted her to believe him when he said, "Don't you understand how devastatingly alluring I find you?"

* * *

SHE DIDN'T BELIEVE HIM. She couldn't believe him. Everything in her past contradicted his silly little statement.

Only his eyes. His eyes didn't lie. His eyes displayed

earnestness, honesty…pleading. He desperately wanted her to believe him. But why?

Pain blossomed in her chest, and she wanted to retreat. She wanted to think about Mr. Smith and what a calm and ordered life could be found with him.

But she couldn't look away from Austin. Couldn't look away from the desire in his gaze.

Desire.

Oh dear God.

Things like this only happened in Penelope's novels. They didn't happen to plain girls like Jane. And yet, here it was. Here he was. Standing right before her. The emotion clear on his face.

He wanted her.

She swallowed and said the only thing that came into her head, "I want to save the doctor."

Oh. Lud. Heat poured into her face so quickly she didn't know why it simply didn't alight with flame. She wanted to avert her gaze or maybe close her eyes or better yet, just run from the room, but she couldn't move.

How had this happened? How had a dangerous marquess come to matter so much? He wasn't a part of her plan. John Smith. She was to marry John Smith, and everything would be—

Everything would be the same for the rest of her life.

She expected Austin to laugh at her, and he didn't disappoint. He erupted in laughter, and her stomach plummeted to the ground. With the sound of his laughter, she could finally move, and so she did. She turned her back on him and strode to the door. Only she didn't get far.

He caught her by the shoulders and spun her around. He shook her in time with his laughter, and for a split second, she struggled to free herself. Tears threatened at the backs of her eyes, and her stomach rolled over and over on itself until she knew she would be sick.

But then she stopped. Stilled. Watched.

He wasn't laughing at her. He was laughing because he was happy. Joyful. What she'd said had made him…elated.

She stared, unable to do much more until he finished shaking her.

"Why is that funny?" she finally asked, but her stomach had settled, the fear vanishing only to be replaced by curiosity, which was entirely far worse.

"I finally got an honest response from you, and it's brilliant. When do we attempt to rescue the good doctor?"

He had gone mad. "We can't rescue him."

He stopped laughing, but he didn't release her. His grip was warm, solid…good. "Why ever not? We know where the man is. We've seen what it takes to get to him. Why not plan a rescue mission?"

"Because we don't know from whom we are rescuing him or if he even needs rescuing. That was what I was trying to tell you. Not everyone requires rescuing, and at this point, we simply have conjecture and no real proof."

His smile was wide as he took her in, his eyes alight with a childlike glee. "Ah Jane, you have such a sharp mind hidden behind all that fringe, I could simply—"

The blasted man didn't finish the sentence. He just smiled obnoxiously at her until she was forced to ask, "You could what?"

He shrugged, and his eyes searched her face as if deciding something. "I know I promised I wouldn't, and a gentleman would hold to his word, but I'm really no gentleman."

Before she could decipher his cryptic words, he kissed her. Full on the mouth with both of his strong arms wrapped tightly around her. She forgot to breathe. She forgot how to stand. She forgot to care, because oh my, it was exhilarating to have him kiss her.

He was so warm and so big and so everywhere, and she melted against him even as a tiny voice in her head cried for her to beware. Men like Austin didn't marry girls like her. She couldn't fall for him. She mustn't. She was marrying Mr. Smith. She was—

Dear Lord, was that his tongue?

He let go of her so abruptly she stumbled the smallest step only to be caught up against his broad chest as he held her steady.

He smiled down at her, his expression just as childlike if not as wide. "What were you saying about conjecture? I fear I let myself get carried away."

She'd forgotten what she'd been saying about conjecture as well. "You're a horrible man."

He raised an eyebrow. "Have I led you to believe anything else?"

"I don't suppose you have, but you could surprise me every once in a while."

"You don't seem like the type of person to like surprises, Jane." His tone was so dry, she knew he dared her to contradict him.

She raised her chin. "I hate them, in fact, so if you think you can woo me with the niceties other debutantes of the season desire, you will be met with unpleasant consequence."

"Are you giving me permission to woo you?" His smile lifted mockingly on one side.

"No!" The word came out sharp and entirely too fast. She stumbled on the next word. "What I mean—" She pushed both hands against his chest to free herself, but he wouldn't let go. "That is…I—"

He kissed her again, freeing her from the obligation of coming up with any more dratted words.

This kiss was different. Gentle. Calm. And yet brimming with anticipation and need.

But the relief. The relief at not having to say another treacherous word swamped her, and she fell into the kiss. She let her arms slip up and around his neck. Pull him closer. He made a guttural noise in his throat as his arms tightened around her, and he pressed her backward.

She clung to him as he dipped her into his arms and deepened the kiss. Heat seared through her along the length of her body where it pressed to his, up her arms where they looped around his neck, and where his lips met hers—

"Why on earth would you go into the library right now, young man?"

They sprang apart at the shouted words. Jane toppled backward as she'd been unaware Austin was leaning her back into a chair. He reached for her, but she swatted his hands away as the sound of the knob turning ricocheted through the room like a gunshot.

"It's my library, Mum," Uncle Alec's voice came through the crack in the door. "I must see to all those ducal duties that are required of me at the ducal desk in the ducal den of—"

"I always did like Nathan better," Lady Jane's voice interrupted.

"We are all aware—"

Jane slipped over the edge of the chair until somehow she landed on the floor behind it. Her mind raced for an explanation. Anything that would explain Austin's presence. In the library. With her. Unchaperoned. Oh God, she needed to get a hold of herself and start thinking in complete sentences.

"Evanshire."

Damn and blast, Uncle Alec was in the library.

"Lofton." There was a noise as if the men shook hands, which seemed odd. Had Austin gone to the door to greet her uncle? What was happening? Why was she still hiding on the floor?

The time to come out had long since passed, and if she emerged now, they would all know something was amiss.

"Evanshire, lad, what a pleasant surprise!" Her grandmother spoke far too loudly, and Jane had the sudden suspicion the woman had seen Austin come into the library. Knew they were in there. Alone. Together.

Complete sentences! She could think of something that would explain what was happening. In complete sentences. But why was she on the floor?

"Jane, I found—" Footsteps. Pause. "Oh, hello. Back from the club already, Uncle Alec?"

Elizabeth.

Elizabeth's voice. Where had her sister come from? Lizzie mostly kept to herself when they were in town, having even less interest in the goings on of the season than Jane. So why had she suddenly emerged from her studies? Why had she appeared in the library?

"I lost the button on my fencing glove, and I thought it was in here. Evanshire and Jane were helping me to look." Pause. "Where did Jane go?"

Yes, that was it. Jane popped up so fast her head swam. She was certain her face had turned red. From exertion, embarrassment, the threat of being caught.

Austin's kiss...

"You found it?" The words came out far steadier than she could have imagined, and she wanted to whoop in triumph. Instead, she smiled softly and folded her hands at her waist.

Uncle Alec stood just inside the door of the library next to Lady Jane. Lizzie stood arrested on the threshold, a fencing glove, indeed, held in one hand.

And Austin.

Austin stood on the other side of the chair looking as guilty as she herself likely looked.

Lizzie smiled. "I did. Thank you. I'm sorry you had to go through all that trouble. I appreciate your help. Yours as well, Evanshire." She gave a little bow to the marquess and turned about. "Back to my Latin then." She strode out of the room, her exit appearing far grander for the fact she sported trousers and with her ever increasing height, her stride swung with some authority.

Jane had utterly no idea what had just occurred, but from the dubious expression on her uncle's face, she was fairly certain he wasn't accepting the ruse.

"Grandmother, Evanshire and I were hoping you were feeling up to some tea and conversation." Jane smiled again, but the expression was becoming cumbersome.

Lady Jane wrinkled her brow in return. "Tea and conversation or are you planning to hound me more about the Seymours?"

"It would be the latter, I'm afraid," Austin put in.

Lady Jane shrugged. "If it gets me some of Cook's lemon cakes, then I am happy to oblige." She gestured to the door. "Shall we? The sun is lovely at this time of day in the green drawing room. We can leave Alec boy to his ducal duties." The last words dripped in sarcasm and not with a measure of mockery.

"Did you give Father this much gruff about seeing to the estate?" Uncle Alec asked.

"Your father was never so pompous about it." Lady Jane made for the door.

"Do you receive such grief from your family, Evanshire?" Uncle Alec joked with a wry twist to his lips.

The oddest thing happened then. Something dark passed over Evanshire's face. If she'd not been so acutely aware of him, she would have missed it. His expression closed though, and the laughing, effervescently happy man who had kissed her not minutes before appeared to have utterly vanished.

But still he said, "Not at all," with some convincing frivolity before turning to Jane. "Shall we?"

"Of course." She started for the door, but her uncle stopped her.

"May I have a word before you go, Jane?" His tone was light, but she'd seen the expression he wore on her father every time her father had cause to instruct Lizzie on the proper behavior of a young lady.

Jane swallowed. "Of course." She looked to Austin. "Would you mind escorting my grandmother to the drawing room?"

Austin gave a true smile now, and her mind itched to know what it was that had turned him so dark for a moment. "It would be my honor." He slipped out the door after Lady Jane as she turned back to her uncle.

"What are his intentions?" The question was blunt, and truly, she had expected nothing less.

"I assume they are to find the villain before he can cause greater harm."

"You know that's not what I meant, and don't believe for a moment, that just because I am your uncle and not your father, I wouldn't toss him out on his ass if he tries anything untoward with you."

She raised her chin in defiance. "I am appalled you think I'm not capable of doing the same."

She was out the door, but she didn't miss his return or the sigh of resignation in his voice as he said it.

"The women in this family will be my death."

CHAPTER 9

"I would ask what your intentions are regarding my granddaughter, but that is rather overdone, isn't it?" Lady Jane settled on a couch upholstered in a slippery looking olive shade at the center of the green drawing room. "So I would ask, are you in good financial standing, what are your views on wifely duties, and how do you treat your mother."

He took a seat in an equally slippery looking chair to the right of the dowager. "I am in good financial standing, and I would be happy to provide references who can attest to my credit. I have never before thought on the matter of wifely duties, but if you should like an opinion, I would say at the outset that I believe a wife should make a good partner, because if she does not, there is no hope for an amicable union. And my mother is deceased."

Lady Jane gave no outward reaction to this but he hadn't expected one. "I am very sorry to hear of your mother. It must be difficult growing up in a household without a mother. Did your father remarry?"

Something inside of him clenched at the word father, but

he swallowed until it eased. "No, he did not. The previous marquess was not inclined toward social proclivities, which prevented him from securing another match. As he'd already gained an heir, I believe he saw no need to stress himself."

She pursed her lips at this. "You grew up in a cold, heartless home, didn't you?"

The question was bold, but coming from the dowager, it did not seem out of place. And more, he found himself shaking his head before he knew he would answer. "No, it wasn't like that at all. It was—" The words stopped as his lips snapped shut, and they tumbled over one another in a scattered attempt to spill forth.

In his mind, he saw Mrs. Rowling as she had been the morning he'd left. She stood on the stoop until he crested the rise in the drive and disappeared from sight, but he'd never lost that image of her. He cleared his throat. "No, it wasn't cold," he finally said.

Lady Jane's expression softened, and although she did not smile, he knew she interpreted more from his words than she'd let on. "I see," she said but was prevented from saying more as Jane entered.

Her cheeks were still red, and her gaze was a little unfocused. He stood immediately, but she waved him off.

"Please sit," she said as she took another one of the chairs in the seating arrangement. "There's no need to stand on ceremony when it comes to such business as this."

Lady Jane smirked. "You always were one to be a stickler for tasks. Always finishing your studies with your governess first."

Jane folded her hands in her lap and squared her shoulders. "Of course," she said. "Why ever would I not?"

This was something about Jane that he was becoming to admire a great deal. While everyone else in the Black family seemed to bend to the will of the dowager, Jane simply did not. She met barb with barb and never backed down from the matriarch.

"Of course," Lady Jane returned and settled into the couch. "Now then, I suppose you want to ask me more questions about the Seymours."

"Dr. Seymour visibly reacted when I told him of Grandfather's death," Jane said.

The dowager straightened. "He did?" She shook her head and massaged the head of her cane. "Poor Milton. That most certainly was a shock to him."

"It would suggest that he is of sound mind though," Austin said.

Lady Jane met his gaze. "It would at that. And you would like to know more about the relationship between Milton and Richard?"

"More specifically about the circumstances of the book. When did Dr. Seymour give it to Grandfather?" Jane kept her hands neatly folded in her lap, but she radiated with a near tangible energy.

Lady Jane pressed a folded hand to her chin as if puzzling out the answer. For a moment, he wondered what it would be like to have eighty-odd years of memories through which one was required to sift.

"Let me see now," the dowager murmured. "It would have been October or November of that year. In 1815 that was." Her gaze cleared as the answers seemed to tumble together. "You were born in December of that year, of course, and we wanted to be ensconced at Bedford before you made an appearance." She looked pointedly at him. "That's the country house Richard always favored. He did enjoy spending the holidays in the lush greenery of his estate." She smirked then and cast a knowing glance at Jane. "But we all know just how quickly he returned to Lofton House." She paused and looked about her, and again, he felt the sweep of time as if it carried weight.

In that thought, he let his own mind slip. An error he stopped immediately but not before it captured the memory of the green hills of Peregrine Hall. The way they had looked before he had left.

"He always did prefer this house." These words the dowager spoke more to herself than anyone else, but soon her gaze focused again. "Milton would have given the book to Richard sometime before the holidays. Your mother and father left for Bedford long before we did, however, so it would have been just your grandfather and I here at the house." She smiled tremulously but not in any kind of sadness. It spoke of her honest appreciation of how hard it was to pry through all of those memories. "You would think I could recall, but it's just so much." Her smile straightened then. "But I remember the day you were born as if it happened yesterday." The look the dowager exchanged with Jane was something he'd never witnessed before, and likely for the first time in his life, he felt the true loss of growing up without a mother. At least, not a real mother.

Jane leaned forward and took her grandmother's hand into her own. "We've had quite a time of it since then."

Lady Jane laughed, and the weight of time vanished. "That we have, child. That we have." She settled and squeezed Jane's hand with a quick shake. "I just wish I could remember more about when it was that Milton came to the house. I know your grandfather had the book at Bedford when you were born. He began reading to you straight away, even before you could keep your eyes open."

Jane smiled but he could see the tension at the corners of her eyes. Her grandfather's death was still so fresh, and he was beginning to learn just how much the man had meant to her. "Did Grandfather ever say anything about the book?"

Lady Jane went to shake her head but stopped. "Come to think of it. Do you know he only read that book to you?" Lady Jane did shake her head now. "Of all the grandchildren, it's quite odd that he should have only shared it with you."

"He didn't read to Emily?" Jane asked.

Lady Jane scoffed. "Emily wouldn't ever sit still long enough. And Ashley was more interested in their walking adventures through the park. Ashley is Alec's elder son," she added for his benefit. "I only wish the twins had had more time with him. That's the youngest set for Alec," she again added.

"Surely he must have spent time with Lizzie." Jane released her grandmother's hand as the woman gave out a wonderful bark of laughter.

"Who do you think it was who gave that child her first foil? Those two were thick as thieves from the outset but never over some book." The look on the dowager's face was eerily similar to one he'd seen a number of times on Mrs. Rowling's face, and a tightness sprang to his chest.

"So why was it only me?"

Lady Jane shrugged. "We all know your relationship with Richard was different and special. You were, after all, the first grandchild whose birth he witnessed."

He shifted in his seat as the two women exchanged a look that reminded him of the day they'd paid a call to Mrs. Seymour. There was something unspoken between the dowager and her granddaughter, and he thought it likely had something to do with this vow Jane refused to explain.

"Did you keep any of your late husband's correspondence?" he asked.

Lady Jane cast him a quizzical glance. "Not much, I'm afraid. Most of what Richard wrote was confidential War Office material and was either destroyed or—" She stopped so abruptly he tipped forward in his seat as if relying on her words to steady him.

"Or what?" Jane pressed.

Lady Jane seized her cane with both hands. "All correspondence relating to War Office matters was either destroyed or kept on file at the War Office."

"Kept on file?" He shifted uncomfortably in his seat once more. "What does that mean exactly?"

"All correspondence is archived by agent in case any of their work is ever called into question. Their correspondence acts as a record of all of their missions." Lady Jane's expression oozed enthusiasm now. "We could get Richard's archive and see what really happened in the fall of 1815."

"They would release that kind of material to us?" He felt rather dubious about such a thing, and his suspicions were confirmed when Lady Jane deflated at his words.

"Well, no, not to us. But they would release it to a high-ranking agent or someone in a supervisory role. You know how the Office is with all of their ranks."

"Like the military one would assume," Jane added.

A quiet unease passed over him as he recalled the words of the informant at The Bent Broom. He stood and gripped the lapels of his jacket. "A high-ranking officer or perhaps a duke?"

Lady Jane stared up at him before a smile slowly spread across her face, and she stood with her cane held triumphantly in front of her. "I'll go ask him immediately." She paused, a frown coming to her features. "Oh dear, we haven't had our tea."

He bowed to the ladies before turning to the door. "No worries, Lady Jane. I must be going." He gave Jane one last look and at her questioning expression, he resolved it was time to discover just what sort of vow she had made.

* * *

"Miss Black, you have a caller."

This pronouncement from Crane, the latest butler at Lofton House, was enough to render the entire room silent. Emily dropped her tirade about the inability to acquire good silk these days (Jane had no idea why this seemed to be a problem), and Lizzie stilled her practice with her foil.

While Lady Jane, of course, felt no such compunction toward silence at all when she declared, "Why on earth would Jane have a caller?"

They were gathered in the green drawing room as they usually were at this hour to receive the day's callers, but as they were under strict guard from an overly concerned brother, callers were few and infrequent as Crane had been instructed to tell guests that the ladies were not in residence if the caller was not of a certain circle.

So Jane had to agree with her grandmother's assessment. Why, indeed, would she have a caller?

Emily dropped her hands from where she had been demonstrating the proper handling of good silk and turned toward the butler. "You must be mistaken, but you needn't worry. You're new. My father will simply replace you if you are all that terrible. Please show the gentleman in. I would be most pleased to accept a caller." She smiled, but the emotion didn't find its way to her eyes.

It was an expression that often unsettled Jane, and it was no different now except she felt a pang of sympathy for poor Crane. He was rather new, and she had witnessed a few hiccups in his transition to the household. But all in all, he was a fine butler.

But then her gaze settled on Emily.

She had been avoiding Jane since the slap, and Jane couldn't very well say she minded.

"I don't think Crane is mistaken," Lady Jane said, her tone giving no room for argument. "Crane, lad, did the gentleman provide a card?"

The poor man's face tightened, and Emily glared at him as if evaluating the opportunity to strike once more. Except no opportunity came because Crane's next pronouncement was quite a bit more astonishing.

"That's just it, Your Grace. It's the Marquess of Evanshire. As he's inquired after an audience several times in this household, a card was unnecessary, but he did wish me to specify that this was a social call."

If she had not been a more composed woman, Jane was sure she'd have fallen out of her chair at that moment.

A social call?

Austin.

No need for a card because she already knew him.

Intimately.

Austin.

Instead of filling with domestic theories, her mind raced to an unbelieved conclusion: she had done this by kissing him yesterday. Had she kissed him or had he kissed her? She couldn't remember anymore. But perhaps her actions had misled him. Men like Austin didn't marry young women like her, she reminded herself. But what if they did?

Oh God, was he courting her?

It was several moments before she realized the odd rasping sound in the room was her own labored breaths. She shut her mouth and focused on breathing in and out through her nose.

"Well, show him in then," Lady Jane said with a great deal of enthusiasm.

She wasn't sure when it had happened, but suddenly Lizzie stood behind her. And she only knew then because of the flash of light that glinted off the broad edge of her foil.

Her sister leaned down and whispered, "If he does anything you don't wish him to do, you only need say the word. I've punctured many opponents in my time. Titles make no difference."

Such a bold statement pronounced in such a bawdy drawl made Jane turn around and eye her little sister. Only her sister wasn't so little anymore. She was tall like their father. Perhaps, too tall, but her carriage was lovely, and the bones of her face...well, she was pretty where Jane wasn't, and she found the thought made her smile with pride.

"Yes, of course, Your Grace." Crane completed a small bow and exited.

"This will not be tolerated!" Emily shot across the room so quickly, Jane had no time to react.

But it needn't matter because Lizzie had not been lying. Her sister vaulted over Jane's chair, coming down on the other side with her fighting arm extended, the tip of her foil vibrating ever so much in the stillness of the room.

That was the tableau the room presented when Austin entered. Lizzie, her foil at the ready. Emily frozen in mid-pounce, arms flung wide as if in complete disbelief. Aunt Sarah half out of her chair as Nora reached for Lizzie as if to pull her back.

Lady Jane was the only one who hadn't moved, and she smiled at Austin now. "Good day, my boy. You've caused a ruckus, I'm afraid."

Austin's lips thinned. An expression Jane was coming to realize meant he was doing his best to hide a grin. "I must apologize then. I meant no such interruption."

"Oh, it's quite all right." This from Jane's mother, who still held her hands out as if to catch Lizzie. "This happens more often than you would think."

"One would only hope that we would cease to do it in front of guests." Aunt Sarah gave a half smile before she completely stood and took hold of her daughter. "Emily and I were just off to pay a call on Lady Mildred."

Emily's face lost all color. "Mother! I didn't touch her. I don't deserve—"

The rest of the sentence was lost as Aunt Sarah dragged Emily from the room.

Lizzie, though, had not let her arm drop. Now her foil pointed directly at Austin's chest. Again, not an uncommon sight, but her words were quite unexpected. "I'm sure my brother has inquired after your intentions, but if you place one foot out of line, I will be forced to demand you name your second."

Austin's face moved as if he were to smile, but he stopped it abruptly and turned to the side as if peering around Lizzie to look at Nora. "She's serious, isn't she?"

Nora finally dropped her arms and nodded. "I'm afraid she is."

Austin straightened and returned Lizzie's glare with one of his own. "I'm afraid my second would be your brother."

"That's of little consequence to me." Lizzie's foil did not twitch.

"I think it might be to him." He had the courage to raise an eyebrow then.

Lizzie lowered her foil. "I think I'm going to like you."

"Well, thank God for small miracles," Lady Jane said. "Please, Evanshire. Do sit down and join us."

He hesitated. "I was actually hoping I may enjoy Miss Black's company for a stroll in the park."

Jane was not one for much novel reading beyond her sister-in-law's works, as she felt authors too readily fell to the dramatic in their tales, but just then, Jane absolutely knew that a human heart could stop beating entirely.

"A stroll in the park, you say?" Her grandmother cast Jane a sideways glance. "It is a rather fine day for it, but I think—"

Jane shot out of her chair before her grandmother could finish the sentence. "I would love to."

Far too many words were tripping from her lips of late without her clearly thinking them through. She would need to do something about that. But later. Right now it was all she could do to draw normal breath.

And then the blasted man smiled. "Excellent. It's a beautiful day. Rather warm for March."

"You're not going to waste this opportunity speaking of the weather, are you?" Grandmother pressed her lips together and raised both eyebrows. "Because then I must object."

He looked to Jane's mother as he replied. "I shouldn't want you to worry that your daughter will suffer a chill."

"Of course," her mother replied with a smile of her own.

"Would you really ask my brother to be your second?"

Jane had almost forgotten Lizzie was there even though the girl stood half in front of her.

"I would indeed," Austin returned without hesitation.

"Does he know this?" Lizzie went on.

"I would assume so."

Lizzie's face clouded over then as if her thoughts lay heavy about her. Jane made a mental note to ask her of it later, but not just then. Just then she needed all of her composure to get through this little outing with Austin.

She stepped forward. "I'll just have my maid fetch my wrap, and then we can be off."

"Excellent." Austin gave her a small bow as she passed.

They were in the foyer only moments later, Jane properly encased in her wrap, with Wendy, Jane's maid, a few discreet steps behind her. Austin bowed in the maid's direction and gave the young woman a friendly smile. It was a titled man who had the blessing of servants, but it was a true gentleman who acknowledged them. Her grandfather's words struck

Jane at that moment with such force, she actually faltered. She recovered quickly though and didn't think anyone had noticed.

She had never had cause to wonder what this would be like. Engaging in social niceties with a gentleman. With Mr. Smith, everything had been so straight forward and planned. No need for these inanities. But with Austin, it didn't seem so frivolous. And for once, she wanted to be just a little silly if it made her blood thrum like this.

They made it through the door and across the way into the park without further incident, and for one blissful moment, Jane let herself believe she was being courted by a devastatingly handsome, caring gentleman.

But only for a moment because then Austin said, "I think it's time you told me what vow you made and why it's likely going to get you killed."

CHAPTER 10

The pain came swift and sharp, and the air rushed from her lungs so quickly, she choked on it.

It wasn't the question itself or the blunt way in which he'd asked it. She was used to such a frank manner of speech. Having been raised in the bosom of the Black family, it was simply unavoidable.

The thing which caused her much distress was deeper than that. Truer. Cleaner. Disappointingly accurate.

This wasn't a social call.

He hadn't meant to truly take her for a stroll in the park. He hadn't meant to parade her around on his arm in front of the other debutantes of the season. Show her off. Make it known he was courting her.

Courting her.

Ha.

She'd had it all wrong.

He wanted information from her. Information regarding the investigation.

Wendy had stopped several paces behind them, and they may as well have been alone.

The coil of energy that had been wound so tautly within her vanished, whatever hope she may still have possessed disappearing with it. She faced Evanshire.

"I promised my grandfather I'd take care of my grandmother." The words were said with so little emotion, she could only imagine the emptiness of her features.

Could he tell he'd just cut her where it could most hurt her? In that secret place where she still believed she deserved to be loved?

She had known from the first moment she'd realized she wasn't beautiful like Emily. She'd realized the first moment she wasn't vivacious like Lizzie. She'd known. And she'd accepted it. That she'd never be quite enough to attract a man's attention.

Until him. But she'd been wrong.

He stared at her now, and the tension around his eyes suggested he hadn't comprehended her words.

"My grandfather." She spoke more clearly now as if he were hard of hearing. "When he knew his time was drawing to a close, he made me swear to protect Lady Jane."

Had it all been a lie? Those charming words? The kiss? Had it all been to manipulate her for information? Men like Austin *didn't* marry women like her. She'd been right all along.

Evanshire shook his head. "Yes, I understand that. But why? Surely, your grandmother is well protected by all the members of the family." He paused and made a sweeping gesture with his hand. "Your own brother is an inspector with the Metropolitan Police Force. He practically has Commissioner Mayne in his pocket. If anyone should be more protected—"

He dropped off his words as she shook her head. "No, no. That's precisely why Grandfather made me swear."

Evanshire looked about them now, and she suddenly realized they had stopped on the path. They were drawing curious glances but not at all for the reasons she had expected.

He reached for her arm as if to guide her into resuming their walk, but the strangest thing happened.

She pulled her arm out of his reach.

It was there one moment. Perfectly poised under his extended hand, and then—

She couldn't have said what came over her. What compelled her. What…gave her the courage, but she pulled away.

A gaggle of young ladies was just passing behind them, trailing in the wake of their gossiping mothers, and it was as if the whole world had stopped with her single, sudden movement.

The ladies halted with the scrape of gravel. The mothers ceased their gossiping with a strangled chirp.

Jane realized her arm hung suspended awkwardly between them, and anyone still watching (which was a great many people considering the hour and fine weather) could easily see that she had just affronted the Marquess of Evanshire.

Little Jane Black.

Little plain, unattractively smart Jane Black.

With more composure than she believed she possessed, she lowered her arm carefully to her side and raised her chin. "My grandfather swore me to the task because he knew I was the only one who could bring Lady Jane to reason."

There. Now he knew. Perhaps he'd leave her alone now.

But apparently she wasn't finished because the young ladies and their gossipy mothers still watched with rapt attention. So she did what Lady Jane would have done.

She stared back. Her lips pressed into an unyielding line. Her shoulders drawn back, which she knew made her look boxy but at the given moment, made her look rather impassable. She stared at the mothers who blinked and hastily averted their gazes and at the young ladies who as if pulled by an unseen force, tripped back into their march across the park.

Jane turned to the path and indicated for Evanshire to resume their pace. If she must have this conversation, she'd really rather have it with occupied limbs. Walking would be a welcomed distraction.

"I hadn't realized you would have been the one your grandfather would select for such a duty," he said once they'd gone a few feet down the path.

"I am the eldest grandchild after Samuel, and the first Lady Jane held as one of her own." She eyed the marquess sternly, so he would understand just how important such a fact was. "To say nothing of being named for her."

Evanshire's face closed as it had done the previous day in the library, but he said, "So you would have me believe you are embarking on a course of events so utterly uncharacteristic of your natural countenance that it may even be dangerous to your person on the vow you made to your grandfather?" His tone carried no small measure of disbelief.

Her feet crunched satisfyingly along the gravel even as her hands remained stalwartly clenched in front of her.

"Of course," she said with a degree of fortitude calculated to overwhelm his disbelief. "It was my grandfather after all who swore me to the task."

His expression turned so bleak then, and she stopped him on the path.

"Evanshire, please do not tell me there is no one in your family to whom you would swear such an oath."

"Of course, there isn't." His reply was automatic.

She tilted her head as the sun had begun to dip, and the

shadows slipped over his face before vanishing. "Well, that's just awful."

He crossed his arms over his chest. "I don't see why you would say so. I should think it's rather more common for a person not to find such a trusted ally amongst one's blood relations."

"If you should not, then what is the point of family at all?"

He flinched. His eyes sharpened and his mouth pinched for the briefest of moments, but in that slim piece of time, she felt a rush of horrible, awful, inconceivable joy.

She had struck a nerve.

She had delivered a blow as cunning and lethal as he had done to her only minutes before. She hurried on. "Perhaps it is rather unusual that I should find myself sworn to such an oath, but I have and I am. So I will press on with this mission if it means securing my grandmother's safety."

"But aren't the other members of your family better suited to the task?"

She had nearly turned to continue along the path, but this stopped her like a careless miscalculation in a row of figures. "I beg your pardon?"

She knew he realized his mistake because he appeared to swim away from her. A slight leaning back of the torso as if by slipping out of her range, he could avoid the retaliation. "It's just that the other members of your family are—"

"Men," she supplied. "Are you saying I'm not suited to this task because I am a woman?"

"I'm not saying that at all." His words came so quickly they nearly fell atop one another. "I'm just saying—"

"You are saying the male members of my family are better suited to the task of discovering this villain and ensuring he is unable to harm another person. That is what you're saying."

"I do not appreciate you speaking for me." His words were clipped.

"I am not speaking for you. I'm finishing the sentence you do not seem capable of finishing."

"I'm perfectly capable of finishing a sentence." His nostrils flared.

"Well, I would love for you to finish this one. I'm sure it has a remarkable conclusion."

"It has a perfectly fine conclusion if you would only—"

"Oh, a perfectly fine conclusion, is it? Just like when you concluded it would be perfectly fine to trick me into thinking you cared for me when all you wanted was to force my secret from me?" The last words slammed against her teeth so hard, she finally realized how much they had both raised their voices.

"Miss."

Jane turned to see Wendy had approached. She stood not three feet away with a single hand extended, her brow knit with worry. "Miss. They're watching," she hissed.

Jane swung her gaze beyond the maid and around the marquess, her eyes soaking in the stunned faces watching the spectacle in which she currently found herself. She snapped her jaw shut and folded her arms over her chest.

She already had a husband picked out. A future secured. And none of it relied on the judgment of a few, tawdry members of London society. She raised her chin.

"Perhaps you'll remember that the next time you call upon a young lady and act more the gentleman you proclaim to be."

The volley slammed home, and Evanshire actually took a step away from her. He might as well have stepped clear to the Continent as the gulf between them wrenched open with that single step.

And when she expected the void to be filled with Evanshire's weak words of remorse, she found it filled with something else entirely.

Clapping.

Exaggerated, sarcastic clapping.

She turned and found Professor Mesmer standing behind Wendy, delivering a round of applause for her bold performance. She squared her shoulders ready to take him down as well for she had no more room—

But he raised his hands in supplication.

"I come in peace," he called across the space. "Your brother requests you return home at once."

She eyed the marquess. "At least that is an honest demand if a rather bullying one."

Mesmer let his hands drop. "The doctor has been attacked in Bedlam."

* * *

"YOU'RE certain it was a deliberate attack?"

He watched Jane from the other side of the Lofton library as she asked this and wondered where it was he'd gone wrong. He had been so certain a bold, direct approach was the way to handle the situation. He had truly believed if he asked her forthright, she would confess. Confess a number of things he could have only imagined and none of them had compared to the reality.

A vow to her grandfather.

To protect her grandmother.

This in itself was unsettling but not more than the following accusation.

Please do not tell me there is no one in your family to whom you would swear such an oath.

It was that more than her revelation that had struck. The

tone in which she'd asked it, so startled and perplexed that he may find himself without such a situation.

A family.

A family that cared about him, yes, but more, one about which he found himself caring in return.

He crossed his arms over his chest and settled against the bookcase behind him. It needn't matter that he had no one to whom he'd swear such an oath. Not everyone had to be smothered in the bosom of a loving family.

But even as he thought it, a pain shimmered in his chest, and he thought of Mrs. Rowling. With no small amount of surprise, he realized he'd swear an oath to her. Instantly and without regret.

He surveyed the room about him. Alec and Sarah, the current Duke and Duchess of Lofton. Mr. and Mrs. Black, Jane's parents. Each stood next to one another, touching in some small way. For the duke and duchess, it was a press of arms as they sat next to each other on a sofa. For the Blacks, it was a hand to a shoulder as Mr. Black stood behind his wife's seated figure.

Even Samuel hovered over his new bride.

The pain in his chest grew more certain.

He really had thought being direct with Jane would have gained him some sort of favor, but he'd clearly been wrong. She thought he had tricked her into revealing her secret when nothing could have been further from the truth.

For the truth was, he had craved privacy with her.

He straightened away from the bookcase.

"The atmosphere in which we found the doctor did not appear overtly friendly," he added as he stepped into the periphery of the group. He settled next to Professor Mesmer as it seemed prudent to stand in solidarity against the great cohesion of the Black family.

"My contacts within Bedlam have confirmed it."

Samuel's hand absently found his wife's shoulder, absently mimicking his father. "He had been checked at final call before lights out, and when the nurse returned in the morning with his breakfast tray, he was found unconscious on the floor."

"What was the damage?" the duke asked.

Samuel's brow creased. "Extensive. The perpetrator appears to have centered his attack on the doctor's face."

"He wanted to ensure someone saw it," Mr. Black supplied.

Samuel nodded. "It would appear so."

"What do we do now?" Sarah asked.

Samuel stepped away from Penelope and began to pace. "We've stepped into something we cannot fathom. It has roots the ends of which we cannot see, and a reach that is untold."

"We've concluded the doctor is truly hiding something, and now we've put him in danger?" Alec stood and paced away from the group as well.

"Yes, exactly," Samuel replied and stopped to face Jane. "You're certain the doctor registered your revelation of grandfather's death?"

Austin didn't miss the look Jane slid his way before responding. "Yes, I am certain."

"Then we have certainly put the doctor in serious danger." Samuel returned to pacing.

"How do you figure?" Mr. Black asked.

"The doctor was safe until we showed up asking questions," Jane answered.

Mrs. Black straightened and sat forward in her seat. "But who could have known?"

"That's exactly the problem," the duke muttered from where he'd taken up a perch at the window. "We can't seem to get our arms around this thing. Whoever he is, he's watching us with terrifying precision while we run around in the dark."

"But what if we weren't?" Austin said before he realized he was going to speak. Every eye in the room turned to him including Lady Emily's, but as she batted her eyelashes at him and plumped her lips, he ignored her. He stepped around the sofa in front of him and joined the group proper. "What if we weren't running around in the dark? What if we weren't running around at all?"

Sarah shot up from her seat. "Are you suggesting we run away? A Black has never—"

Samuel cut her off. "No, not run away. Remove the bait."

He nodded. "Precisely. There's nothing for this fiend to watch if there's nothing there at all."

"By concealing what he presumes is a threat, you're going to force him to make a move," Sarah said, her body stilling as she watched him. "You're going to make him desperate if you take away the thing he's been watching. He could do something dangerous."

He regarded her. "I would think that's something you would find appealing."

The duke snorted from the other side of the room. "It is precisely something she would find appealing."

"You think the villain will make an overt maneuver if we remove the thing he seeks. Which is what exactly?" Mr. Black offered.

Jane had been leaning against the great desk at the side of the room, but she straightened now and paced along the opposite side of the group from her brother. "We know he's watching the doctor, and we know the doctor, or at least his wife, is afraid of whatever this man is capable of."

"Which suggests the doctor has some knowledge that is potentially lethal to this man," Austin interjected.

She cast him a glance but otherwise continued. "So it would suggest that removing the doctor would upset him."

"But would it be enough to make him act?" Penelope added as she selected a chocolate from the box perched on her stomach. "This man is incredibly passionate about whatever it is he seeks. He's not going to react unless it's something that strikes home."

"Why do you say he's passionate?" Samuel eyed his wife.

She sucked on a chocolate. "He tried to strangle me. That's an act of passion. It's personal. He had to touch my body. It's not like shooting someone. The gun would have removed him from the act."

Samuel's face darkened, but he turned to the group. "I think she has a point."

"Of course, she has a point," Lady Jane finally spoke up. "We should at least try this. We won't know unless we try it, and we can't just sit here while he picks us off one by one." She looked to the duke. "And no luck with Richard's correspondence at the War Office?"

Alec shook his head. "I'm being stopped at every turn. There's someone in the War Office who doesn't want that information released."

"But how do we remove the doctor? He's a prisoner of Bedlam." Sarah looked around the group.

"Didn't Bethany say he went in himself?" Lady Jane asked of Mrs. Black.

The small woman shook her head. "She intimated as such, but I don't believe she actually spoke it."

"Perhaps she can get him back out, and then we can steal him away." Lady Jane massaged the head of her cane.

Samuel shook his head. "Then we'd have Mrs. Seymour involved. We can't open the playing field anymore than it already is. Too many people are in danger."

"So we close the playing field," Jane said. "We snatch the doctor from Bedlam."

"We?" Austin found himself saying as he took a step toward her. A step that was quickly aborted when she turned an icy glare on him.

"Yes, we." She looked to her brother. "We've already successfully entered the hospital. How much more difficult could it be to enter it in disguise?"

"You mean infiltrate the staff?" Mrs. Black offered, and Austin didn't miss the play of a smile at her lips.

Jane returned her mother's near smile. "That's exactly what I'm saying. If we infiltrated the staff, we could easily get to the doctor."

"And slip him from the premises," Samuel added.

"Precisely. It should be simple. We must only let it go no farther from this room so no one else is in danger, and those that know of it—"

"Are restricted to those he's already watching," Samuel finished. "I think this might work." He looked to his father. "But where could we hide him? We must assume the villain is watching the house."

"Eaton Park, perhaps?" Mr. Black offered.

Jane shook her head. "It can't be a property of the family. We must assume he's watching those as well."

"Then where can we take him?" Lady Jane asked. "Doesn't the War Office maintain bolt holes in London? Couldn't one of those be used?"

The professor stepped into the fray at this. "I think including the War Office is of extreme danger considering where the man who inquired after my person at the astronomy club went after leaving the premises."

Lady Jane frowned. "I suppose you're right. Then our choices are getting rather narrow."

"We could rent a facility under an assumed name. Keep him out of sight," Sarah put in.

"It's too dangerous," the duke said. "He knew Jane and Evanshire entered Bedlam under assumed names. He'd find us out in a moment if we tried to hide under an alias."

Austin's stomach tightened as the conversation bounced from one member of the family to the other. He knew the solution. He knew where the doctor would be safe. But he couldn't. He couldn't make his mouth move. His heart thundered even as his mind settled on the realization that it must be done.

"We could go to the Continent. Surely this man's reach isn't infinite." Lady Jane clenched her jaw as she clearly grew more agitated. "I can't believe this thing stretches that far. That it could go all the way back to that incident with Seymour when we were fighting Napoleon. It just can't be."

Jane stepped over to her grandmother and perched herself on the arm of her chair, wrapping one arm around the older woman in a sign of comfort he had not seen Jane administer to any other family member.

Her grandfather had been right to swear her to such a dangerous oath.

He didn't have a choice. As he watched Jane, he knew that.

"There's somewhere else we can take him," he said before he had fully realized he was going to do this. "Somewhere no one could possibly know. He'll be safe there, and we can force the villain out."

Samuel eyed him. "Where is this exactly?"

Austin shook his head. "It would be better if no one knew just in case..."

He didn't need to finish the sentence. The possibilities hung in the air around them. The possibility that one of them would let it slip to an unfriendly ear, and they would be found and killed. The possibility one of them might be captured and tortured until he or she revealed the location.

No, he had no choice, because for once, something else mattered more than his need to flee his past.

Samuel nodded. "You're right. If you're certain the location is secure, we'll proceed with the plan."

Austin nodded in reply to Samuel but his eyes were on Jane. "Yes, I'm sure," he said.

And with that, he was going home.

CHAPTER 11

"They're always sending me the bony ones, ain't they?"

Jane tucked her elbows in closer as if to hide this so called boniness of which Mrs. Dregsmoore was accusing her. Mrs. Dregsmoore was in charge of the scullery maids at Bedlam, and while she managed the staff with an iron fist, it was clear the woman lacked certain faculties in common sense. Samuel's contacts had been right to suggest infiltrating the maids. It was all too alarmingly easy.

A simple bribe to one of the other scullery maids, who had made a well-timed suggestion to Mrs. Dregsmoore of a lass good enough for the post, and it had secured a position on the roster for Jane, who had only to appear on the scheduled day in uniform with mop bucket ready.

Again, alarmingly easy.

The rest was appearing to not be so.

To begin with, Jane was used to a certain degree of manual labor. Keeping the ledgers was no idle task, and she'd experienced several cramped necks in her tenure. But scrubbing floors was an entirely different sort of manual labor. One she did not wish to join into again.

"Ye've got to scrub, ye do." Mrs. Dregsmoore hovered over Jane's bent body as she attempted to dislodge what she hoped to God was mud from between the floor and the wall. The wooden planks ran right up against the door jambs here, and mud caked the lot of it.

She peered up at Mrs. Dregsmoore through the fringe of her hair.

"I is scrubbing, ma'am." Oh, see, that was good. Wendy had been practicing with her, and although she could never master the girl's Welsh lilt, Jane was marginally progressing at dropping her h's and employing the improper verb tense.

"Ye's getting the floor all wet is what ye's doing." Mrs. Dregsmoore bent one arm against her knee and drew back one arm as if to imitate a scrubbing motion. "Ye've got to put your weight into it, girl."

Jane watched the woman and tried to determine the difference in weight between the two of them. She figured it was quite a bit and resigned herself to never scrubbing floors with any kind of aplomb.

"I'll do just as ye say, Mrs. Dregsmoore."

The woman screwed up her face with a puzzled eye. "Ye say ye're friends with ol' Sally, like, eh?"

Jane nodded, not daring to speak another word. Sally was the maid who had been too happy to accept the bribe.

The woman humphed an acknowledgment. "It's just Sally's all Cockney, ain't she?" Mrs. Dregsmoore crossed her arms over her chest. "Where is it ye say ye're from?"

Jane's mind raced. She wasn't supposed to have interacted with Mrs. Dregsmoore this much. The plan was for Jane to slip in and obtain the ring of keys kept in Mrs. Dregsmoore's office for cleaning the individual cells. She should never have had this much conversation with the woman.

"I's not Cockney," Jane said then and tried her best to think of Wendy, but there was absolutely no way for her to pretend to be Welsh. So she tried the next best thing she knew. "Me mum's the housekeeper at Gregenden House in London." Jane let her eyes fall and her shoulders slump. "Well, she was, eh." She peered up at Mrs. Dregsmoore as if to suggest the worst.

The truth of the matter was Nora had been the housekeeper of Gregenden House, and she, in fact, become with child, but not in the way Jane intimated.

The old woman straightened and rubbed her hands into the grime along her apron. "Oh, aye, I see then, girl." She fidgeted some more before finally staring directly at her. "Well, ye doing good for yerself then. Get back to work." The woman waddled off, and Jane took up her scrubbing brush.

Until Mrs. Dregsmoore turned the corner. Jane waited a few beats before dropping her brush back into her pail with a soft splash and springing to her feet. She retraced her steps to where she had first encountered Mrs. Dregsmoore that morning.

It was a small office underneath the rear stairs. Jane peered up those stairs now and listened for any telltale sounds. This set of stairs was different than the one they'd taken that day they'd met the doctor. These were wooden and narrow, the treads warped in places. But they were also quiet and dim, which suggested they were only used by the cleaning staff and not for the medical staff or patients.

Down the corridor beyond the stairs was the rear entrance through which all the maids had traipsed that morning. Jane had met ol' Sally as Mrs. Dregsmoore had called her at half six that morning around the corner so as to appear as if they'd arrived together. The guard hadn't even looked at her as they'd entered, and then Sally had taken her directly to Mrs. Dregsmoore's office.

It was all Jane could do to pay attention to what Mrs. Dregsmoore said while also trying to locate the keys for the patients' cells. She thought she'd answered well enough as Mrs. Dregsmoore, again, had more grit than sense.

Watching the guard carefully, Jane rounded the corner of the stairs and walked up to Mrs. Dregsmoore's office. She expected the guard to at least look her way, but as she neared, she realized the man was asleep.

He'd wedged his head against the wall and the beam of the stairs. His eyes were shut but his mouth lay open with a soft snore tumbling out. She frowned but continued making her way to the office.

Mrs. Dregsmoore didn't lock it, although Jane hadn't expected the woman would. She slipped through the door and stopped, waiting to hear a shout of detection that never came. She rushed forward then, the skirts of her serviceable gown swishing softly against her legs. The keys were supposed to be hung on the wall behind Mrs. Dregsmoore's desk, but all Jane found there was the woman's tattered coat and a shawl, browned with age and torn with moth holes.

She turned to the desk, but it was rather empty as well. A quick search of the drawers proved nothing, and Jane stopped, hands on hip and scanned the room. Where else could the keys be kept? The contact hadn't said Mrs. Dregsmoore kept the keys on her person.

Oh God, but what if she did?

Jane's heart beat a little faster as she realized Austin would be meeting her at the rear entrance at any moment. Or at least, he expected to meet her, and she still didn't have the keys. Damn and blast, now was not the moment to allow her fears to consume her. She closed her eyes and thought of her grandmother.

Emotions be damned. She had a job to do.

She looked about her again, but there was simply nowhere for the keys to hide in such a small, cramped place.

She stilled, the sounds of the guard's soft snores trickling down the hallway to her. She peeked out into the hall and there she saw it.

A ring of keys dangling from the guard's belt.

Those weren't the ones she was meant to obtain, but surely, they would do.

She continued to stare as she doubted the likelihood of her being able to remove the keys without waking the guard. But then, Evanshire had planned to enter through that door. How was he planning to avoid the guard's detection?

Blast it. There had been so many meetings. So many plans of strategies. Samuel had run so much correspondence between his contacts here at the hospital.

But Jane had focused on her mother and Wendy's training. She knew exactly what it was she needed to carry out her length of the mission and nothing more.

Nothing more in case something went wrong.

Her stomach lurched when Austin appeared in the window of the rear door. He was outfitted all in black from his hat to his cravat to his shirt to his coat. The look should have been austere and cutting, but she drank in the sight of him. Despite what he had done to her, he was still a good agent, and she had a vow to fulfill. He would know what to do.

She waved a hand at him, but he ignored her and walked right in. The blasted man.

The guard!

The guard who now awoke with an aborted snore, blinking his eyes furiously as the wind swept through the now open door.

"Eh, you there—"

But he didn't finish the sentence.

Austin was on him. Both arms went around the man so quickly, Jane jumped, her own cry strangling in her throat, but her hands flew to her mouth as if it would escape and give them both away.

But wait—

Austin hadn't attacked the man. He was holding the guard's limp body in his arms, a telltale flash of white in one hand.

Both of her eyebrows shot up as she scuttled to meet him.

"You drugged him!" she hissed.

He had the gall to grin at her. "I borrowed a little of your Madame LeFevre's special potion."

Jane snapped her arms across her chest. "She's not my Madame LeFevre," she hissed.

"Regardless, the stuff works wonders. Shall we get out of the hallway before someone sees us?"

She backed up immediately as Austin carried the prone body of the guard down the hall to Mrs. Dregsmoore's office. He set the guard in the chair and spun about the room.

He held up a hand and jangled two closed fingers in the air.

Jane shrugged and shook her head. "They weren't here."

He frowned but only for a moment before bending to the guard's body. There was some rustling and rummaging before he straightened and held out his hand. A ring of keys dangled in his grasp.

Jane shook her head. "He'll know what we're about when he wakes up and finds his keys gone."

Austin stepped incredibly too close as he bent his head to hers with another grin. "He'll know what we're about when he wakes up no matter what. What's the harm in lightening him of his keys?"

"He may simply believe he's had a bit too much drink and dreamed the whole thing up."

Austin shook his head with a sorrowful grin. "Not when I'm finished with him." And with that he shed the guard of his trousers, coat, and hat.

He made such quick work of it, she suddenly wondered if he had undressed an unconscious man before. She gaped at him, but he only held up the bundle of clothes to her.

"For the doctor." He stuffed them at her until she wedged them into the pocket of her apron.

"Someone will notice." Although to be honest, the voluminous folds of the skirt did hide the bulk well.

He pushed her to the door. "We haven't much time. The guards make their rounds on the hour."

She jolted as this was yet another piece of the plan she had not been instructed on, but then Austin was here for that. She followed him into the corridor and up the servants' staircase.

They came out on the floor above to a deceptively silent corridor. She paused and reached out a hand to stop Austin from moving forward.

She shook her head and pressed a finger to her lips. She didn't know what it was, but something indeed was not as it was supposed to be.

"May I help you?"

The voice came from behind them, and she jumped, reflexively springing behind Austin, attempting to appear the demure maid.

A man stood there. He wore a frock coat and held a ream of paper in one hand. The hallway was too dark to see much more than the general features of him—a full beard, spectacles, and a hooked nose. A rather homely man but his eyes were intense.

So she said the only thing that came to mind. "Oy, look 'ere!" The thickness of her accent startled her enough to forget the rest of her words. She swallowed and tried again.

"I's just doing as Mrs. Dregsmoore said. I's pleasing the visiting doctor with the what for just as he asked. Ain't no business of mine, and I's just do as I's told."

Later she would congratulate herself on not blushing straight to the roots of her hair. It was enough that Austin coughed uncomfortably before turning to the other man.

"I beg your pardon," he said, his voice completely steady. "The name's…Smith. Dr. John Smith. I'm up from…Kent."

He really was a rogue.

"I wasn't aware of a visiting doctor on the ward." The man held one hand above the ream of papers as if he'd been looking through them when he'd stumbled upon them.

"I wasn't properly announced. I'm here to see a specific patient, and the family has asked to keep the matter quiet. You can understand."

The man rocked back on his heels and gave a low whistle. "I see then. You must be speaking of the Brimstone boy. Tragic case."

Austin slid her a glance before replying, "I'm sorry, doctor. I'm not at liberty to confirm. As I said, the family would like to keep it quiet."

The man gave a quick bow. "Of course, Dr. Smith. If there's anything you need while you're here—" He cast an unsavory glance in Jane's direction, and she wanted to throttle him. "Our facilities are at your service."

Evanshire returned the bow but kept his mouth grim. "Indeed."

The other man walked away, his shoes ringing on the stone corridor. They both stood utterly still long after it was safe to move. Jane sucked in air tainted with the salt of weeping stones before turning to Austin.

"That wasn't funny."

"I found it particularly adroit."

He didn't give her time to respond as he started down the

corridor to the intersecting hall that contained Dr. Seymour's cell. As they drew closer to the intersecting corridor, the sounds returned. Moans and chatter, the scraping of a chair against wood.

Without hesitation, Austin walked to Dr. Seymour's cell and began inserting keys in the lock even before Jane had caught up. The doctor scuttled from the darkness within the cell. She heard the rustle of fabric and the rasp of breath, but she could see nothing as the doctor's lamp was not lit.

Her heart clenched at the thought of just how badly he had been injured when he suddenly emerged from the darkness like a phantom, sweeping down to thrust his arms through the bars of the cell and clamp them onto Jane's hands.

"Go, child!" he screamed in a whisper. "He mustn't find you here!"

She recoiled at the sight of him. She couldn't have helped it even if she'd been warned. The right side of his face was mottled purple and yellow, the eye swollen shut. Dried blood crackled at his chin, and the hands with which he gripped her were painted with grime and crusty blood.

But in his one good eye she saw not fear for himself but concern for her. She returned his grip. "I swore to my grandfather to protect that which he loved, and I will be damned if anyone will stop me from doing so."

Austin stilled at her words, and she turned her head to stare at him. He only quietly smiled at her before inserting yet another key into the lock. There was a click, and the door swung open. The doctor let go of her and shrank into the shadows.

"No, no, no," he mumbled. "He'll catch you. He'll kill you."

Austin rushed in but stopped before grabbing the man. "We're taking you somewhere safe. We're going to find who did this to you."

The doctor shook his head. Jane heard it more than saw it in the dimness.

"No," he murmured again. "He'll kill you."

"Over my dead body," she muttered and reached up to her cap. She pulled it from her head to reveal a crimson velvet hat, entirely too chic for her but which perfectly suited her next character.

Austin reached up and pulled the cravat from his throat. Only it wasn't a cravat at all. The fabric unraveled into a plume of vibrant blue silk backed by supple black velvet. He handed it to her, and she swung the shawl over her shoulders, tying it with a snap. She pulled the guard's clothes from her apron and handed them to the doctor even as her other hand went to the ties of her apron.

"It's your turn now, Dr. Seymour."

He stared at the bundle, his one good eye wide. "You really mean to do this?"

She nodded as her apron loosened, and she swept it off, tucking it under the mattress of the bed. It would be discovered, but they would be long gone by then.

"Yes, we do," she said, straightening to fix her hat as any lady would.

The doctor stared at her and then at Austin.

"But how?" he finally stammered.

Austin pointed at the guard's clothes. "Straight through the front door."

* * *

"I MUST SAY, it isn't every day we get a gent from the likes of Kent." Dr. Seymour's laugh might have been brittle if anyone had been listening too closely.

The day was cloudy, which worked to their advantage. The front entrance of Bedlam was a grand affair with a robust portico and all leading down into a courtyard often riddled with visitors coming to and fro. Their best chance at escape was to get lost in the crowd, and the gray light was a boon for hiding Dr. Seymour's features.

The doctor walked in front of them, his arms swinging confidently for all the world as if he really were a guard at the hospital. The procured guard's hat sat low on his face to hide the evidence of his recent encounter, but he'd thrown his shoulders back to give himself a pronounced stomach, which Austin found quite remarkable as the man had appeared to be no more than skin and bones. Now he appeared for all the world like he enjoyed several pints a day.

"Well, it was fortuitous that my schedule allowed me to break away from my studies to attend to this matter. The family is rather an old acquaintance. It would have been remiss of me not to make an effort."

"Is that right, ye say?" the doctor called over his shoulder.

A couple passing on their right looked briefly at them before returning their gazes to the steps in front of them, their faces impassive.

"If only we'd had lovelier weather. I would have enjoyed a turn at the shops."

Austin slid a glance at Jane, who perched rather delicately on his arm as they descended the steps. He marveled for a moment how simply she'd transformed the maid's uniform into something so acceptable as a lady's gown. The silk of her shawl and the velvet of her hat were rich fabrics that anyone would spot right off as being the marks of a lady. And yet...it had been so easy to hide.

Pondering on Jane's intellect had him recalling their walk in the park and remembering dimmed the euphoria of their rescue. He hadn't had a chance to speak to her and set things straight, and he didn't know when next he would. But right then, he needed to get them out of there.

A carriage sat ready for them at the bottom of the steps, the sides emblazoned with the crest of a now defunct title. A nice touch Samuel had devised. Should anyone be watching, it would take some time for them to match the crest with the name and realize they'd been fooled. By then, they would be long gone from London.

His chest constricted with his inner torment, and he pressed ahead as the doctor opened the door to the carriage.

"Are you not staying in town then?" he asked.

Jane shook her head as he handed her up into the carriage. "Oh, I'm afraid not, my good man. Dr. Smith must return to his studies posthaste, you know."

The next several things happened so quickly even Austin wasn't sure all that transpired. A laborer passing by on the steps behind them collided with Austin at the same moment the doctor was replaced. The good man popped into the carriage as another man sprang outward. For concealed in the carriage was a real guard at Bedlam. Another man easily bribed into doing one's bidding, and at the exact moment of greatest confusion when the laborer struck Austin, the men switched places in the chaos.

"I say here!" Austin yelled just as the real guard gained his feet on the pavement.

"Oy! The 'elp is to use the rear entrances see!" the real guard yelled above them all.

Some more visitors were going up the steps just then, and a gentleman turned, raising his quizzing glass to them. He frowned ponderously before shaking his head and moving on.

"Begging yer pardon, sir," Samuel said under his laborer's garb. He leaned in just enough to whisper, "I'm trusting you to take care of my sister," before casting a wink at Austin and trundling off.

Austin tipped his hat to the guard and sprang into the

carriage. "Thank you, man. Good day to you." He snapped the door shut, and the carriage sprang into motion.

"I'm afraid you'll need to change again, Dr. Seymour." Jane was already pulling a sack from the bench. She extended a new set of clothes to the doctor. "I'm sorry for the lack of privacy, but I'm afraid the necessity of the situation precludes such comfort."

The doctor accepted this new bundle, but his eyes searched Jane's face. "I do not like this, young lady." He shook his head and doffed his guard's cap. "I do not like it at all. Richard was a good friend to me, and I can't see to putting his granddaughter in such harm's way. You have no idea—" He cut off though before saying anything else.

Austin leaned forward as the carriage rocked its way to the main thoroughfare. "That's just it, doctor. We do not know. You must tell us who it is that holds such power over you."

But even as he was speaking the doctor had begun to worry the new set of clothes in his hands, shaking his head, and then his whole body as he rocked back and forth with the carriage. Austin looked to Jane, but she, too, carefully watched the doctor, and for a moment, he wondered if they both thought they'd made a mistake. Perhaps the doctor was truly mad.

Jane slid forward on the bench then and took hold of the doctor's arms. "You mustn't say anything now." She kept her voice low, like a mother speaking to a frightened child. "We are taking you somewhere safe, and in time, we hope you may realize you can reveal your secret to us."

While he couldn't agree with her that time was not of the essence, Austin realized Jane's method was likely the only one to garner them the results they wished. Whomever it was that so haunted the doctor must be of truly significant danger for such an intelligent and respected man to have fallen so far.

The doctor stared at Jane now, but Austin's attention was pulled to the outside of the carriage. Traffic had picked up considerably, and he peered out the window to determine their location.

"I'm sorry, Dr. Seymour, but you'll need to change quickly," he said, returning his gaze to the poor man. "We'll be nearing the switching point soon."

Jane turned her head to the window before turning back to the doctor with a reassuring squeeze. "He's right, I'm afraid. Let's get you switched into your next costume, shall we?"

The doctor only stared at her, so Jane took the clothes back and began to unfold them.

"It will be a simple switch, you see?" Here she held up the large black garment that would conceal most of the doctor's person.

Something in the doctor's gaze shifted then at the sight of the garment, and for the first time since they'd encountered the man, a genuine smile began to play at his lips.

"I did always fancy a turn at playing God," he said and reached for the cassock.

CHAPTER 12

That was the last thing the doctor said for the next nearly twenty-four hours.

Jane sat across from him, her back having long gone numb from the constant tumble of the coach as they rounded another bend in the seemingly endless road.

They had switched to the coach on Marlborough. They'd stopped at Madame LeFevre's now defunct modiste shop and gone through the front doors as if they were patrons. They continued straight through the shop and out the back where an unmarked coach waited. She was only mildly surprised when Austin himself jumped up into the driver's seat.

That was the last she'd seen of him for the past interminable hours other than for the occasional stop to rest the horses and attend to the necessities. They hadn't stopped at a posting inn when darkness had fallen, and again, she was only mildly surprised. She knew Austin would press on until they reached wherever they were going. He still hadn't shared that knowledge with her, and she doubted he would.

The doctor, meanwhile, continued to trouble her.

While she knew he wasn't mad, she was beginning to

understand madness came in many degrees. And whomever the villain was behind all of this, he'd somehow managed to sink his claws into the doctor to an alarming degree. The poor man had not settled in the entire of the trip. His gaze remained locked on one window or another until Jane had drawn the curtains and told him to rest.

He hadn't done so, of course. Instead, he'd begun an odd little counting game on his fingers, traipsing up one hand and down the other. Jumping from digit to digit as if deciphering some complicated sums using only his hands. She would have liked Austin to witness it, but he'd hardly spoken to her except to ask after her well being and need for the necessary.

She once again could not believe she had been seduced by a rogue.

Except something wasn't quite right.

If Jane was anything, she was observant, a rather fortunate symptom of being a wallflower. And with every mile, she thought Austin grew more cross. His answers clipped, his manner short. His smile having all but vanished. It was a curious and unexpected turn of affairs for someone who had been so jovial since the day she had met him. Even after she had accused him of being a lying rogue. Something was wrong, and it grew worse with every mile they drew closer to their destination.

She wanted to ignore it, preferring to maintain the professional air she so ardently wished, but her natural need to fix and mend was getting the better of her.

If he had been a ledger, she would have set him to rights already.

It was then that she became aware of a murmuring in the carriage that had nothing to do with her own rampant thoughts.

The doctor had begun murmuring to himself as he

counted from finger to finger. She listened, trying to extricate words and even sentences from the nonsense the poor man uttered at his hands. By the fourth go round, she had parsed together several phrases, none of which made sense.

"The cat and mouse can play together." Next finger. "Mary's child, though. Oh, Mary's child." Next finger. "The wolf, the wolf. He's not as bad as he seems. And faithful John. Oh yes, John is faithful." Next finger. "But is it a wonderful musician or a good bargain? I like a good bargain." Two more fingers fell. "I like a good bargain, indeed." Another finger. "Ragamuffins and Rapunzel!" The last word shouted as he struck the next finger.

There was only one finger left, and she realized this one caused him the most trouble. He worried over it. Examined it. Muttered and muttered and muttered. She couldn't hear the words.

She mustn't startle him. She mustn't even let him know she was there. He'd fallen into a kind of trance. His words and fingers, the constant rocking of the carriage, it all swam together.

Slipping carefully along the bench, she bent forward, just out of the doctor's direct line of vision. So focused on that last finger, he didn't see her. She was close now. So close she could smell his stale breath.

He hadn't eaten. She'd offered him so much of what they'd brought. Cheese and bread and ham. Even cold pie. He'd refused it all with only a shake of his head.

But he hadn't needed food. He'd only needed this game he played.

Suddenly, the words collided in her ears. The words. She knew them. She knew what he was saying, although she couldn't quite place it. Somewhere, somewhere in her memory. It was right there. It was—

She sat up, not caring in the least if she broke his trance.

If she upset him at all.

She knew what he said.

He worried that last finger. "The Frog Prince, the Frog Prince, the Frog Prince. It was the Frog Prince all along. We didn't know it. We didn't know it. But I know. I know. He won't let me tell."

The game started over again.

It was several moments before she realized she was shaking, and her lungs struggled to take in air.

The Frog Prince

Beware the Frog Prince.

Without further thought, she reached up, her fingers fumbling on the ties of the curtain before finally getting it free. She raised the cloth and her hand went to the window. The glass was cool from the dark of night, and she leaned forward, pressing her cheek to it, her forehead.

Beware the Frog Prince.

But they didn't know who he was.

She straightened when the cold of the glass began to burn against her cheek, and she peered into the breaking dawn. It was that moment when the darkness of night was first penetrated with the encroaching sun, and although there was no sunrise yet, the world appeared strangely lighter.

Shapes turned into trees and shrubs. Colors defined into greens and blues.

The country swept past them as the coach rolled on, and she trembled, thinking of Austin out there through the whole of the night. She could only imagine how tired he grew. Tired and cold.

The coach tipped again as they rounded a curve, and the road fell away into cultivated fields. They must be coming into a hamlet for the fields on either side of the road until now had been untamed.

Trees were sparse now, and long rows of neatly tilled soil

traveled off until they disappeared at a point on the horizon. The sky continued to lighten, and she waited for that moment when the first orange rays would spill over the edge of the world, illuminating all one could see. It was a time of day with which she was very familiar as she often rose early at Eaton Park to oversee the seeding and harvesting. Tend to the teams fixing fences and seeing to livestock.

It was her most favorite time of day, really. The anticipation of it. The way the sun seemed to drench the world in its blessing for a brand new day.

And now, staring out the window, her senses calmed at the familiar sight.

Until she realized it was too familiar.

She straightened like a bolt, both hands flying to the sides of the windows.

The doctor hiccuped in his game, startled out of his trance and snapping around to face her.

They were in Kent.

More specifically, they must be near Maidenstone, the closest village to Eaton Park. She knew these fields. She knew these tress. She knew—

Dear God, where was Austin taking them?

They were passing the Holston estate. She could tell by the bent oaks along the drive. Next would be Featheringtone's Park. With the elms at the front gate. Yes, there they were!

She snapped back from the window to meet the doctor's astonished gaze.

"Everything is all right," she said far too quickly, ruining any assurance her words may have brought. "It's only just that I recognize where we are."

"You do not know where he's taking us?" The doctor's voice was gravelly as he'd not truly spoken, except for muttering at his fingers, in hours.

"It's a precaution," she said and something flickered in the doctor's eyes.

Once upon a time, Dr. Seymour had been an agent with the War Office, and that telltale flicker suggested he still found some thrill in the chase. But his body was not as young and vibrant as it once was, and she felt a stab of pain at the loss of his youth. Swept away with any possibility of something more by this villain known only as the Frog Prince.

She needed to wrest the villain's identity from the doctor. But not now. The past hours had proved just how fragile the doctor was. It would take time to draw out the truth, and time they did not have.

How long would it be before the Frog Prince found them?

Her gaze drifted back to the window, and just as she'd expected, the quiet edifices of Maidenstone sprang up along the road beside them.

The church with the broken bell, the pub with the sign that only hung on one hook so it swung perpetually lopsided in the wind. The blacksmith's shop, smoke already pouring from its chimney at this hour. The milliner's and the bakery. It was all just as she'd left it mere weeks ago when they'd left for London.

The coach slowed and turned off the main thoroughfare, climbing into the hills beyond the town. They were heading in the opposite direction of Eaton Park, and while she knew this was safer, she felt a pang of regret at not seeing the land that brought her so much joy.

The coach rolled on for another mile or so before it slowed again and turned neatly into a drive lined with towering elms. Their branches had just started to bud, and she knew in full summer, they would provide a magnificent canopy over the drive. It would be a sight to see.

She swallowed, hoping she wasn't still there come

summer. Her eyes darted to the doctor, and she hoped for his sake as well.

The drive swept up to a vista as they made the bend, and she could take in the whole of Maidenstone below. The curls of smoke from morning fires popping through the trees, and there. There in the distance was the first spill of sunbeams. Her heart clenched just as the coach rolled to a stop.

She turned about as the house, if there was one, must have been on the opposite side. She didn't wait for Austin but sprang for the door, wrenching it open as she stumbled outside.

The house was magnificent. Great slabs of cultivated stone made up the center part of a house that was rightly not a house but a monolithic mansion. Four stone columns supported the portico over the front door while two sweeping staircases rose up to meet it. On either side, the house spread in its majestic grandeur only to seep into the manicured gardens that surrounded it.

There was even a lake, for heaven's sake.

Jane stared until Austin touched her elbow. She started as she hadn't heard him jump down from the seat.

"Welcome to Peregrine Hall," he said.

Peregrine. But that was his family name. Her eyes drifted to the big house again before returning to face him, a smile already coming to her face. But the smile fell away as she registered the dark look on his features.

Austin's home brought him pain.

The thought left her breathless. She hadn't expected that. He had always appeared so happy as if nothing in the world could touch him. But that wasn't true. There was something dark in Austin's past.

Eaton Park meant so much to her. It grounded her. Gave her life. But for Austin, home didn't appear to hold such power.

"Austin," she said before she realized she was going to speak.

Something sparked in his eyes then, but it was quickly swamped by the foulness that had come upon him. "We must get inside."

She wanted to say more. She wanted to push the darkness from his shoulders. Shake him. Fix him.

But he wasn't hers to fix.

She nodded and turned to take the doctor's arm as he carefully stepped onto the drive. He winced, and she worried just how taxing the long journey had been for him.

"We must get you inside, and you must rest," she said.

The doctor did not object, and they climbed the stairs to the house just as the sun struck it full in the facade. She stood transfixed as the sun washed the stone in brilliance, and she wanted nothing more than to see the sunrise from within.

The thought was entirely too domestic, and a flash of pain seared it from her mind. She focused on getting the doctor up the last few steps just as the front door opened and a head peeked out.

It was a woman, soft with age and yet demanding in the set of her mouth, chin, and shoulders. She squinted at them until something seemed to register. The door slowly opened wider, and she took a hesitant step forward.

She was round, but pleasantly so, as one would expect from a caring nurse. She wore the uniform of a housekeeper, pristine if out of date as if her garb meant very little to her. Her white cap sat upon a crown of neat gray curls, and a small brooch sat pinned to her chest.

She lifted a hand to shade her eyes from the sun just as Austin said, "I apologize for not giving you notice, Mrs. Rowling. I have brought guests as well, which is entirely inexcusable, but you see, the matter was of some delicacy."

The woman's stern mouth trembled and for an odd

moment, Jane feared the woman would burst into tears.

That was until she said, "Puddles? Is that you?"

* * *

IT WAS as if he hadn't left at all.

The gloomy face of Peregrine Hall had struck him as soon as he'd crested the hill of the drive. It's imposing face just as gray and dark as it had been the day he'd left. The cold drive had crunched under the wheels of the carriage, and he'd tasted wood smoke on the air. Mrs. Rowling already had the house up and stirring, preparing for the day.

He hadn't planned to arrive at dawn, but they'd made good time on the road, and he didn't think they'd been followed. He'd been careful to switch routes after leaving the city proper, heading north only to double back along a less well-traveled route to the south. They'd made Rochester by night's fall, and he'd known he could press on until Maidenstone.

It wasn't even as if the cold night bothered him. The thought of where the horses headed, what lay at the end of the road, all of it, had encased him in some bizarrely numb existence. Once resolved to it, he'd only wanted to arrive. Get it over with.

His homecoming.

He wasn't ready for a rumpled Jane to emerge from the coach when she had. God, the only thing he'd thought to say was to welcome her to Peregrine Hall. What an idiot, he was. He'd just been deadened to it all, and the sight of her...it had wrestled something loose inside of him. Only not enough, and he'd sounded inane.

Then there was Mrs. Rowling.

She hadn't changed. Not a bit. There might have been more lines around her eyes and mouth, but as she'd always had thick gray hair since he was a child, she appeared to have not suffered the passage of time. It was the same warm, brown eyes that had shone on him in his agony. The same doughy bosom to which he'd clung when—

Without bidding it, his head turned toward the lake. Its inky surface glistened like a sheet of ice this morning, but he knew it not to be frozen. It was too late in the spring for that. Its murky depths were awake. Ready.

He turned away, taking Jane's elbow as he led her to the door. The way was slow as Jane held up the doctor, whom now appeared slightly the worse for wear since they'd smuggled him from Bedlam.

The bruises along his face were turning more yellow and green now, and he walked with a decided limp as if favoring his right hip. They needed to get him to a proper bed. Jane had said he wouldn't eat the food they'd packed. He'd need tea and at least bread then, as well. He mustn't give up now they were so close to unmasking the villain.

"Is that you, Puddles? Is it really?" Mrs. Rowling's voice was even the same. Lilting and pure, reminding him of the tumble of the brook that ran the length of the property to the southwest.

Again his head turned involuntarily, and his gaze fastened on the spot through the trees where he'd run as a boy to the quiet solitude of the brook. Deep into the woods. Far enough away that he couldn't hear the yelling.

He tried a smile but found it wouldn't come as easily as he had wished it would for the woman who had raised him when there had been no one else.

"Mrs. Rowling, it is truly I, and I'm afraid we mustn't tarry on the stoop like this. My companions are in serious trouble, and I wish there had been some other recourse than to bring this danger to your door." He glanced at Jane to find her watching the housekeeper.

Mrs. Rowling snapped her jaw shut and reached for Dr. Seymour. "You're not to apologize for coming to your own home, Puddles. Inside with you then, and we'll see about tea and bread. Hurry now." She took the bulk of Dr. Seymour from Jane, and Austin didn't miss the sigh that escaped the poor man's lips as he leaned into Mrs. Rowling's warm embrace.

Austin had sighed like that many a time in his youth and knew just exactly the kind of comfort the doctor drew.

He grasped Jane's elbow more firmly and ushered her through the expansive double doors at the entrance. The dimness of the foyer shrouded them at once, and he was oddly grateful to have the mocking glare of the sun pushed away. But the space inside had him pausing, and Jane made a noise. He'd forgotten he held her elbow, and he must have squeezed it without knowing when he saw his childhood home once more.

The front hall was just as it'd been we he'd left. The walls rose on each side to a towering height as the double-floored entry melted into the imposing twin staircase that flanked either side. Dripping in plush, red carpet it had beckoned the guests every spring for the country ball his mother would host for the local gentry. The marble of the floors resounded under Mrs. Rowling's footsteps, and the air sparked with the scent of lemons.

"This is painful for you."

His head snapped around as once again he'd forgotten Jane was there. The look of utter concern on her face had his knees buckling, and he released her arm, afraid to touch her any longer. But she advanced on him.

"You haven't been here in quite some time, have you?" She went on. "There must be a reason why. A man doesn't just leave his home for no cause." She paused to look back the way they'd came, but a maid had closed the door behind them. She regarded the paneling of the doors, but Austin knew she was seeing something else. Something beyond those doors.

And when she looked back at him with wetness staining her eyes, he knew he was right. Just beyond those doors was Eaton Park. Her beloved Eaton Park.

She knew only too well the attachment one could derive from a place that was once home. Only for her, it still was.

As he looked about him, at the gold trim of the balustrades, the satin imprints of the red wallpaper, he felt nothing. Nothing except the haunting shadows of what once was.

"Come," he said, choosing not to acknowledge Jane's insight. "We must get food and rest."

He followed Mrs. Rowling's retreating figure into the center of the house where once again, the ceiling disappeared to rise up through the heart of the mansion. Here a much more modest staircase wound itself around a central shaft where balconies from every floor to the top let out into the open space. He caught up with Mrs. Rowling just as someone else did.

"Mary." He spoke the name before he thought better of it.

It was hard not to when suddenly faced with the grown version of one of his childhood friends. Only then they'd just been children. Now, he was a marquess, and she was—

He took a quick survey of her dress to find a uniform complete with apron. His gaze snapped to her clear, green eyes. She was now a servant here at Peregrine Hall.

Mary curtsied. "Your lordship."

His gut twisted. Mary shouldn't curtsy to him.

"This is my girl, Mary, Dr. Seymour. Her mother was a healer, and she'll take right good care of you." Mrs. Rowling turned to Mary. "Take him to the east suite. I'll have a tray sent up at once.

He stared, he knew he did, but he couldn't stop himself. It was the same Mary only...taller. Her yellow hair was tied into an intricate knot now instead of messy braids, and no dirt smudged her brow but it was the same Mary.

She dipped a bow to him. "It's nice to see you, Marquess."

No, no, that wasn't right. He was Austin and she was Mary, and they'd meet at the brook to catch tadpoles. She straightened from her bow before turning.

"Welcome to Peregrine Hall," Mary said, dipping into another crusty.

Jane.

Jane stood beside him. He should make introductions. It was only proper.

Jane reached out a hand and took Mary's. "It's Miss Jane Black. No need for ceremony."

Mary smiled hesitantly. "We don't have much company around here. It's nice to test out my social skills." She gave Jane a playful wink.

And Jane laughed, the sound so airy and free. "I know better than you can imagine. Would you mind coming to fetch me when you have the doctor settled? I shan't like him to be alone."

Mary's brow furrowed. "Of course, miss. I'll have one of the girls sit with him at all times." She took the doctor onto her arm. "Come along then, sir. We've a lovely room for you. You look like you've had a time of it. No need to worry any longer. I'll get you fixed up right quick. My mum was the healer in these parts when Dr. Struthers couldn't make it in time. She's taught me everything I know." Her voice faded as the pair climbed the stairs.

"She married Ben, you know." He started at Mrs. Rowling's voice. She laughed at his expression, chagrinned. "I always suspected you didn't read my letters, but I guess that confirms it."

Mary. Married to Ben. But Ben…

Ben had taught them how to string a good fishing line. How to find the wild blueberries that grew along the banks of the brook. How to—

"He's the game keeper here now. Does a splendid job of it." Mrs. Rowling picked up her skirts. "Let's get you fed now, and I suspect you'll need a lie down. I've sent the maids to make up the master suites. You'll—"

"Oh, it's not like that, Mrs. Rowling," Jane spoke up. No, he should have been the one to explain. Jane needn't be burdened with this. "Evanshire and I are partners on a mission for the Metropolitan Police Force. We're here in hiding until the culprit at hand can be smoked out and captured. I'll only be taking a guest room, thank you."

A guest room? No, she was…what was she?

His.

He drew himself to look at her and only found what he'd expected. Nothing at all. Her expression rested completely neutral.

She thought him a seducing rogue.

"Oh, I beg your pardon. You're not—" Mrs. Rowling faltered when he had never known her to before. Her eyes moved between him and Jane, before she said, "That is I thought when Puddles said you were in trouble that it was—"

"She is not with child. At least not my child." The words came out so forcefully he was surprised Mrs. Rowling did not recoil in shock. But he didn't want her to assume the wrong impression of Jane. Not his Jane.

He looked to her then. He just needed to assure himself he'd not slighted her, but instead he found her standing not entirely unlike she'd been that day in the park.

She had raised her chin, and her eyes flashed. He was making it worse.

"I see," Mrs. Rowling said. "Well, you'll still want tea then.

Cook makes the most luscious bread. It looks like you could use a slice or two." Mrs. Rowling took Jane's hand. "A mission for the Metropolitan Police Force. Well, I'm not surprised. I always anticipated Puddles would seek out danger when he left here."

Jane tugged at Mrs. Rowling's hand. It was all as if he were watching some sort of play, and he wasn't a part of the cast but merely an observer.

"Puddles?" Jane asked.

Mrs. Rowling patted her hand. "He used to like to jump in them. Every time it rained, he'd come scampering into the kitchens and tug on my skirts to take him into the yard. He'd spend ages jumping from one puddle to the next. Was always worried he'd catch his death, but he never did. He was a strong lad." She eyed him. "He's turned into a strong man, it seems." She made a tsking noise and turned back the way they were headed. "And here I missed all of it."

"You took him into the yard to play as a child? Didn't his mother wish to do that?"

The question was so innocent, and now that he'd encountered the warm bond of the Black family, he knew only too well why Jane had asked it. But her words cut directly to his heart like nothing else could.

His mother.

No, his mother hadn't wanted to be the one to play with him. It just wasn't done.

Mrs. Rowling slid him a glance, her eyes tense, before she reached some sort of decision and patted Jane's hand again.

"Oh, it wasn't like that as such," she said. "I do hope the weather holds so you might see the gardens. We have the loveliest roses. Do you like roses, my dear?"

Mrs. Rowling prattled the entire way to the breakfast room while Austin could only maintain his stony silence.

CHAPTER 13

"I will kill her myself when she gets back. She's ruined everything." Emily heaved, wrenching herself over into Harlow's lap as though she were a puppet whose master had suddenly let go of her strings. "You can't imagine, Harlow, my love. It's so unfair."

He smelled. A lot. Like stale tobacco and liver oil. But that was why she pressed her lavender scented handkerchief to her nose. She always kept extras in her reticule when she knew she was to meet Harlow in the park. Old men certainly went bad like food, and the stench was far too much.

Except—

Lady Emily, the Duchess of Merritt.

Oh yes, that was quite worth the odor of liver oil.

"There, there, my dear," Harlow patted her back in blocky slaps, his bony, arthritic hands striking her spine so she had to adjust her position. "I'm sure it's not all that bad."

When she was sure a few tears had stained her cheeks, she straightened and peered at him, allowing her lip to tremble to just the right degree. "But it is, don't you see?" She dabbed at her eyes without actually mopping up any of the tears. It was a great effect, and one she'd practiced to some length. It drew attention to how wide and beautiful her eyes appeared when damp with tears. "We're not accepting any invitations now. None." She allowed a sob to catch in her chest. "I shan't be partaking in the rest of the season. The whole season, Harlow." Another sob.

Harlow patted her hand. "Oh, my love, that is inconceivable! How dare they subject you to such treatment? It's not as if your cousin's actions should cause recompense to be paid on you."

She squeezed his hand in return. "Oh, my darling, I knew you would understand. If only someone would rescue me from the clutches of this family. Then I could live the life I deserve." She let her eyelashes flutter, and as they were wet with tears, she knew the effect was mesmerizing.

Only Harlow didn't seem to notice. "But surely you know where your cousin has gone. Perhaps you can write her a letter so she's aware of the heinous consequences of her actions."

This man truly was daft. She eyed him, wondering if she had misjudged the situation. She thought snaring an old one would be easy. Obtain the title and wait for him to drop over dead. Judging by the decaying crepe of his skin along his jowls and that fetid smell, it shouldn't be much longer. Why wouldn't he simply offer marriage already? She couldn't make it any clearer that she was amenable to his suit.

"That's just it. I don't know where she's gone. The family is being so secretive about it. Something about a doctor or something and needing to get away somewhere safe. It's all nonsense. And why does Jane need to be involved? Can't they see what this has done to me?" She bit the inside of her cheek, and a fresh torrent of tears sprang to her eyes.

But Harlow didn't react. In fact, she wasn't sure he saw her any longer. His eyes had gone cold and flat, and his mouth had thinned to a near transparent line. Carefully, she pulled her hands back from his.

"Harlow, my love, did you hear me?" She mewled a little for effect.

These old ones. One never could tell where their mood was going to shift.

He blinked, and his eyes focused on her again. "There was something about a doctor. How strange. Did the doctor have a name?"

Why in God's name did the doctor matter?

She lifted a single shoulder coquettishly. "I don't know, my darling. He might have, but what does his name matter? It's all—"

He grabbed her so quickly she didn't have time to pull out of his reach. She steeled herself, forcing her heart to slow and her mind to concentrate. These old ones were dangerous. They were just unpredictable, and a girl had to understand how to handle herself. That was all.

"Harlow, you're—"

"What was the doctor's name, Emily? You must tell me." He spit when he said the words. How utterly distasteful. She really hoped the end was near for him because being his wife was looking to be less and less pleasant.

"Of course, he had a name, but I didn't care to learn it. It meant nothing to me, and the season is already ruined and—"

He shook her. The stupid, old man shook her. "You must have heard the name. You must have heard where they were going. Where was it?"

This was entirely too much. There were plenty of dukes out there. Even old ones. Drat. She'd wasted so much time cultivating this prospect, and just look where it had gotten her.

She smiled, plumping her lips and tilting her head to appear the perfect confection. "Harlow, dear, I think you're overwrought. Perhaps this is too much for you." She patted his hand where he gripped her. God, his grip was getting entirely too tight. The nerve of the man. "I think it's best we say adieu."

He shook her again, but this time it was so hard her teeth rattled. Well, that was entirely enough. Without hesitation, she threw up her hand, palm out, and connected solidly with his nose. His head snapped back, blood spurted forth like a sick kind of waterfall. She was already on her feet and to the other side of the clearing before Harlow stood, sputtering and madly trying to stem the flow of blood from his nose.

"You need a rest, my dear," she said and straightened her cuffs. "Good day, Your Grace." She passed through the trees and into the park proper, regretting ever having wasted so much time on the man.

CHAPTER 14

Dr. Seymour padded his toast with eggs before taking a bite. He also preferred coffee in the morning instead of tea. With a drop of milk, of course. And he nibbled with his front teeth more than chewed. But at least he was eating.

This was what Jane told herself on the third morning after they had arrived at Peregrine Hall. She had been carefully scrutinizing the doctor's eating, bathing, and sleeping habits since they'd arrived. He'd bathed nearly upon their arrival, but she thought this had more to do with Mary's gentle prodding and a driving desire to be rid of the stench of Bedlam.

Mary proved quite adept at healing and soon had the doctor bandaged from top to bottom in salves and creams and stuffed into bed with a warmer. This then had brought on a near dead sleep for the next day and a half.

Jane sat next to him, unable to leave his side for a moment even though a prickling curiosity had started to grow inside her. With every glimpse through an open door, with every step down a new corridor, her mind wandered.

So this was where Austin had spent his childhood.

She didn't know why she hadn't thought of it earlier. Why it never perplexed her so. That Austin might have come from something. But now his past lay all around her, and questions begged to be answered.

Who was Mary really? Why had he had such a strong reaction to seeing the woman?

And Puddles. Apprehension always stole over her when she thought of the pet name the housekeeper had given a young Austin. Why had it been a servant to place such devotion on the small boy and not his own mother?

But her vow kept her beside the doctor, watching him in his sleep. So still. So quiet, she kept checking to see that he drew breath.

Until he woke with a start in the evening of their second day at Peregrine Hall. He sat straight up in bed and stared at her, proclaiming, "Bethany! He knows!"

His shout had brought Mary and Mrs. Rowling, but Austin was notably absent.

Not that she cared. Especially after his careless remark about her condition (or lack thereof) upon their arrival.

No, she was not with child, and she would certainly not be with his child.

The thought sent a spike of pain through her chest, but she was getting better at ignoring it.

They settled the doctor back into bed with assurances that no one knew anything, and he was not in harm's way any longer. He gave up his struggle all too quickly for her liking and let the pillows engulf him once more.

Mrs. Rowling coerced him into some tea and broth, but he refused all else. After only a few sips of each, he fell asleep again. But this sleep was not like the healing slumber from before. This was a fitful sleep, and it was all Jane could do to keep him abed through the night.

It was nearly eleven when Mary came one last time to check on them both and found Jane holding the doctor up where he'd tried to tumble from the bed. He muttered in his sleep, and it was the same muttering from the carriage.

"Mary's child, though. Oh, Mary's child. The wolf, the wolf. He's not as bad as he seems. And faithful John. Oh yes, John is faithful. But is it a wonderful musician or a good bargain? I like a good bargain. I like a good bargain, indeed. Ragamuffins and Rapunzel!"

With Mary's help, they were able to get him back onto the bed. Mary cast a questioning glance at Jane, but all Jane could do was shrug. She didn't know of what the doctor spoke any more than Mary did. And then Mary did the strangest thing.

She sat down. She pulled a chair to the opposite side of the doctor's bed and sat.

"I've seen this a time or two with Mum," she said as if they were speaking of knitting patterns. "They are always worse the second day. She says it's the body's way of telling everyone it's healing. Leave it alone. You know when you have a cut or a scrape, and it begins to heal?" She peered at Jane as if expecting an answer, so Jane nodded, hoping that was enough. "It's like that. Like a healing scrape begins to itch, a healing body begins to twitch." She worried her lip as she shook her head at the doctor. "I think this poor man has a great deal of healing to do."

She settled back in the chair for all the world as if she intended to stay the night.

And she had.

Every time the demons became too much for the doctor, Mary had been there to help keep them back and the doctor abed. Mary held the doctor's head while Jane tried to spoon water through his cracked lips. Mary had refilled the bed warmer with hot coals while Jane had washed the doctor's face and neck.

And Mary had talked. She spoke of Peregrine Hall and her husband, Ben. She told stories of Austin and them as children, running wild across the acres of the estate to a brook on the far boundary of the property.

"Oh, it was such a beautiful time of our lives." A soft smile came to her features. Mary was rather beautiful, but not in a way that made Jane aware of her own plainness. It was more in the way that Lizzie was beautiful. "You know, you spend the whole of your childhood wishing you were big. Prancing around like a lady or a gentleman. Settling down to business of the manor." She shook her head, the soft smile still at her lips. "And then you're grown, and all you wish is to be that carefree child once more. Just once more." She looked to Jane then, a golden warmth in her green eyes. "Do you have memories like that? Oh, you must, having grown up at Eaton Park."

Jane started, but Mary quelled her with a laugh. "You didn't think we'd recognize you here? Eaton Park isn't so far, and tales of the smart Miss Jane Black travel readily in these parts." Mary leaned closer across the bed. "Is it true you can do sums and such so as to keep the ledgers for your father's estate?"

Jane opened her mouth, but sound did not emerge. In fact, her face flushed. She could feel the heat of it burning in her cheeks, and she hoped the dim light of the lamps would prevent Mary from seeing it.

"Yes, I do keep the ledgers for my father's estate," she finally said.

Mary waved a hand at her. "Oh, you're a modest one. Mrs. Rowling and I said as much as soon as we saw you."

They had spoken of her? Without her knowledge? Jane swallowed. "Is that so?"

Mary nodded and leaned back in the chair as if settling in for quite a chat.

"Oh, yes." She paused as if to change track in thought. "Well, actually, we'd rightly hoped you were the new marchioness come to Peregrine Hall to set up your home." Her face crumpled dramatically. "We were right sorry to hear you weren't. Mrs. Rowling and I, we liked you straight away." She raised a single eyebrow, and a playful smile tripped across her lips. "Are we sure there's no possibility of that? You know, in future? When this business with the Metropolitan Police is all over, of course."

Mary's face was so alight with hope, Jane felt the very breath squeezed from her lungs. There was no point in it really. She'd only let herself believe for a very small space of time that Austin should have any interest in her beyond the mission while she'd spent the whole of her life believing exactly the opposite. That no man could take an interest in a plain girl with such a tenuous connection on society and far too much intelligence.

Yet it wrenched anew to have to let Mary down. Jane shook her head. "I'm sorry, but there just isn't."

Mary leaned forward again, her elbows on her knees as her expression changed to one dangerously close to curiosity. "Is it him?"

The question was so blunt Jane's mouth opened again without sound. She gurgled in quite an unladylike manner before finding any words at all. "I beg your pardon?"

"It is him," Mary said with some satisfaction as she sat back and pressed her opened palms to her nose. "The idiot. Mrs. Rowling and I suspected as much. He can't recognize a wonderful thing when it practically sits in front of him." Here she threw her hands at Jane as if encompassing the situation. "I blame his mother for this. Sure as the day is long, I blame her."

As Mary shook her head, a faint echo of something

stirred in Jane's chest. Not hope. She was done with that. It was more curiosity and a measure of concern.

Regardless of how he felt about her, Austin was still her brother's closest friend. And if she had proven anything in her life, it was her loyalty to those who fell under the Black family's protection.

"His mother?" Jane finally dared to ask. This was the second time his mother had come into conversation since they'd arrived and yet, in the time she'd known him, Austin had not once spoken of family.

Mary frowned, and a line appeared between her eyes. "It's a terrible thing, and I'm sure he's never spoken of it to you."

Jane shook her head as Mary seemed to require a response.

"It's not my story to tell, I'm afraid, but I can at least relay enough so as you have the facts of the matter." Mary put her elbows on the arms of her chair and steepled her fingers. "His mother met an unfortunate end when he was all of thirteen." She paused, and Jane was glad as she absorbed this information. "It was not entirely unexpected, but he was never quite the same after it happened."

"It was not unexpected?" Jane puzzled over this. "Was she ill?"

Mary's frown deepened. "I'm sorry to say she wasn't."

The words were spoken so quietly, so gravely, Jane thought she'd misheard. But if she wasn't ill and her death was not unexpected then—

"Oh, God." The words came out before Jane realized she'd have such a reaction.

"Precisely. God rest her soul," Mary whispered, and then her eyes drifted to the doctor. "Austin has been saving people ever since."

Mary's last words settled over Jane like a peculiar blanket.

Austin. Saving people?

He had chosen to be a soldier when custom dictated he needn't have. She remembered the hardness of his face in the carriage when she declared her intent to continue on this mission. The unyielding harshness in his eyes when he'd told her he was going with her.

Jane swallowed. "I suppose that makes sense." She paused, considered. "Was his father…" She didn't know how to finish the sentence, but Mary seemed to understand.

She waved a hand again and scoffed. "The previous marquess was not endeared to his family as such. It wasn't that he was cruel. It was just—" Mary seemed to weigh her words. "It was just how he'd been brought up himself, you know? I think it was hard on him. The way things were after the marchioness…did what she did." Mary stumbled over the last words as she kept herself from revealing another's secret even if Jane had already figured it out. "And Austin didn't help the situation. Never was there a more rebellious young man. Not even my Ben was so rash." Mary gave a soft laugh. "Oh, I suppose I must call him Evanshire now. As he's the marquess and all." Another soft laugh and a shake of her head. "It seems so odd to think it. He was always just Austin when we were little." Mary raised her gaze to Jane then. "It's odd, isn't it? How society has a way of disrupting the natural order of things?"

Jane thought of her mother's tutelage when it came to being a maid and smiled. "My family isn't so good at adhering to society's rules."

The night had passed quickly then with Mary sharing stories of their youth. Of a playful, young Austin before he'd been weighed down by events he could not have foreseen. Although curiosity poked at her, Jane had not pressed Mary on the circumstances of the marchioness's suicide. It wasn't her place.

And it never would be.

As Jane watched the doctor take another bite of eggs, she wondered how long it would be before the villain was roused out of hiding. Before they could return to London. She hesitated in her thoughts. She was so close to Eaton Park. And perhaps, by the time this was over, she needn't return to London at all. She felt quite certain that she'd ruined Emily's season beyond repair, and what was the point in prolonging the matter?

Mrs. Rowling opened a window behind them, and the smell of freshly turned earth cascaded over her at precisely that moment. Jane sat up in her chair and poured herself another cup of tea.

"I think we'll try a walk today, Dr. Seymour."

The doctor only moved his eyes to her but continued his rhythmic tiny bites.

She smiled, hoping to coax a similar expression in return. "The Kent air is just the perfect thing for healing."

He didn't smile, and she couldn't admit the doctor wasn't the only one in need of that Kent air.

* * *

THEY ENCOUNTERED Mrs. Rowling again when they reached the foyer.

"Oh, having a turn about the grounds, are you?" she said without missing a moment in directing a pair of maids in moving what appeared to be a marble bust in an attempt to clean underneath it. "Will his lordship be joining you?"

Jane paused but kept a steady hand under the doctor's elbow. She had seen the same pair of maids making up their rooms when they'd first arrived and then again at every meal they had taken in the small breakfast room.

It wasn't her place to ask but something tickled at the

back of her mind, and she asked anyway. "Mrs. Rowling, do you not have footmen to employ in such heavy lifting?"

The housekeeper paused to give Jane her full attention. "Footmen?" Her brow folded in puzzlement. "Oh, my dear. I had forgotten for a moment your prowess with matters of a domestic nature." A smile came to her face now, and she seemed to warm to the topic. "We don't have footmen on staff, as it were. With his lordship's preference for his London home, it is rather unnecessary to maintain a full staff here at the hall."

"But what if footmen are required?" Surely a house of this size could not rely on a staff made up of so few persons.

Mrs. Rowling shook her head. "When the need arises, we hire men from the village. There is always someone willing to perform a task for a shilling or two."

It was a rather odd arrangement but not entirely unheard of in the realm of keeping country estates. She tucked the piece of information away and adjusted her hold on the doctor, remembering Mrs. Rowling had asked a question of her.

"I'm afraid I'm unaware of his lordship's current situation. I have not been privileged with his company these past few days," she said.

Mrs. Rowling's face became guarded so quickly it was like the sky turning black before a late summer storm. "He hasn't been in the doctor's sick room?"

Jane shook her head as the doctor took a very small step closer to her side. She eyed him, and he returned her look with one of his own. It was the most he had communicated directly to her in three days, and she felt a small boost of hope.

"He has not been in the sick room with us, I'm afraid. Did he indicate he would be?" Jane knew perfectly well the marquess had indicated as such, and the fact that he had not been present in three days suggested only one thing.

He was hiding.

Thinking it, she felt a wave of sadness wash over her, but then, she likely would have tucked herself away with a ledger if faced with the same pain returning home had obviously caused him.

The realization did not have the same effect on Mrs. Rowling as the woman spun neatly on her heel and headed for the stairs without a word in parting. Instead, she gave out many words, muttering under her breath as she went.

Jane managed to catch, "a gentleman of the realm" and "like a scared, little boy in short pants" and her favorite "box his ears for this."

She smiled at Mrs. Rowling's motherly concern for her employer, but at the same time felt that same twinge of sadness. It should have been his mother going after Austin. Not the help.

She pushed away thoughts of the marquess and turned to the matter at hand. Namely, the doctor.

"Shall we?" she asked, gesturing to the door.

The man came readily enough with her, and she understood even he wished to have a spot of fresh air, regardless of the torment that must be eating him up inside.

Spring had come to Kent, and it hit her full in the face as she stepped out onto the portico. The air was full with the smell of turned soil and the sound of birds calling to one another as new nests were built. The trees along the drive had begun to bud in earnest, and even the grass surrounding the lake had erupted in a robust green to suggest the cold of winter would not dare to return.

She eased the doctor down the front steps until their feet crunched gravel.

"Do you suppose we should take a turn about the lake?"

She raised a hand to her forehead to shield her eyes from the midday sun as the sound of voices in the distance drew her attention.

The landscape was sparse here, and it was evident the land had been cleared on the other side of the water where a sweeping knoll spread down into the valley, seeming to reach all the way to the hamlet of Maidenstone. She realized with a jolt their proximity to Eaton Park and wondered suddenly how her path had not crossed with the marquess's before now. But at the same time, she remembered Mrs. Rowling's reaction to their appearance and doubted if Austin had been in residence much in the past ten years or more.

Her eyes finally discovered the source of the voices at the same time the doctor stepped away from her. There was a team of men at the very bottom of the hill, surrounding a newly turned field. She couldn't quite make out what they were doing, but she didn't miss the telltale sign of dirt shifting. She wanted to learn more, but the doctor had wandered away from her by then.

She forced her eyes away from the men at work to find the doctor had reached the small lake already. For a man so beaten just days previous, he appeared awfully spritely just then. They'd had to find clothes for him to wear when they'd arrived at Peregrine Hall and luckily, Mary had procured something from one her younger brothers. Close, but not perfect, and the doctor waddled a little with the overly baggy trousers.

But when he reached the lake, he simply stopped, sitting down directly onto the grass. She went after him and stooped to ensure he was all right.

"How are you feeling, Dr. Seymour?" She had asked him the same question so many times over the past few days, she no longer expected an answer. But to her surprise, he gave one.

"Bethany," he said. The word was spoken like an oath, scared and quiet.

Jane sat at once, rounding her shoulders so she was at eye level with the doctor.

"Your wife has been taken into Lofton House. She's safe." It had been her brother's idea to get Mrs. Seymour. It had not been an invitation, and in fact, it had been a rather frightening interlude for the woman.

They had made it look like a horrible kidnapping.

Samuel, her uncle Alec, and her father had snatched the woman in the middle of the night. They'd done a good job of smashing up the place to make it look authentic. According to Samuel, it could be fairly certain none of the staff would carry on at the house or perhaps in service at all after the incident.

"She's with my grandmother, Lady Jane," she went on, and for a flash, something appeared in the doctor's eyes.

"Jane." This word was even more of a whisper, but it was so sure, so certain, as if a memory had just shifted to the very front of his mind. "Bethany and Jane." He smiled but it was more of a twisting of the whiskers about his cheeks. The doctor needed a shave. She hadn't thought of that. If Austin had been in the sick room as he had claimed he was, perhaps that would have been seen to.

She glanced back at the hall, wondering if Mrs. Rowling had found her quarry.

"Richard knew."

The words had her snapping her attention back to Dr. Seymour, but she didn't dare utter a single word. The doctor sat, transfixed by the surface of the water, his eyes behind his spectacles searching and searching but not for something that sat before him. Not wanting to break the trance, she sat as still as possible, the wind ruffling her fringe beneath the edge of her bonnet.

The doctor's lips moved, but no sound emerged. Still she waited. Waited.

A bird called. The voices of the men down the hill traveled up to them.

Still she waited.

Finally, Dr. Seymour looked at her. "I know what he's done. I can't prove it though." His tone was filled with such sadness. Such despair.

She reached out, closed her hand over his. "You needn't worry about that. It's my brother's job to find the evidence. He needs only to know where to look."

His lips moved again without sound, but she knew this time he wasn't trying to speak. It was more of a helpless gesture. She squeezed his hand again.

"You think this villain is stronger than the Black family?" She asked the question with a smile, hoping to lighten the mood, but the doctor grew more forlorn.

"Richard. My friend." He spoke the words even as his gaze drifted away, and she knew she'd lost him again.

She squeezed his hand one more time and stood. He didn't notice when she walked away. She looked back twice as she rounded the lake, but he continued to sit exactly where she'd left him, his lips moving with no sound coming out.

Her shoulders sagged with the weight of it, but she wouldn't let the temporary defeat swamp her. This was going to take time. She knew that. There had been so many years of torment and fear. It would not be undone in a day.

She picked up her head and drank in the sight of the Kent countryside. Soaked in the neat rows of turned fields. The dipping valleys and rolling hills. So lush now in early spring.

She'd missed this. For the past two years, they had gone to town at the turn of March. How she'd hated leaving just when the earth was crawling back to life. Just as everything gave that final heave through the cold and thawed, shaking loose the last clutches of winter.

She stopped at the brink of the hill and put her hands to her hips in order to expand her chest, and she drew the deepest breath she'd had in a very long time.

The mission was not over. She didn't even know when she would realize it was. But for now, she was home.

She peered over her shoulder at Peregrine Hall.

Well, almost home.

Shouts from down below drew her attention again. One of the work party, a tall gent with broad shoulders gestured wildly at a bunch on the east side of the field, pantomiming digging.

Whatever was going on down there, it seemed to not be progressing well.

She took a step forward and stopped.

This wasn't her place. It wasn't Eaton Park, and her father was not here to give her leave to intervene. She'd just stay where she was. Observe but not interrogate. Peregrine Hall had nothing to do with her. It was Austin's duty after all.

But Austin was hiding.

Hadn't even been here in years.

The tall gentleman began to shout now and gesticulate with a good degree of force. For a frightening moment, she expected actual violence. But then the man threw up his hands and marched off down the drive to where a cart had been stopped along the line of trees.

She turned her head and peered back up at the hall. It sat much as it had that first morning they'd arrived only now the front lay in shadow as the midday sun was beginning to fade.

Austin really was hiding. Of that she was certain.

She looked back down the hill. The tall gentleman puttered around the cart, and the work crew had ceased even pretending to dig. She dropped her arms.

This may not be her home, but it was someone's home.

She made her way down the rest of the hill, her feet sinking slightly in the squishy soil. She was glad she'd had the foresight to pack her walking boots in her trunk. She hadn't known where they were going, but she liked to be prepared for anything.

As she drew nearer, she realized the men were digging trenches along the boundaries of the field. They were not overly deep but they were well-sculpted, suggesting they might be used for irrigation. She approached the man at the cart.

"Excuse me."

The poor man started and looked about as if he'd been touched by a ghost.

"I'm very sorry," she went on. "I don't mean to disturb."

The man swung about and nearly collided with her. She stepped back quickly and wrenched her neck up as the man was a great deal taller than he'd first appeared from a distance. She was met with a craggy face, weather beaten and grooved, but his eyes were youthful and a smile came to his lips. Or rather, she thought it was a smile, but his beard was so generous, she couldn't be sure.

"You must be the lady whose come to the house!" His tone was deep and warm.

Her stomach rolled at the term *lady,* but she pressed a return smile to her lips. "I'm afraid it's just miss. Miss Jane Black."

The man's smile seemed to grow wider now and threatened to shoot his eyes clean of his face for the mirth in them. "I thought as much. I am certainly glad to see you."

She stilled. What was this?

He gestured behind her to the work crew that was doing everything except working.

"I don't know a thing about these irrigation ditches, and

these ones is to be put in before the seedings happen. I don't see as how we're going to make it in time." He took off his cap and swiped a sleeve along his brow.

She looked between him and the half-dug ditch. "I do beg your pardon, but I don't truly understand what's going on here."

The man's smile faded somewhat, and then an understanding came to his face as his eyes lit. "Ah, I thought my Mary would have explained. The name's Ben. Ben Higgins."

"You're Mary's husband." This was obvious, but she stated it anyway.

Mr. Higgins gave a laugh. "Lucky bloke that I am." He laughed harder before gesturing back to the ditch. "That's why I'm having such a time with this."

She turned back to the ditch and realization finally struck as she recalled what Mrs. Rowling had said the day they'd arrived. "But you're the game keeper. You shouldn't have anything to do with managing the fields."

His smile widened, shifting the dense beard along his jaw. "That's just it, Miss Black. The steward left coming on four months now. Worst possible time for him to go, too, but it couldn't be helped none. His daughter was in a bad way with a babe, you see, and he and the missus went off to Surrey to care for her." Mr. Higgins' brow clouded with worry. "But that leaves us with an irrigation ditch that won't very well dig itself." He looked at her, and his expression cleared. "But I've heard tales of you and your exploits at Eaton Park. Have you any knowledge on how we should go about this?" He pointed again to the ditch.

But Jane's mind was somewhere else. "Your steward left four months ago, and the marquess hasn't found a replacement?"

Mr. Higgins shifted uncomfortably, and his eyes darted

everywhere but at her. "Well, it's not like that exactly, you see."

She crossed her arms over her chest and pinned Mr. Higgins with her best lady of the manor glare. "And just how is it exactly?"

CHAPTER 15

"I'd thought you'd given up hiding in favor of running away."

From anyone else, such a statement would be grounds for immediate dismissal. But as Mrs. Rowling said it to Puddles, Austin could only stare and appreciate the accuracy.

"You have excellent aim, Mrs. Rowling. I fear I may have failed to appreciate that in my youth." He closed the book he'd been reading. Well, not reading exactly. More like staring at the pages of familiar sketches and tales. A ratty and torn edition of pirate tales his nanny had found for him and smuggled into the nursery.

He'd not been a keen student of Shakespeare and Homer as a child, and reluctant to read, his nanny had thought more interesting tales of adventure were in order. And so it was *Captain Henderson's Tales of the Masked Pirate Gang* had come to find a beloved spot under his mattress, hidden from the judgmental gaze of his father. Future marquesses did not read pirate tales, so it was said, but Austin thought the world would be a much better place if they did.

"There are many things you failed to appreciate in your

youth, but that is neither here nor there, is it?" She came fully into the room and took up a seat opposite him. "I'm surprised to see you still fit."

He had fled to the only place he had sought sanctuary at Peregrine Hall and often found it. At least within its walls. Outside he'd had the brook and Mary and Ben. Inside, he had the nursery. So here it was he'd come three days previous. He'd wedged himself onto the window bench where he'd spent many a childhood night staring up at the stars and wondering.

Wondering if other children had mothers who loved them. For whom they cared.

Wondering what would happen if he simply ran away. Would she notice? Would his father have him apprehended and hauled back?

Wondering…

As a grown man, he'd done much the same, but his pondering had narrowed somewhat in focus. Mainly to that of Jane and what he was going to do about her.

Never in the nearly ten years since he'd been of an age had he contemplated marriage. He'd never really given it a thought. If the title died out with him, who was there to care? There was no one left but him, and he'd hardly noticed the damn thing.

But now, suddenly, he didn't find marriage so repulsive. Not if it was with Jane.

And with this he realized he didn't know how he could go back to the way his life had been. Alone. Empty.

He most certainly couldn't go back to this, Peregrine Hall, no matter that circumstances dictated just that at present. He couldn't go back to his townhouse in London. He couldn't go back to his quasi-partnership with the Metropolitan Police Force.

Mrs. Rowling's aim was deadly accurate. He was incredibly good at running away.

If only he could pinpoint what it was from which he was running.

"It's rather tight, but I've managed. I suppose Miss Black ratted me out?" He raised an eyebrow, but Mrs. Rowling only adjusted her perch on the trundle bed.

"Something to that effect. I can articulate a number of things that would have you scuttling back to your nursery, but it would be easier if you were to simply tell me." He'd been wrong about Mrs. Rowling. She had aged. Not overtly. It was subtle. In the creases along her brow, the sagging skin at her once demanding jaw.

"I'm not sure," he said, his voice weaker than he'd expected it.

"Perhaps if you read any of my letters you would have been more prepared for the state of the place."

He looked sharply out the window at the neat fields and outbuildings. He turned a questioning glance on the housekeeper. "What do you mean?"

She shook her head and folded her hands against her apron. "You always did see things the way you wish."

"Why do I sense you're no longer speaking about the estate?"

She took a moment before answering, and in that pause, his mind conjured up a number of things she could toss back at him. But she only smiled and shook her head. "It will come in time. You cannot push a person to change his perspective when he's not willing to change."

"That sounds rather ominous." He dropped his legs from their perch on the window seat. "If you have something to say, you might as well say it."

Mrs. Rowling stood with an efficiency that belied her age.

"It will do no good to say it. I've been saying it since you were a boy of thirteen, but there's one thing no one can ever cross."

"And just what is that?"

Mrs. Rowling leaned in, a single finger pointing accusingly at him, and once again, he was that boy of thirteen, having tracked in a slough of mud from the yard. "The bond between a mother and her son."

Well, that was too far. He surged to his feet and pushed the accusing finger aside. "There was no bond between mother and son as far as I'm concerned."

Mrs. Rowling frowned but didn't back down. "That's the problem precisely." She turned and headed for the door without allowing him a response. "Miss Black has taken the doctor for a turn about the grounds. If you're to be protecting them, you should probably be aware of that."

Fear shot through him, but he swallowed it down. They were in Kent, for Christ's sake, and no one knew they were there. A turn about the grounds was harmless. Still. Mrs. Rowling was right. He was supposed to be protecting her.

Them.

God, he needed to get away from here.

And go where, exactly?

He pushed his hands through his hair and followed the retreating Mrs. Rowling only he didn't make it far. He collided with the woman who plagued his thoughts within seconds of stepping into the hall.

An apology sprang to his lips, but for one blessed moment he stopped. She had so neatly collided with him that her body pressed along the length of his. She was warm and smelled of the outdoors, fresh spring air and earth. She was tall, perfectly so, and her lips were so close to his.

For a moment, one blissful moment, he recalled her kiss. The softness of her lips. The surprise in her taste. His stomach clenched, and he realized he'd missed touching her.

But he dipped his head and took in the rest of her. Her firm jaw, her slanted eyes. He stepped back, reluctantly allowing his hands to slip from her arms and the heat of her body to disappear.

Whatever she had been about, she'd been about it in a hurry. She was clearly dressed for the outdoors in a wool gown and sturdy walking boots, but it was the bonnet haphazardly trailing down her back that suggested she had entered the house in some haste. He took another careful step back.

She breathed heavily, but from the flare of her nostrils, he didn't think exertion plagued her. He steeled himself for whatever was to come while surreptitiously peering behind her to see if Mrs. Rowling was nearby. But the blasted woman was nowhere in sight.

"Well, you've apparently searched me out for something, Miss Black—"

"Mary told me where you liked to hide." He cringed at her harsh tone, but her words hurt more.

"Mary?" He raised an eyebrow, but she ignored him.

"Do you have any idea the current state of your property?" Her nostrils had stopped flaring, but he knew she wasn't done being angry.

He glanced back at the nursery, remembering his conversation with Mrs. Rowling. She had said something similar, and a tickle of apprehension licked his neck.

"Explain." He crossed his arms over his chest and regarded the windswept quality of Jane's hair. God, she was beautiful when she was like this. Caught up in whatever it was that had drawn her determination.

"Do you know the estate is without a steward? And heading into the planting no less." The gall blasted woman crossed her arms over her chest, returning his stare with equal measure.

For a terrible moment, a smile worried his lips, but he forced it down, assuming a serious mien. "I was not aware."

"I'm sure Mrs. Rowling informed you in one of those letters you failed to read."

"You're incredibly observant."

If her expression could get any colder, it did in that moment. "You're incredibly frightened."

He jolted, not expecting her to lay such a bold claim with such cunning. "I beg your pardon?"

She dropped her arms. "I don't understand it fully, but I know enough of it. There's something about this place that frightens you." She gestured to the nursery. "That's why you hide. That's why you haven't read Mrs. Rowling's letters. That's why you haven't been here."

She took a step forward, and damned, if he didn't take an involuntary step back. Her eyes softened, her mouth relaxing into something that, horribly enough, looked like sympathy.

"I had the blessing of growing up in the bosom of a loving family with parents that sought out opportunities for me." Ah, God, her brow furrowed, and she almost looked like she would cry. "I can't imagine what it is you lived through here as a child, but I'm beginning to get a picture of it." Her brow relaxed. "But that is no excuse to allow such a beautiful estate to go to ruin." And then she poked him. With one solid finger to the arm he still had crossed over his chest. "You might not like it here and wish the whole place would go to rot, but there are people that rely on Peregrine Hall for employment. Think of Mary and Ben and Mrs. Rowling. Would you have them turned out because you allowed the place to go to ruin?"

A retort was ready on his lips, and he'd even opened his mouth when he stopped. Eyed her. "Ben?" he asked when he was sure he hadn't meant to. "You met Ben?"

Her hands went to her hips. "Of course, I did. Did you

know he's attempting to act as steward? The man doesn't know a parcel map from a pitchfork. But he cares about Peregrine Hall, and he's doing his best to keep it going."

Ben was acting as steward?

He looked back at the nursery again. Something was amiss. Something…

He snapped his attention back to her. "Where's Dr. Seymour?"

For once, he'd caught her off guard. But it was momentary, and not nearly as satisfying as he'd hoped.

"I left him by the lake. Mary was going to sit with him for a bit. He seems taken by the water."

Her words were harmless, and yet, deep within him a pain spurted forth as if it were freshly delivered.

The lake.

He had always meant to have it filled in.

"Is he talking?" he asked, not liking how hard it was to pry his teeth apart.

"Not much, but more than he was." She shook her head. "He keeps repeating the same nonsense over and over. He's listing characters from the Grimm tales, and he always stops at the Frog Prince." She shook her head. "He knows who it is, but he's terribly frighten. More than you can even imagine. It's going to take time." There it was again. That look of bone-deep sympathy.

In the space of a few minutes, she'd mastered every emotion that had the power to render him a useless sap.

"Well, there's been nothing in *The Times* for the past three days, so I think our ruse worked well enough. We'll have the time to give the good doctor."

She tilted her head in question. "Are you really confident that you'd find a message hidden in *The Times* if Samuel were to plant one?"

He gaped at her. "Your lack of confidence in my abilities as an operative are appalling."

"I've seen the current state of your property." Her tone was duller than a butter knife.

He pulled uncomfortably on the lapels of his coat as he cleared his throat. "Well, it seems we have the time to address that. Where shall we start?"

Her eyes widened until her whole face lit. "Are you serious?"

He stilled. In the nearly year and a half since he'd met Jane Black, he'd never seen her this utterly happy. This effervescent. This…content.

He'd showered her with any number of compliments. Engaged her in earnest conversation.

He'd kissed her. Attempted to seduce her.

But an offer of allowing her to assist in repairing his estate had this effect on her?

God, he was going to need some help if he were ever to convince her he was more than a rogue.

"Deadly serious," he said and took her arm. "Lead the way."

* * *

"You should light a match and start over when the smoke has cleared." That was the bluntness she usually reserved for her father, but the words were out before she could stop them.

They stood in the very center of Peregrine's stables. Or rather, what was left of them. It was oddly comforting to know Austin conjured such loyalty in his staff that they would carry on as best they could despite his inattention to the estate.

She regarded him now as he stood, hands on hips, slowly

turning a circle to take in the ruin of the building. He was dressed simply as the situation dictated, but he still commanded a presence with his broad stature and dark features. Even the scar on his cheek looked particularly daunting just then.

And for a moment, she allowed herself to remember what it felt like to be in his arms for that brief moment when he'd caught her earlier coming down the corridor to the nursery.

She swallowed as she thought of it. Not of the physical intimacy, but of the realization this grown man hid in his childhood nursery. That Mary so readily offered the information suggested this was quite a common occurrence when Austin had still been in residence. It saddened her at the same time it made her wish to pry him open like an oyster and discover exactly what had happened to this man.

The Austin she knew from London was always so jubilant. If not carefree, at least...happy. This Austin was not. Shadows haunted his eyes, and it was almost as if he'd startle at the merest touch. It must have been something truly awful to leave such a scar on a man who faced danger so easily and frequently without a care.

She thought of what Mary had said about his mother. Austin had never mentioned his mother as far as she could remember, and from what Mrs. Rowling had indicated in her story of how he'd acquired such an interesting pet name, it didn't appear as though the bond between mother and son had been that strong.

She had wanted to keep her dislike of him steadfast if only to guard her heart, but with every new piece of his past she discovered, it grew harder to stay mad at him.

Her hands fisted at her side before she knew what she was about. There was more to the Marquess of Evanshire than she'd originally believed. But this did not mean she must change her mind about her feelings toward him.

"When was it that Ben said we stopped bringing in new horseflesh?" Austin kicked a discarded saddle with his foot.

"Nearly three years now. There are only the two work horses and the two for the cart Mr. Higgins sometimes takes into town. There's truly no horseflesh suitable for riding any longer." She made her own survey of the space. "But then, there wouldn't be a suitable place to keep them."

He looked into one of the empty stalls. "Where are the four remaining horses kept?"

"Ben has them in stalls at the gamekeeper's cottage."

Austin turned sharply. "He's caring for them himself?"

She nodded. "Without the addition of new horseflesh there was no need for trainers or grooms, so they were dismissed. Well, except for the stable master. He left of his own accord when it was determined his services were not needed."

Austin's expression didn't change, but she knew he was mulling over her words. It couldn't have been easy to hear a member of one's staff had vacated a position because he himself felt he was not needed.

He placed a hand against the stall door and leaned forward until he stared at the ground. "And when did the stable master leave?"

"More than two years ago."

Austin said something she'd never heard him say, and she stared at him.

She had not anticipated enjoying this sojourn, and she certainly hadn't expected to enjoy being in Austin's company. Not after he'd tricked her. But now.

Now she was almost enjoying this.

That morning when they'd arrived and the rising sun had lit the face of Peregrine Hall, something had moved inside of her. Something base and instinctual. The need to preserve a legacy. The need to cherish the land that had nourished a family for generations.

It was the same pull she had whenever she surveyed Eaton Park. It was perfectly reasonable that she should fall back on it now. Surely it had nothing to do with the marquess.

Austin muttered another interesting epitaph before stomping his foot into the stall. This childish manner was rewarded with a scolding neigh from farther down the row of stables. She did try very hard not to laugh when he jumped, his head turning in the direction of the noise.

He turned back to her, his brow furrowed in accusation. "You said there was no more horseflesh here."

She bit the inside of her cheek to keep from smiling before she replied, "There is no serviceable horseflesh." She indicated a stall farther down the way with a nod of her head. "That's just Harold."

His expression did not relax. "Harold?"

"A rather dapper old gentleman, or so Ben tells me." She moved past him to reach the farthest stalls. "Harold is rather past the age of doing much and has taken up a life of leisure here." She stopped at the end of the row and extended her hand toward the last stall. "You're disturbing his peace."

He hadn't followed her, but he eyed her wearily now. "Harold?"

She nodded and gestured again with her hand. "Yes, Harold. He's actually quite pleasant for an old sir." She fished in her pocket for one of the apples she'd retrieved from the kitchens when she'd gone in search of Mary to find where Austin might be hiding.

She held her hand out, palm up with the delicious treat, and the old horse leaned his head forward, scooping the treat up with his dexterous lips.

Austin approached her. "We're keeping a horse in luxury during his retiring years in a falling down stable?"

She cocked an eyebrow at him. "You can understand the urgency of the situation then."

He didn't meet her gaze as he reached out a hand to scratch between Harold's ears, but she could see something brewing in his eyes. It wasn't quite pain. It wasn't sorrow. More like resignation. It wasn't what she hoped for, but then, she hadn't realized she was looking for a particular reaction from him.

It was just…well, Eaton Park was in her bones, in her blood. She just couldn't fathom how someone could not feel the same connection to his home.

Austin turned so sharply she didn't have time to step back, so he was far too close, his eyes far too intense when he said, "My mother killed herself. She tied herself to a rock and walked into the lake. She had dismissed the servants for the day while my father and I were in Maidenstone. We found her when we returned that evening."

There was no feeling to his words. In fact, there was a stark absence of feeling as if he were reciting the lines of a play. Or perhaps, relaying information that he believed she should have but over which, he had no opinion himself.

The air caught in her throat, and she nearly coughed. She'd known his mother had taken her own life, but she hadn't realized…she didn't know.

She laid a hand on his arm and said, "I'm sorry." Stopped, shook her head. "That isn't right. One cannot feel sorry for such a terrible thing. It's just too…terrible." She couldn't meet his gaze as she searched for the right words, the right thing to say. She pulled her hand back and looked at him squarely. "There's nothing I can say right now that would be the right thing, and for that, I'm sorry."

He straightened, and as he stepped away from her, she felt

like she'd lost him somehow. Which was ridiculous. He wasn't hers to lose. He'd already proven that.

"There's nothing for you to say. I simply wanted you to know, so you would understand why it is I've neglected my duties." He faced away from her as if taking in the wreck around them. "It's not an excuse. I can see I shouldn't have allowed my emotions to exceed my responsibilities to Peregrine Hall."

It hurt, hearing him say that, and she hated herself for it. Had she been expecting some sort of shared intimacy between them? He'd made perfectly clear how he felt about her. She knew that. But still. Hope had a funny way of never leaving.

She gripped her skirts in her hands with resolved efficiency and stepped forward. "A past neglect can always be put to rights in these circumstances. Peregrine Hall is not so far lost as it cannot be repaired." She peered through the open doors of the stable to the hills beyond.

It was waiting.

All of it.

The fields, the stable, the hall itself. It was waiting for its person to return. To bring it back to life. To nurture it. To love it. That was the thing about land. It never left you even if you left it.

It was a moment before she realized he watched her. She raised her chin. "If you're amenable to engaging in some much needed improvements to the property, I would be happy to lend my assistance. After all, we are stuck here for the foreseeable future. We might as well make the most efficient use of our time."

His expression was unreadable, or at least, confusing. His eyes almost appeared hurt or perhaps lost while his mouth was stubborn and indifferent. She waited, no longer compelled to speak of personal matters when he'd made it clear he shared only when it was a necessity.

He seemed to shake off the conflicting mood and crossed his arms over his chest. "What is it you have in mind?"

She stepped out of the stable and into the fading afternoon light. The sun was behind them, and Peregrine was cast in wavering shadows. "Ben has industriously started on the irrigation improvements needed for the eastern fields. That's a priority as planting gets underway, and he assured me it is the only urgent update to the fields needed for this year's growing season." She turned to ensure Austin had followed her outside. Satisfied he could hear her, she went on. "However, the evidence of decay in the stables would suggest there is more throughout the property, and all outbuildings should be checked along with the current yields and conditions of the tenant farms. Do you know how many there are?"

His empty stare suggested he did not.

She pursed her lips. "Right then. Well, there's only one place to start." She brushed her hands down her skirts. "Shall we?" She gestured to the hall, but he didn't move.

"Where is it that we'll be starting?" he asked, his voice none to sure.

She smiled, feeling a measure of confidence for the first time when in the company of this man. "With the ledgers, of course."

CHAPTER 16

"This can't be right," Jane said from where she sat at the marquess's desk in the marquess's study in the marquess's estate.

He glanced over his shoulder at her now. She looked so at home there, hunched over all of the ledgers of accounts they had been able to obtain from the steward's cottage with Ben's help.

It had been a shock to see Ben. He had always been big when they were boys, but he'd grown into a behemoth of a man complete with a burly beard and a deep, ponderous laugh. But what had been more shocking was Ben's greeting. It was as if Austin had never left. Had never run away.

Ben had simply grabbed him. Propriety be damned, apparently, because Ben crushed him in an embrace that carried with it years of separation. And Austin suddenly wondered why he'd been hiding in the nursery.

At the sound of his childhood friend's voice, a flood of memories came back to him. Not bad memories. Good ones, actually. Warm, golden ones. The early mornings at the brook, hoping to catch tadpoles. The middle of the night excursions to fetch Mary and climb to the highest point of Peregrine, collapse on the grass, and watch the stars until they all winked out one by one.

His chest tightened, and he feared it was a symptom of nostalgia. Not something he had ever imagined feeling for Peregrine, but there it was.

And there she was.

Jane.

As if she'd been here her whole life, staring at these very ledgers.

"Has the grist mill never received a single repair in the thirty years since it's been built?" She looked up at him, and there was an adorable line pressed between her eyes.

He couldn't bring himself to say he didn't know for what was surely the hundredth time in three days, so he just shrugged, not wanting to shatter her moment of numerical bliss.

She shook her head in response and muttered something he didn't quite catch. Something about things being just not right. He didn't know how she could equate such emotion to inanimate things like grist mills, but she'd been doing it for three days.

First, it was the neglect of the stables. How could such mistreatment be inflicted upon such a beauty? Where she'd seen beauty, he'd seen neglect and rot. Then it was the kiln. Why hadn't it been allowed to expand? Clearly, there was room for capacity. Was no one seeing to its needs? As if it were a person.

He returned his gaze to the window and the grounds beyond. The marquess's study was in the north wing, so he was at least grateful he didn't have to gaze upon the lake. He waited for the roll of nausea that came whenever he remembered what had happened, but it didn't come. There was only the echo of something he knew had once been much worse.

When he looked out the window, he saw the stables, and inexplicably, his mind drifted to Harold, the poor old horse spending his retiring years in a run down shell of a building. They'd barely even gotten the doors open. God forbid, the fire Jane suggested should happen. He didn't know if they'd be able to get Harold out in time.

He turned. "We must first find a new home for Harold. If a temporary structure should be erected, then we'll have it done. We can't leave that poor horse in there."

She had raised only her wide eyes to him. "I'm sorry?"

He gestured over his shoulder to the stables. "The old gentleman still in the stables. We must move him immediately. He doesn't deserve that."

God, he was starting to sound like her now.

A smile slowly spread across her face, and he suddenly didn't care if it made that kind of happiness spring to her features.

"I think that can be arranged." She shuffled through some of the ledgers. "Ben and his men should be finished with the irrigation ditches by the end of tomorrow. I can see if there is a team available to erect a paddock for Harold's temporary quarters." She regarded him. "Are you planning to rebuild the stables? If so, that will affect our decision in placing the temporary paddock. We won't want it to interfere with any of the new construction."

Our decision.

The sound of that hit him like he couldn't believe it held the power to, and his mind skittered across the question that had been plaguing him for days now.

If he wasn't a rogue, what was he then?

He swallowed and sank into a chair.

"Yes, we'll rebuild the stables." He watched her as he said it, and he knew she understood what his words meant, as reluctantly as they'd come. If he invested the funds required to rebuild the stables and replenish them with horseflesh, it would be financially irresponsible of him to then let the estate flounder like he had for the past ten years.

Jane's assessing expression seemed to be mulling over the same conclusion as he was. She finally said, "When would you like the rebuilding to commence?"

This was better. Straight facts. Logic. No emotions needed. "As soon as possible. At least by this summer, I would hope."

She regarded the ledgers again, shifting one for another. "We must put together a schedule then of the needed improvements, determine their priorities, both real and subjective, and then deduce required funds, the readiness of said funds, and the availability of workmen needed to complete the task." Again, she lifted only her eyes to him. "Have you ever undertaken a project of this sorts?"

He shook his head. "I can't say that I have." But he was beginning to realize she was a project if he followed his thoughts where he feared they were going.

She sat back in her chair. "It's going to take a great deal of patience, you know." She gestured to the pile of ledgers. "With the state of things here, it's likely going to take an enormous about of patience. And I mean more than what you may have encountered as a soldier or in the House of Lords." She paused but he knew she wasn't finished. "When one assumes a project of this size, it can be expected that one shall encounter unforeseen obstacles."

He had already realized that. He attempted a straight face when he replied, "That is something with which I have a little experience."

She cocked an eyebrow. "You do? Well, that is certainly helpful." She held up another ledger. "Would you like to begin on the household accounts?" She opened the cover. "I must say, Mrs. Rowling does a fine job—"

"Let's take a walk." He couldn't stand another hour in this room with her, mapping out a future as if they were married when with every word she uttered she'd nearly convinced him of his rakish state.

"Right now? But we've only—"

He stood and cut her off. "We've been at this for three days. I think we've earned a turn around the property." He gestured to the books. "Besides, we can get a first hand account of some of the items you've articulated from the ledger."

"Are you attempting to flatter me?"

He froze with one arm outstretched. That wasn't at all what he had been about, but as he assessed the earnestness on her face, he thought it likely was a sort of flattery for her.

He grinned. "Is it working?"

She frowned, and he lost his grin. "Hardly." But she stood. "My competence with household accounts is not anything remarkable. All young ladies are taught to manage the house. It's something required of a woman when she becomes a wife." She, of course, stated this at the exact moment when she made her way around the desk and stepped directly in front of him.

The tension could be felt as if it were tangible, with snaky arms that had wrapped around them both. He stared into her brown eyes, gone wide with realization of how close they stood to one another. That blasted fringe drooped into her eyes though, and he wanted nothing more than to push it from her face, cup her cheek, and kiss her properly.

But as much as he yearned to taste her once more, the memory of her rebuke in the park was entirely too fresh. So instead of pulling her into his arms, he took a step back and held an arm out to the door.

"Would you like to see the rose gardens? Mrs. Rowling is correct. They are quite lovely from what I remember."

She hesitated for a moment, but her expression wasn't wary. God, it was closer to calculating than anything else. She seemed to come to a conclusion because she shook her head and stepped in front of him in the direction of the door. "The doctor and I have already traversed the rose gardens extensively. They're rather lovely early in the morning." She eyed him almost as if she were unsure of how to phrase the next piece of her observation. "Did you frequent them often as a child?"

His teeth clenched, but he knew she was doing her best not to overstep. She was too polite for that.

"My mother didn't like roses." Jane's head snapped up, and he smiled at her curious expression. "Not that I recall anyway." He opened the door and gestured for her to continue. "My mother and I were not close, as you have likely gathered. My parents' marriage was not a love match. I believe their fathers had arranged the suit before either of them had reached the schoolroom." He stopped on the threshold of the front door. "I actually believe the arrangement had something to do with horseflesh." He felt an honest smile come to his lips. "There's irony for you, considering the current state of Peregrine's stables."

The late spring day was surprisingly warm, and he found himself turning toward the lake. Jane followed after him without hesitation, and he would give her credit for that at least. He hadn't been down to the lake yet. Had avoided it even if everyone had forced him out of hiding.

But now he faced it with the soft breeze of the afternoon caressing his face. He heard shouts almost immediately, and his gaze drifted down to the workmen in the eastern field repairing the irrigation ditches. He raised a flattened palm over his eyes.

"It looks like they're making steady progress."

"Indeed. As I said, they should be finished by tomorrow."

Jane had stopped several feet from him on the shore of the lake. The sun was at her back, and with the wide rim of her bonnet, her face lay in shadow. He wondered for a moment what she felt when she looked over this land. She'd grown up in Kent. Not far from here, he understood.

Which gave him another ludicrous idea, but he was feeling just punchy enough to act on it.

"Tell me, Miss Black. Where is it that your dear John Smith resides?" He looked about in an unnecessarily dramatic fashion before tossing her a grin. "Can we see this house from here? Perhaps I can tip my hat to him."

* * *

"YOU CAN'T, I'M AFRAID."

Although she was trying very hard to distance herself from the man, he had a way of being humorous when it was least expected. He was annoying like that, but she was learning to take it in stride.

They had been at Peregrine Hall for more than a week, and there had been no word from Samuel in *The Times*. Silence was either a good or terrible thing. Good in that they hadn't been found out. But terrible in that they hadn't unmasked the villain as of yet. She wondered for a moment how Samuel was getting on in London. How her mother and father were and Lizzie. And even for a wild moment, how her cousin Emily was faring. She pictured them all shut up in Lofton House per Samuel's bidding.

And here she was. Standing on a knoll in Kent, letting the afternoon breeze stroke her cheeks and the fading light warm her shoulders. The doctor hadn't improved much in terms of voicing his thoughts, but he grew sturdier, more robust in their morning walks. His eye had healed rather nicely under Mary's care, and it was wonderful to see both of his blue eyes so keen on his surroundings while they made their way through whatever landscape they had chosen for that morning.

Most mornings he was silent except for an odd comment about a flower or bird or the state of a cloud in the sky. But she never pressed him on the urgency of their situation for she wasn't certain herself what that urgency was. One day seemed to fade into the next at Peregrine, and she welcomed the attention required to focus on the needed improvements.

It was something familiar, something she could fall back on without fear.

Fear.

She glanced at Austin from beneath her fringe. It wasn't fear she felt when she was around him. Not now. Not anymore. It was an unsettling. An unsettling that could never find peace, and which she could not displace with rudimentary work. The precise calculations of ledgers. The logical figuring of schedules and outcomes. It was all comfortable. Known. Predictable.

But not Austin.

Once Dr. Seymour recovered enough, trusted them enough, he would reveal the secret locked in his mind. Then she would be free. Free to return to Eaton Park and the life she had planned with Mr. Smith. It would be just as it should have been all along.

She regarded Austin now, surprised again that he had agreed to the scheme of improvements. When she'd found him hiding in the nursery, she really hadn't thought he'd give a care. But as he seemed to do with alarming frequency, he did the unexpected.

She really did want to think him a rogue. To think him a seducer of innocent women. But he was making it terribly hard for her to believe that.

"Ah, you can't see the house from here then? Or is it that

we're to be in hiding, and my gesture would give us away?" Austin scanned the horizon as he spoke, but she caught the smile in his voice.

"Oh, it isn't that all," she said and waited until he looked at her so he could see her grin. "It's that you're not currently wearing a hat."

When he'd suggested the walk to interrupt their efforts on the accounts, he'd clearly been in a hurry as he'd walked right through the front door without coat or hat while she'd scrambled to get her bonnet and wrap.

He stared at her for several seconds before his mocking grin collapsed into a satisfied smile. "Well played, Jane."

She nodded. "Quite. Now then, didn't you say we may see to some of the issues uncovered in the accounts by embarking on this walk?"

"I did say as such, didn't I?" He scratched at his chin in mock confusion before sweeping about. "Should we start in the eastern field? I'd like to see where the new irrigation ditches will cut through."

"I think that's a marvelous idea." She picked up her skirts and began the hike down the hill, but not before Austin offered his arm. She raised her chin. "I'm quite fine, thank you, and I do not think the situation calls for such manners. It is the country after all." She marched past him without caring to see how her words effected him.

For they probably didn't.

But she didn't miss the hesitation in his following step. She'd nearly rounded the lake before she heard his footfalls behind her. The ground was firming up well with the progression of spring, and they would need to begin the planting soon. It was critical the irrigation project be completed without difficulty, or the planting would be delayed. From what she'd seen of the accounts, Peregrine couldn't take such a hit.

She kept her eyes focused on the workmen when she asked, "Did your father ever go over the ledgers with you?"

Austin made a noise of disbelief. "Hardly. My father and I never really got on." He hesitated, and she thought he wouldn't go on as he had proven how difficult it was to reveal this part of himself. "It wasn't that he was cruel or anything. He just wasn't there." His gaze had drifted somewhere off on the horizon then.

"I'd be happy to instruct you on deciphering the accounts and which ledger goes to which revenue source on the estate. It's quite simple once you learn it, and then when this is all over, you'll be able to handle your accounts quite proficiently."

He stumbled, and she reached out a hand automatically to catch him. But the way he had stumbled caused his hand to clasp her shoulder, and this turned her far too close to him. She smiled as banally as possible and turned out from under his hand once she knew he was steady again.

But not before she caught a strange look in his eye. Almost like…hurt.

She gave herself a mental shake. There was nothing in her words that would have hurt the marquess. She was stating simple facts.

When they reached the eastern field, Ben raised a hand in greeting.

"You've emerged from the den of ledgers, have you?"

Jane was still surprised by the man's towering size, and she peered up at him through her fringe with a smile she wasn't quite sure of. Ben was a wonderful man. Warm and open, just like his wife. But she'd had very little experience dealing with men who were quite so friendly to her. She was just so used to being ignored.

"It's only a temporary expedition at his lordship's insistence," she said.

"Oh, his lordship's insistence, eh?" Ben let out a bark of a laugh as he slapped his old friend on the back. "I've a mind to tell her how you feel about snakes, your lordship." Ben whined the last two words as a child would taunt an enemy before bursting into another peel of laughter.

"Then I shall have to tell her how you feel about dolls."

Ben stopped laughing so quickly, she feared he'd swallowed his tongue.

"You wouldn't dare."

Austin crossed his arms over his chest. "In a second."

Ben turned a surprising shade of red before coughing and turning back to his men. "The line to the road is nearly finished, your lordship. We should have a test of it by noon tomorrow at the latest."

She felt herself fighting a smile at the banter between the old friends, and briefly, she speculated just how deep Austin's childhood scars ran. While he hadn't spoken poorly of his father, it was clear he'd been rather absent. And Austin had obviously had friends. Good friends, if their current camaraderie, taken up so keenly after such a long separation, were evidence of such.

But if she were honest, she knew where the truth of his issues lay. He'd told her himself and so had Mrs. Rowling in her own way.

His mother.

Lud, she didn't even know the woman's name, and yet the mere ghost of her held so much power over this man. This man and these people. This land. What had she done to haunt it so?

"That's splendid to hear," Jane said, cutting off any scalding remark Austin might have for his friend. "His lordship is keen to start a new project as soon as is possible. Had you anything slated to begin once the work here is finished?"

Ben scratched at his forehead beneath the brim of his cap.

"Well, the plantings are to begin soon, and some of the men have their own farms to look after." He gestured with a hand behind him in the direction of the town. "But there are men in the village seeking work. What is it you're looking to do, Evanshire?"

Austin looked to her as if she held control over the improvements schedule. It was an odd feeling that zipped through her. One of confidence, trust, and reliance. It was a feeling she'd only ever shared with her father when he'd waved a hand at her over some statement regarding the accounts and said to do as she thought best as he'd never doubted her capabilities. Surely, such trust was accepted between father and daughter, but from an outsider?

Well…

She shook the strange feeling and faced Ben. "His lordship would like to have Harold relocated to a temporary paddock until the stables can be properly rebuilt. Do you think such a structure could be erected?"

Ben's eyes went wide, and he gave a low whistle. "You're taken with Harold now, eh?" He gave a friendly tap to Austin's shoulder, and the marquess actually bounced a little on his feet from the impact but cast a mocking grin to his friend.

"He's a debonair gentleman. I can relate."

Ben guffawed so loudly it drew the attention of some of the workmen. "In that you're both long in the face, eh?"

"At least our faces are still visible."

Ben clapped two hands to his face. "It's rather incredible, isn't it? Not a whisker on my chin until nearly twenty years, and then this sprouted up nearly over night. Damn near terrified Mary."

Austin's eyes shifted to Jane.

Ben shuffled his feet. "I'm begging your pardon, miss."

Jane shook her head. "No need. I've heard far worse."

"From that brother you were speaking of when first we met?"

"No, from my little sister actually."

This sent Ben on another round of laughter, and she caught Austin smiling at her.

This would simply not do. Undertaking the needed improvements at Peregrine was to ensure emotions would not play a role in the time she was forced to spend here.

This feeling of acceptance was…unexpected.

And unwanted.

She snuck a peek at Austin again and felt less confident about that last one. She had found such surety in her resolve in the park when she'd called him out for being a rogue, but now…

He was charming her. If she didn't know better, she might even think he was wooing her. Which was certainly not true. He'd made that abundantly clear. And even if he was, wasn't he just showing his true rakish colors?

"So a paddock for old Harold, you say? And you're going to rebuild the stables?" Ben gave his friend another pat. "Mary will be right pleased to hear it. Will you be bringing back the horseflesh, as well?" Ben's eyes gleamed, and she wondered how deep the man's love of animal husbandry went.

Austin nodded. "Yes, I will, but I'll require your input on the subject. I can't for the life of me remember what it was my father had installed in the stables."

Ben shook his head. "And you think a dunderhead like myself would remember? Nah, I wouldn't think it. You'd best ask Mrs. Rowling."

"Mrs. Rowling would be a very good source of information." Jane addressed this to Austin, but his gaze had traveled beyond their little group, and she turned to see where he was looking.

In the distance the thatched roof of a cottage billowed smoke as a woman stood in the yard beating out what was likely a rug. At this distance it was hard to decipher the details, but the collective was quite domestic and comforting.

"Who is that?" Austin asked of no one in particular, but Ben answered straightaway.

"That's Mrs. Maddox."

"Maddox?" Austin asked. "Who in God's name is Maddox? I don't remember them being on the estate."

Ben scratched under the brim of his hat again. "They took up that tenant parcel nearly five years hence. Been doing a fine job of it, too. He's even fixed up that cottage some."

Austin shifted on his feet, and she could feel the tension roll off of him. "Attending to the cottage is the responsibility of the landlord."

"Well, the landlord hasn't been here, has he?"

The statement was bold, and she knew Ben only got away with it because he and the marquess were old chums.

That, and it was true.

Austin's frown was grim as he turned it on her. "I think it's time we visited the tenants, Miss Black."

CHAPTER 17

"The rose gardens again this morning?"

The doctor only raised an eyebrow at her question and wandered out the doors off the breakfast room in the direction of said gardens. It was becoming something of a habit with him. He rose early. Took his breakfast with Jane and then went into the gardens. But it wasn't as if it were a person going for a morning stroll. The doctor always seemed to drift wherever he went. Like he wasn't entirely there, and the wind more than anything else was pulling him in another direction.

This morning was no different, and so she dabbed her napkin to her lips, leaving her unfinished breakfast as she followed him out into the gardens. She was bone tired from traveling from tenant to tenant with Austin for the past two days, and today would likely be much of the same.

It was a mental exhaustion as well a physical one. Visiting the tenants was the marchioness's duty, and with every introduction came another explanation that she was not, in fact, the marchioness. No matter how many times she explained it, it still hurt.

She was greeted with another warm morning, the sun making its way over to this side of the house. They had had only spots of drizzle here and there since they'd come to Peregrine, and the earth continued to awaken around them. There were blooms on some of the varieties of roses now, and she found she walked more slowly, taking them in.

The doctor never seemed to waver, and she didn't think he really noticed the roses. But without fail, he would go into the gardens every morning, so there must be something about the place that he found comforting.

The passages of roses wound their way to the heart of the garden where there was a stone terrace and several benches set round a circle. The doctor always took the bench facing north. He would sit like that for hours if she let him, but as the rose gardens sat at the edges of the morning sun, she always brought him inside lest he grew chilled.

She sat on a bench opposite him and waited. He never spoke. He only stared into the cultivated blooms. She hadn't heard him recite his fairy tale rhyme in some days, and she wondered if that marked an improvement. Was his mind settling, no longer in need of the hypnotic cadence of the words to quiet his thoughts?

He sat hunched over as he usually did, his hands worrying themselves in his lap. His eyes fixated on something in the greenery, but overall, he assumed a rather quiet facade.

She turned her attention to the fountains that lay on the other side of the stone circle. She wondered if they were still operational, and if the gardeners would turn them on when the weather truly warmed. They would be so beautiful in—

"You have a lovely home."

She snapped round at the words.

The doctor hadn't moved, and his gaze remained fixed on the flowers about them.

"I'm sorry?" Her voice was weak, but she was surprised to find sound emerging at all.

The doctor still didn't move, but he said, "Your home. It's lovely."

She looked about her. "Oh, it's not my home. It's the Marquess of Evanshire's estate. He's the gentleman who brought us here."

Dr. Seymour met her gaze, startling her. "You're not the marchioness?"

He asked it so innocently, but her insides roiled. "No, I am not."

He straightened his gaze, becoming quizzical. "But you act the part so confidently. I assumed you belonged here."

Her throat threatened to close at his words, but she swallowed and remembered her resolve. Austin had no interest in her in that regard, no matter how humorous or charming he appeared to be. How understanding and accepting he was of her eccentricities. He was the worst kind of rogue because he made her believe she deserved such attention.

She shook her head. "No, I'm afraid I've selected another match for a husband. It's a good family from where my family has its own estate."

"We're in Kent, are we not?"

If she didn't know better, she would think the doctor had been lucid this entire time. "Yes, we are in Kent."

Dr. Seymour nodded. "Then Richard gave his son the estate at Eaton Park."

Dr. Seymour would have been acquainted with her grandfather at the time he'd deeded the land to her father. "Yes, that is correct."

"Then isn't Evanshire a suitable match from a good family near your family's estate?" He even raised an eyebrow now as if they always conducted such personal conversations during their morning walks in the gardens.

She opened her mouth twice before finally managing, "He would be, but he's not interested in a match as such."

Dr. Seymour actually smiled, and she nearly fell off her bench. "Ah, but I think he is."

She wanted to jump to her feet and return to the breakfast room, to find another witness to the doctor's sudden display of lucidity. "I'm sorry, but he just isn't, I'm afraid. And I've already made plans elsewhere."

Were the doctor's eyes twinkling now?

"You make it sound like choosing a husband is like marking an item off on a list of things one must do. Marriage doesn't truly work like that, Miss Black."

"Please. Call me Jane." It was the only thing she could say to avoid any of the other explosive tidbits he'd just laid at her feet.

He straightened now and looked everything like a respected doctor of the ton. "Do you really not see how much the marquess cares for you?"

"I'm afraid the marquess has the reputation of a rogue. He is quite convincing."

"Yes, but actions are never false. He's returned to a place that brings him great pain to help you fulfill a vow."

Her heart stopped beating, and a cold shudder sprang through her chest.

"How do you know that?" She hadn't meant to whisper it, but the air sat heavy in her lungs.

Dr. Seymour clasped his hands together. It was the first time she had seen him refrain from fidgeting. "When you were born, your grandfather told me you were the one."

She stared, not quite believing what she heard.

The doctor continued. "He always worried about Jane. That would be your grandmother, Jane. He said he didn't know who would keep her headstrong ways in check once he was gone. And then you were born."

Her stomach heaved. "He knew then? I mean, when I was just a babe?"

Dr. Seymour smiled until it reached his eyes, and never since she'd met him had she seen such happiness light his face. "Of course, he did. You should have seen your grandmother when you were born. It was obvious that another living being finally held power over her. Your grandfather was not a stupid man. He knew immediately what he would one day ask of you." His expression turned ponderous then. "I don't think he would have ever imagined you would turn out so wonderfully fit for the job."

An ethereal calm swept over her at these words, and she realized she clenched her skirts in her hands. She tried to ease her grip but found she couldn't. "I'm not sure I understand what you mean."

Dr. Seymour laughed. The sound was startling in the quiet of the morning gardens. "Ah, I could tell that about you straightaway. For a girl who is so strong, you show a remarkable lack of confidence. It's quite a conundrum. No wonder you are driving Evanshire mad."

She surged to her feet quite unexpectedly. "I am doing no such thing. The Marquess of Evanshire has little to no regard for my person in that fashion. I am simply his partner in this mission."

The doctor raised his eyebrows. "Is that what you think?" He shook his head and got to his own feet. "Tell me, child. Has anyone ever called you plain? Told you your intelligence was unappealing?"

She stilled, the sudden burst of righteous indignation fleeing at the first sign of the familiar truth. She was unattractive, both in her physical appearance and in her countenance.

"I see," the doctor went on. "They have then." The doctor was a good deal shorter than she was, and she looked down at the top of his head as he made an odd clearing sound in his throat and shuffled his feet. "My Bethany and I were unable to have children as such, but I owe this to Richard." When he looked up, his eyes were like crystal behind the lenses of his spectacles. "Let me tell you this, dear. When others encounter someone who threatens them in personality, demeanor, and intelligence, they will do whatever they can to weaken their opponents stronghold. Even if such schemes include lies."

Lies.

What was he saying?

Somewhere deep inside of her, in a place she tried so desperately to keep hidden, she thought she understood exactly what he was saying, but she didn't dare hope.

She thought perhaps she should respond as the doctor continued to gaze up at her, but before she could even lick her lips, footsteps sounded behind them. She turned just as Austin emerged from an arch of roses and shattered the moment.

She straightened, dropping her hands calmly to her sides. "Good morning, your lordship."

He had been about to smile but at her words, his expression faltered. She hesitated, and in that hesitation, she longed for normalcy. Tending to the ledgers. Seeing to the tenants. Helping to improve the estates.

She was staring at Austin when she realized exactly where her thoughts were going, and she must have made some outward sign because his brow furrowed with concern.

"Good morning, Miss Black. Dr. Seymour. It looks to be another fine day." His words were harmless but his gaze probed her, and she worried what he was thinking.

When had it happened? When had the life she had planned to lead, the quiet ordered life as the wife of a landed gentleman turn into the exact life she was leading now? Albeit in an odd sort of half-life.

And more, why had that realization never occurred to her?

But it would be different with Mr. Smith. He didn't do horrible things to her stomach and her mind and…her heart.

It had been weeks now since the marquess had kissed her. Weeks since he'd shown any tangible interest in her person. Weeks since she had first hoped.

Since she had been seduced by his charm.

She forced a smile and squared her shoulders. "The doctor and I quite enjoy the rose gardens in the morning. They are well situated to receive the morning and afternoon light, but there's something about breathing in the smell of flowers in the morning, which does one good. Isn't that right, Dr. Seymour?" She turned, and her face fell.

The doctor mumbled to himself, counting along his fingers. His shoulders hunched, and it was as if he'd drawn back into himself. She regarded Austin, and something unspoken passed between them.

She put her arm along the doctor's shoulders and helped him back to the breakfast room where he immediately wandered off into the depths of the house. Mary always kept an eye on him when he was indoors, and she said he mostly spent the days in the gallery along the upper floor. He moved with the sun from window to window until she fetched him for luncheon.

Jane watched him go now, but she felt Austin step close to her before he spoke.

"Was he better this morning?"

Her chest squeezed, but she managed to say, "Yes. We actually had an entire conversation."

She felt the heat of his gaze on her, probing, wondering. She faced him.

"What did he say?" he asked.

She shook her head. "I'm afraid nothing important."

* * *

THEY HAD LEFT the last tenant just as the sun fell into the western sky. Jane had been unusually quiet most of the day. She was normally quiet, but she was remarkably more so. He wondered what the doctor had said that morning in the garden. The expression on her face when he'd come upon them was something he couldn't name. It was almost as if she were confused by something she had thought she'd known differently.

They crested the drive at Peregrine Hall, and she walked so quickly he had to work to keep pace with her.

"Do you want to tell me what's got you upset? Or do you hope to walk it out of you?"

She stopped so abruptly, he almost collided with her.

He reached out a single hand to take her arm. "Jane. What is it?"

In the time he had known her, she had never been without a feeling behind her expression. Shyness. Guilt. Trepidation. Determination. Annoyance. But he'd never seen her like this. So…lost.

She didn't answer him, and he didn't expect her to. He cast his gaze toward the lake and the trees beyond. Without a word, he turned her away from the house, striking off the path around the lake and into the trees. She gave a noise that might have been protest, but he kept his grip on her arm and pulled her along.

It was cooler in the trees, and the shadows wound around themselves. He remembered the quiet and let it engulf him as soon as he stepped from the path. The ground fell away, but his step had not forgotten the terrain. He held onto Jane, helping her over a boulder and then another before once more finding a foothold in the soft brown earth of the forest floor.

The quiet was soon replaced with the trickling of water, and he knew they were getting close. But even as he understood it, he wasn't prepared when they broke through the last of the trees and came out onto the stream's bank.

For a moment, he forget Jane was with him, and in his mind, he saw Mary and Ben waiting for him on the rocks by the water. A smile came unbidden to his lips, and finally, he turned to Jane.

She looked a little less lost now, but he knew it was mostly from the curiosity driven by their surroundings.

"Ben and Mary and I would come here when were children. It was an excellent spot for doing all those things my nanny thought future marquesses should not do."

This drew a small smile to her lips, but it was reluctant.

"Come." He took her hand this time and drew her along the bank to where a large, flat rock extended over the water. He helped her atop it and then climbed up himself. The surface of the rock had warmed in the afternoon sun, and after the chill of the shadowy trees, it felt good to sit atop it.

He didn't press her to speak. After his mother had died, he had come often to this stream just for the silence, for the opportunity to listen to his own thoughts. He wanted to give that to Jane now. So he sat and waited.

It was some time before she spoke.

"Did you ever realize you may have drawn the wrong conclusion about someone?"

The question was unexpected, and he looked at her. "I cannot say I have."

She didn't respond. Instead she reached up, unknotted the ribbon of her bonnet, and tossed the hat aside. Then she laid down, right there on the rock, her eyes closed against the glare of the sun.

His chest tightened at the sight of her, and he knew

exactly why he had grown to care for Jane when no other woman had ever drawn his attention.

This was the Jane no one saw. This creature who defied society. Defied everything and was just herself.

And she was stunning.

Sunlight streamed over her, warming the freckles along her nose and the browns of her hair as it loosened about her face.

He leaned down and kissed her. He shouldn't have done it, but then, he hadn't realized he was going to do it. He just couldn't have stopped himself right then.

He'd startled her, and she came up against him, her hands going to his shoulders, and he should have stopped. Except her grip on his shoulders changed.

She pulled him toward her.

And he sank, going down on his elbows until he could cup her face in his hands, seal his lips to hers. She made a noise in her throat, deep and guttural, and it licked a fire to life inside of him.

He bruised her lips before sliding down, pressing kisses to the smooth column of her neck, the tantalizing edge of her collar bone, and farther still. He collided with the edge of her bodice and stilled.

He looked up at her and knew he wouldn't stop. Her head was thrown back, her hair undone about her shoulders as the sun captured her in an aura of sensuality. He should have realized she was unschooled, innocent. But instead when he saw her like that, he knew he had to have her.

Tugging at the sleeve of her gown, he brought one shoulder down, and right there, at the first bit of exposed skin, he laid his lips. Softly. Gently. Reverently.

She moaned, and her hands pressed into his back.

Another tug and another piece of forbidden skin. He devoured her until the sleeve had slipped entirely from her shoulder. He stared at her. If he pulled at her sleeve again, he could expose her to him. All of her.

And yet he stopped and looked up.

She opened her eyes, staring up at him.

He didn't know what he had expected when she looked at him. Fear? Uncertainty? Curiosity?

But he did know what he hadn't expected to see there, and which shone from her gaze in abundance.

Trust.

Absolute and complete trust.

In him.

Something in him broke loose, and he hadn't meant to speak. But he did.

"You're beautiful."

The words were so innocent. So overused and not what he had meant at all. He had meant so much more. Something poetic and earth shattering. But instead, that was all he could manage.

Her eyes changed, deepened and narrowed, and something else appeared there.

Belief.

She believed him when he called her beautiful.

The thing that had broken loose struck and shattered in his chest. It flooded through him. Relief. Relief that she finally believed him. That she understood.

That she knew her own worth.

And likely because he was so stunned, she was able to knock him to the side when she suddenly sat up, grappling to right her sleeve, snatch her bonnet back.

"Jane." The only thing he could say was her name, and in it, he poured everything.

She slid from the rock before he could catch her. Before he could say more.

"Jane." Again, only her name would come out as he called after her.

But she had already disappeared into the trees.

CHAPTER 18

"Well, this is rather a change in circumstances."

Austin turned from the window where he had been watching Jane walk along the lake with the doctor.

"How so?" he asked Mrs. Rowling as she came through the drawing room door, tea tray in her arms.

"Someone else is hiding from you." She raised both her eyebrows. "That's quite something different I would say."

"She's not hiding from me." His frown must have been startling because even the stalwart Mrs. Rowling flinched.

"It appears as though she is, I'm afraid." She set the tea tray on a table before folding her hands resolutely in front of her. "Do you wish to speak of it, or do you plan to ignore the matter until it is no longer relevant?"

That sounded frighteningly close to the his own words only days before when—

When he had ruined everything.

He slumped against the window frame. "I wish to make her my wife, but every time I think I've broken through, she slams the door in my face again."

"I see," Mrs. Rowling said curtly. "And what evidence do you have to suggest this?"

"I'm afraid my reputation proceeds me."

She cocked an eyebrow. "Puddles has earned himself a reputation? Is it something sordid?"

"I'm apparently considered a rogue."

"Oh my, that is sordid. And to think it so unfounded."

He paused. "How do you know it's unfounded?"

She cocked the other eyebrow. "Really, Puddles? Must you ask?"

He scrubbed a hand over his face. "There was an incident in London." He was not about to speak with Mrs. Rowling about what had occurred more recently, but there was plenty to mull over without it.

Mrs. Rowling made a muttering sound of disapproval. "What did you do?"

He eyed her. "Why do you think it was I who made the transgression?"

She frowned.

"Perhaps it was my fault."

More frowning.

"It was definitely my fault?"

Her expression relaxed at that, but not in a way to suggest he'd come to the right conclusion, but more that she had resigned herself to some distasteful task. She came forward in the way he remembered from his childhood. It was a ponderous way of stepping as if she were being careful with her feet while she worked over a problem.

"Explain to me what is happening." She paused but cut him off when he tried to speak. "What is *truly* happening."

He glanced back out the window. Jane and the doctor had made their way to the far side of the lake, and although it was hard to tell from this distance, he was fairly certain the doctor had found a seat on the bank and was settling in.

"I think I fell in love with her." The words nearly burned him as they slipped from his throat, but as soon as the truth was in the air, a weight lifted from his chest.

"Then I'm certain you behaved incorrectly."

He threw Mrs. Rowling a scalding glare, but she waved him off.

"Let's start at the beginning," she said and took a seat by the window.

So he did. Starting from the first moment he'd rescued Jane from the pavement in front of that lecture hall more than a year previous. He told of how he'd been charmed by her when for so long no woman had had the power to affect him.

And told of the other bits. The Brownlow affair. The professor. The telescope technology. The hunt for a killer and a traitor. He poured everything out, and when he was done, he collapsed in the chair opposite the only person in the world he had ever seen as a parent figure.

Who now pursed her lips at him.

"That's it?" She cocked an eyebrow. "You haven't seduced her?"

He'd omitted that part on purpose, and still, he hadn't seduced her. Not entirely at any rate. "Is that relevant?"

Mrs. Rowling slowly closed her eyes and opened them again as if searching for patience. "It's the most important bit when it comes to a girl like Jane."

"What do you mean?"

Mrs. Rowling shifted forward in her chair. "A girl like Jane is one that must be handled delicately because her path has likely not been easy. You said she has a cousin. Emily something? Are they close?"

He shook his head, remembering the crack of Jane's hand against her cousin's cheek. "They do not have common interests."

"This Emily is beautiful then?"

He didn't mince words. "And the daughter of a duke."

"Ah." Mrs. Rowling folded and refolded her hands in her lap. "Then yes, I assume Jane has faced a fair bit of criticism from that direction during her precious formative years. And her parents?"

He thought of Mr. and Mrs. Black. "Unquestionably supportive and loving."

"Even of her more eccentric pursuits?"

He thought of the younger Miss Black, Lizzie as the family called her, and her penchant for sword fighting. "They are undoubtedly supportive of any pursuits their daughters express an interest in."

"So she's been encouraged to develop outside of the norms society has decided are most valuable for a woman to obtain while already lacking those that society has determined are irreplaceable."

"What is it you're saying?"

"I'm saying you're trying to woo a wallflower, and you're absolute rubbish at it." She sat back in her seat with a huff. "You're really a terrible rogue."

"I've never been in love before."

Mrs. Rowling stilled, and her face took on a stark expression.

He leaned forward. "Mrs. Rowling." He kept his voice even and low. "I often feel at times that there is something you are keeping from me. Something unpleasant."

Mrs. Rowling had a back that would make a diamond shatter, and she did not flinch at his words. "I am rather uncertain whether or not you are aware of certain things in your past, and if you are choosing to remember them differently or if it is simply that you do not know."

He sat back. "I do not speak of the past."

"Yes, I realize that, and that's rather pig-headed of you, don't you think?"

"You're out of line." The words came out before he could stop them, and even he was disgusted with how much they sounded like a defense. Defense to what?

Mrs. Rowling made to stand. "Very good—"

"Wait." He thrust a hand out to stop her. "Is there something important I'm missing? Something that would help me convince Jane to marry me?"

That was it. The thing burning inside of him. The thing that had him defensive and greedy at the same time. Greedy to know whatever it was that Mrs. Rowling guarded so carefully.

She eased back into her chair. "My lord, you must understand that if I am to speak of this, it is well outside my place. While I believe the relationship we have is rather past that of lord and servant, I am also aware I am an old woman. If you are to turn me out, again something I do not believe you capable of, but with what I have to say being of a volatile nature I wouldn't say dismissing me would be unheard of or unexpected. You know I haven't the funds to live on my own nor the family to support me. I would like your word that you will not take such action. If you find what I am about to say is, in fact, unpleasant, we will pretend I never spoke of it at all. I will continue on in my place here at Peregrine Hall and mind my position until I am no longer able to perform my duties."

Her eyes were so clear. So sharp. He didn't believe her when she said she was an old woman, but the softness of her cheeks and the spots along the backs of her hands told him otherwise.

He gripped the arms of his chair. "Agreed. Go on."

Mrs. Rowling did not hesitate. "There are things which occur between a man and a wife, which can be puzzling to a small child caught between the two, and I am afraid the events of your past have somehow become mixed up in your mind."

His grip tightened until he thought he might shatter the wood beneath his palms. He nodded for her to proceed, his heart thundering so loudly he could not speak over it.

"Your mother and father had an arranged marriage. This I am certain you know."

He nodded again.

"Your mother was quite young when she wed while your father had the benefit of many years behind him. Your father was diligent in his duties to the title and to the crown. His father had chosen a suitable bride from a respectable family. Your grandfather's good work with his title and lands meant his son had no need for money and could marry for pedigree to carry on the line."

"You make my mother sound like prized horseflesh."

Mrs. Rowling made to stand again, and he raised his hand once more. "I beg your pardon. Please continue."

She settled, but her gaze was wary now. "Your father was a remarkable gentleman. The level of his dedication to all of those under his care was rare in men of his rank, and it was because of him that I can say I have worked under this roof for more than forty years." She paused, licked her lips as if gaining momentum. "He worked hard to provide for the tenants. He strove to improve conditions for his servants." Another pause but now her lips parted slightly as if preparing for the thing that would hurt him to hear. "He gave his wife the freedom he believed she deserved as long as she were to provide him an heir."

He stilled and watched her carefully. She didn't go on, and finally, he was forced to speak. "My father respected my mother. Is that what you are trying to say?"

"Respect is not a word I would use. Your father did as

only he knew how." For the first time she fidgeted, a small play of her fingertips against her apron. "Your father was not inclined to love another being, but he was aware of that fact. So he—"

"He gave space where he could not give love." He didn't know where the words came from, but they were suddenly there as his mind cast back into the pool of memories of his father.

Mrs. Rowling was right. His father had never been close to him. Had never told him he loved him. But he had also not been a terrible father. Not like the fathers of some of the boys at school. His father had just been…absent even when he was in the same room.

How could he have missed it? He had always thought his father had been horrible to his mother. Hated her. But in fact, it wasn't that at all.

Mrs. Rowling seemed satisfied with this answer as she nodded. "I think that would do quite nicely, yes."

"Is it that which would cause me to dismiss you?" His stomach tightened. Surely that couldn't be it. But then…what?

Mrs. Rowling closed her eyes, and when she opened them, the darkness there frightened him. "Your mother took a lover after you were born."

No, that didn't make sense. His mother…his mother…he didn't know. He had just thought his father had been…

"She wanted to run away with him, live in France or Italy. Somewhere where they could be together. But your father demanded she stay." Once more her lips stilled, partly open, before she said. "For you. He demanded she stay for you."

No, that wasn't right. His father…his father had been absent. Unloving. Cold. He'd driven his mother to her death. He'd—

"But she couldn't bear it. She had never wanted to marry

your father, and even more, she never wanted you." The words should have cut him. Slain him. Something. But he couldn't feel anything. Just cold. Numbing cold. "Your mother didn't kill herself because your father didn't love her. Your mother killed herself because your father so cared for you."

He couldn't speak as the whole of his past seemed to rearrange itself. But Mrs. Rowling was not done. She leaned in now.

"You will never convince Jane Black you wish to marry her unless you give her your entire self. That is what it will take to convince her of your intent. But I'm afraid you've already given your entire self trying to save a mother you were not meant to save, and now there is nothing of you left to give."

* * *

"If someone stumbled upon us now, they would say you're the one carrying the troubles of the world."

Jane narrowed her eyes at the doctor. He was doing that so much lately. Speaking for all the world as if it were a regular day when no one else was in earshot to hear him. She was beginning to think she was going daft herself.

"It can be certain I'm carrying one," she muttered and was rewarded with a grin from the doctor.

"I often found your line of work rather taxing," he said.

She started until she realized he spoke of spying. "This isn't exactly my…profession." The last word came with a defined hitch, and she peered at the doctor to see if he noticed.

He continued to smile at her, a certain gleam in his eye behind his spectacles. "You're a Black, aren't you? Then spying is always your first occupation. It runs in the blood."

She shivered at the thought. "I'm afraid my pursuits are much more orderly in nature."

"I keep hearing rumors about a lass that likes ledgers. That wouldn't be you, would it?"

His expression said he already knew it was her, but she ignored it and answered anyway. "My father always allowed me to attend to the accounts on our home estate."

"Eaton Park." He said it with a certain amount of reverence, and she looked at him, realizing he, too, must be missing home.

"Yes, Eaton Park."

They fell silent then, each staring off into the distance to the fields that dropped below the rim of the lake. It was quieter today than it had been when they'd first ventured to the lake on their walks. Ben and his team were preparing for the planting, and the field lay quiet about them. But it wasn't the physical silence that unnerved her. It was the stillness of the water and the secrets it held that she now knew.

Her thoughts couldn't proceed a single step without circling back to Austin.

Austin.

That day by the stream. The way he'd looked at her. The way he'd told her she was beautiful.

The way she had finally believed him.

She wished her mother were there. Or Penelope. Or Lady Jane. Someone she could talk to. Someone she could confess to.

To say she'd been wrong.

A bird swooped across the lake in a delicate arch breaking the silence as the doctor looked up quickly.

"A swallow, I should think," he mumbled.

"You care for birds then?" she asked. Every little bit she talked to him, she hoped it would somehow help to heal the damage that had been done.

But the doctor shook his head. "No, no. I fancy birds just like the next man." He turned to her. "They're a sign of life. Of time. Of things marching on." Turned away. Watched the bird reach the other side of the lake and bank east. "For too long stone walls and iron bars were all I saw. It's nice to be reminded things are still moving just as they once were."

He wasn't speaking of birds. She knew that. But she wondered of the many things he could be speaking of. Bethany? His wife whom he had not seen in so many years. Too many years. Of the life they could have had?

This sudden thought had her wrapping her arms around her middle. To think that an unnamed person could wield so much power over another. Condemn another to a life that was less than it could have been. Should have been.

"Horses."

He looked at her with one gray eyebrow raised.

"I feel the same way about horses." She gestured to the far side of the house where the sagging stables peeked from around the corner. "Not fancy horseflesh you see the great lords of society parading about. But the working horseflesh. The ones who pull the plows and carts. The ones that haul the wagons. So much progress, and it's all done on the backs of horses." She paused, her heart pinching a little as she remembered Harold cooped up in a ratty stable during what should have been the most relaxing years of his life. Not yet moved to his new paddock as the planting had taken priority. "The life of a farm would not thrive without horses."

The doctor made a sound of agreement as he scratched at his whiskers. "I think I understand what you mean, lass. You miss your home then?"

She opened her mouth to answer but the words tripped on her tongue. She had been about to say she was home. For, in truth, she was. She was in Maidenstone. That was home enough to her.

The earth moved differently in Kent. The air shifted with greater ease, filled with the smell of the earth instead of the smog of coal fires. The press of time didn't exist here as one day faded into the next, and it was only the call of the crops and the livestock that pulled one about. No teas, no musicales, no soirees. No one on whom to pay reverence.

Only the earth.

So basic. So primal. So pure. So...undemanding.

It was exactly what she had wanted her entire life.

The ball of anxiety she'd been carrying about since that day with Austin tightened in her stomach, and she sucked in a breath to keep from retching.

This was not at all how this was to happen. She was to save the doctor and learn his secret so she could protect the family. Uphold her vow. Marry Mr. Smith and continue with the steady, safe life she had planned.

But even as she thought of Mr. Smith, she pictured Austin.

Austin standing in the middle of the fields. His fields. Peregrine. Surveying the land as if he were seeing it for the first time. She knew what that was like. She understood it. Felt it.

Austin laughing with Ben and Mary as if they were still little children sent out to play to keep from under the heels of the grown ups.

Austin teasing her over the ledgers. Austin goading her into helping him. Austin touching her, his hands on her bare skin. His eyes—

You're beautiful.

No, it didn't matter. She already had her life planned. It didn't matter—

It didn't matter that she had fallen in love with him.

"Oh, God." The words slipped out before she could stop them, and the doctor turned, his brow creased in concern.

"Have you wrestled with those stormy thoughts long enough, child? Have you come to the heart of the matter?"

His face was so kind. His expression so caring. But she couldn't bring herself to say anything. Dr. Seymour carried enough burdens for more than one man. He didn't need her silly quibbles with love.

"It's nothing," she said, but she knew she'd spoken too quickly because the doctor did not stop watching her. She pushed to her feet, turning away as the sting of tears reached her eyes.

She couldn't be crying. Not over this. Not over something so silly. So trivial.

So everything.

The air caught in her throat, and she chocked, hitching her shoulders to ease the pain. The doctor was at her elbow before she realized he had followed her.

"This appears to be more than just nothing, Miss Black." His tone had changed, and the weighty way in which he'd spoken her name carried almost the tone of a concerned father.

She studied the doctor's face, realizing all at once, that not only was the doctor suffering his secret, he was still suffering the loss of his friend. His comrade. His confidant.

She shook her head and tried to force a smile to her lips. "It really is nothing. It's only a silly matter of the heart."

"Matters of the heart are never silly," the doctor returned before doing the most stunning thing. He laid a hand on her arm. In the weeks since they had rescued him from Bedlam, he had been reclusive, shirking human touch whenever it should be a possibility. Withdrawing as soon as the opportunity arose. But now, he touched her elbow, his grip soft, warm, and sure. "This must have something to do with his lordship, the marquess. Has he declared his intentions?"

She shook her head. "No. Of course not." But then, wait. "I don't know."

Dr. Seymour raised both brows. "You do not know?"

Everything inside of her tumbled at his questioning gaze. She thought of that day. Austin's touch. His kiss. His gaze. The way he had looked at her said so much.

With Mr. Smith it had always been so simple. He was always straightforward. Plain in his intentions. He sought a wife who could manage the estate while he conducted his experiments. That was all.

But with Austin.

The way he smiled at her had her questioning the stockings she wore for no reason at all. Nothing in it was simple.

"I don't know," she repeated when her thoughts continued to circle in her head. "I think I've been wrong all along."

The doctor's frown turned ominous. "Then you've fallen in love with him, haven't you?"

The shock that he understood shot through her chest, and she wrapped her arms more tightly about her, backing away. "No, that's not it." Again, the words came too quickly.

Dr. Seymour shook his head and looked at the ground. "This is not at all my area of expertise. Never was. You should have seen my bumbled proposal to Bethany." He laughed then but he still looked at the ground, and she continued to slink away like a wounded dog. "I mucked up the whole thing and yet she still said yes." Another laugh. Finally he looked up, but she was a good five feet away by then. Poised to flee. He frowned harder. "Is there anything I can do to help, miss?"

She opened her mouth but no sound emerged. Not until she managed the words, "If only I could speak to my mum."

And then something happened.

Perhaps it was the bird that had flown past them earlier. Perhaps it was the stark expression of fear she felt on her features. Perhaps it was the way she folded in on herself like a wounded animal. Perhaps…

But whatever it was, the doctor's face cleared like the last of a storm playing itself out from a summer sky. His jaw firmed, and his shoulders unwound. For the first time since she had met him, Dr. Seymour stood at his full height and gripped each lapel of his worn jacket with a steady sure hand. Suddenly, a gentleman stood before her. Not an escapee of Bedlam. Not the tormented shell of a man.

A gentleman.

A doctor.

Her grandfather's friend.

And he spoke. "Harlow Merritt. Lord Crawley."

CHAPTER 19

"I can see why you've kept this to yourself."

Dr. Seymour stood in front of him, appearing taller than Austin remembered him being. He was also not as gaunt as he'd been the day they'd rescued him from Bedlam, and he knew Mrs. Rowling's care had such an effect.

He crossed his arms as he paced to the window of the study and although he looked out it, he saw Jane's reflection. She stood behind him, hunched, and looking everywhere but at him.

"I'm glad you've decided to share this information with us."

Harlow Merritt, Lord Crawley.

The head of the spy network at the War Office.

No wonder Dr. Seymour had fled into Bedlam to hide. It was the safest place he could have gone. Austin's gut twisted, thinking of Samuel in London protecting his entire extended family on his own. He had to get this information to him. He turned and strode back to his desk.

"A notice in *The Times* will take too long. We need to get word to London now." He hesitated before finally peering up at Jane. She stood much as she had since bringing the doctor to him. So guarded. So wary.

He had ruined everything in one unguarded moment of passion. She had grown comfortable around him while they had gone through every blasted ledger at Peregrine Hall. As they had visited the tenants. He had even heard her laugh a time or two at the antics of his tenants' children. And then...

He'd fallen in love with her.

Mrs. Rowling had done little to help him sort the matter, and instead, had muddied the waters a great deal by telling him the truth about his mother. He eyed the doctor and wondered what in God's name was happening to force everyone to spill their darkest secrets all at once.

He stared at the surface of his desk. He still didn't know how to get word to London. Not without endangering their position.

"You must go to London."

His gaze flew to Jane. It was the first words she had spoken since coming into the study. Her voice was firm, unlike the tremble he saw at her shoulders as she spoke them.

She even took a step forward. "You must get to London as soon as possible. Alert my family. Father will know what to do."

"I agree with the miss, my lord," Dr. Seymour said with a gesture to Jane. "Mr. Black will surely be able to handle the situation." He cast a curious glance at Jane. "Isn't your uncle the duke now, then?"

Jane's smile was tremulous. "He is at that."

Dr. Seymour raised his eyebrows. "Then the duke should be able to address the matter. Go right to the top if he must."

Austin straightened. "Dr. Seymour, are you aware of any other titled gentlemen in league with Lord Crawley?"

Dr. Seymour grimaced. "Not voluntarily. There are a few

who have discovered his secret just like I had and chose to go along with his schemes to save their families."

"Do you have their names?"

"Yes, of course," the doctor said as he wrung his hands together. "Would you care for me to write a list?"

"Please." Austin gathered ink and quill for the doctor and moved aside so he could sit at the desk.

It was at that moment Mrs. Rowling entered. She gave a nod before asking crisply, "Do you require a tea cart, my lord?"

Now was not the time for tea, but if he were to leave and take Dr. Seymour's information to London, he would be leaving not only Jane but Mrs. Rowling and Mary and Ben and the rest of the staff, meager as it was, in danger.

"Shut the door," he said far more sternly than he had meant, but Mrs. Rowling, bless her heart, didn't hesitate. She stepped back and slammed the door shut.

"Have you obtained your information then?" she said without preamble.

He wanted to cock an eyebrow in question, but he knew better. Mrs. Rowling always seemed to know everything that transpired under her roof.

"We have," he said, coming fully around the desk to approach her. "I'm afraid I must get to London."

"Then you must leave at once. I'll have the maids ready your things." She moved to the door, but he stopped her.

"There isn't time. I'll need to go on horseback. If I leave now, I can make it before—"

"Before what? The middle of the night?" Her lips pursed in annoyance.

"Something like that," he mumbled and looked back at Jane, but she hadn't moved. "I'm afraid I've drawn you into a spot of trouble, Mrs. Rowling."

A single, thin gray eyebrow shot up. "Indeed, you have.

Go then. At once. The sooner this is over the sooner me and my staff are out of danger. To say nothing of the miss." She gestured to Jane, and he felt a stab of remorse.

He couldn't leave her. Not now. Not when—

The doctor stood, extending a fold of paper to him. "Here it is. All of them that I could remember. Lord, I hope he hasn't ensnared more of them."

Austin took the paper and studied it. "Did Lord Crawley ever say why it was that he chose such a route?"

Dr. Seymour appeared uncomfortable as his eyes darted between Austin and Jane. He cleared his throat and said, "He didn't like all the attention the Black family received for their work with the War Office."

"What?" The single word exploded from Jane.

Dr. Seymour's face fell. "It wasn't any fault of your grandfather's or father's. The Blacks are good. Good at what they do and what they've done for this country. Lord Crawley did not care to see his family live in their shadow."

Jane wobbled, and Austin thought for a moment she would collapse. But it was as if iron itself sprang up through her, from her feet straight through her backbone and up through her neck. She turned an icy glare to Austin that he knew was not meant for him, but still, it chilled him to the bone.

"You must leave at once."

And there it was. The thing he had been avoiding.

He didn't want to leave her.

If he left and something happened, he'd never be able to live with himself. His mother. Oh God. He'd left and she'd killed herself. He hadn't been there to save her.

But even as he thought it, he remembered Mrs. Rowling's words. He finally realized he was in love, and things were more confused than ever.

Jane raised her chin the smallest of degrees, but her gaze

pierced right through him. For the first time in days, she actually looked at him. And what he saw there hit him like nothing else could.

Courage.

Bravery.

Strength.

Determination.

And he fell again.

And yet even though he loved her, everything inside his head remained a tangled mess. He couldn't leave her. Hadn't meant to fall in love with her.

And suddenly, clearly, and most of all—he didn't know if he could save her.

But he had to do this thing. He had to do it for her.

He nodded once, turned, and left.

* * *

SHE SAT down in the closest chair, bumping her bonnet against the back of it. She reached up, her fingers brushing its brim. She hadn't removed it when she'd come in from the lake with the doctor. Her fingers trailed down the stiff edge until her hand dropped to her chest. The lace fringe of her shawl tickled her fingers. She hadn't removed that either.

"I'll get you some tea, my dear." Mrs. Rowling bustled to the corner for the bell pull before returning. "Please, dear, give me your things. Let's get you comfortable. You've had quite a shock, you have."

Jane shook her head. "No, I'm fine really." The bonnet dug in at the back of her neck, and Mrs. Rowling made a tsking noise before reaching forward and simply tugging the hat from Jane's head.

It pulled a little at her hair, but soon it was off, and she could lay her head back against the chair.

The doctor appeared in her vision then, the careworn expression having returned to his face. She reached out a hand to indicate he should sit. Suddenly she worried he would lapse back into his mumblings if she allowed him a moment alone to think.

"I'm sure you could use a cup of tea as well, Dr. Seymour." She was surprised by how strong her voice sounded when she certainly didn't feel as such.

The doctor sat, but a line appeared between his brows. "I'm not sure what it is I am to worry over. There's been so much worry for so long."

She swallowed. "It's all quite a shock to hear what one has believed for so long to not be the truth at all." It was easier to admit to that than the stark worry that soared through her at the thought of Austin on horseback tearing through the English night. Alone. In the dark. In danger.

A maid soon arrived with the teacart. Jane served the doctor before catching Mrs. Rowling trying to slip from the room.

"Mrs. Rowling." Jane paused with the teapot over an empty cup.

Mrs. Rowling turned with a single raised eyebrow. "If we are to be in any sort of danger, I must prepare the staff."

"Of course," Jane said as she lowered the teapot. "Well, then we must be of assistance in some way."

"Yes, you will as long as you stay out of the way. I will return shortly." The housekeeper left with a twitch of her fingers.

She turned to the doctor. "I fear Mrs. Rowling would get along smashingly with my grandmother."

The doctor chuckled. "I think you're correct." His voice was steady, but his teacup wobbled as he brought it to his lips.

"Thank you," Jane said before picking up her own cup.

The doctor hesitated, raising an eyebrow in question.

"For entrusting us with your secret. I cannot assure you this will end well, but I can assure you it will end." She stared into her tea as she spoke the words, realizing she knew the truth of them all along.

Her stomach clenched, thinking of Austin again. He should have taken a guard with him. Ben, perhaps. But Austin wouldn't have left the staff without Ben's protection. Of course, he wouldn't.

She mulled this over in her mind until she was nearly sick with it before she realized the doctor tapped a single finger against his teacup. And then another. And then—

"Dr. Seymour." She straightened to get his attention. "The rhyme that you repeated. The one listing the characters of Grimm's tales. What was that about?"

The doctor eyed her as if he hadn't a clue as to what she was speaking. Perhaps he didn't realize he spoke in rhymes when he was so deeply within himself. She tried another tactic.

"In the book of fairy tales you gave my grandfather, you hid a piece of paper that warned to be wary of the Frog King. Why was that?"

The doctor's brow furrowed over his spectacles. "Richard and I used to speak of other agents at the office in code so others wouldn't understand should we be overheard. Your grandfather always thought Crawley resembled a toad. So we coined him the Frog King."

Jane stared in disbelief. "My grandfather thought his superior officer was a toad?"

"Oh, Crawley was not his superior officer then. It was Crawley's father at the time. But Richard was right, wasn't he?" the doctor quipped before taking a sip of tea.

It was going to be a very long wait for Austin to return.

CHAPTER 20

He heard the distinct click of a gun being cocked as soon as he stepped through the door. He stilled, raising both arms even as they trembled in fatigue.

"It's me," he whispered to his unseen potential assassin. "The Marquess of Evanshire. I bring news."

A lamp flared to life to his right, and suddenly the foyer of Lofton House glowed brightly. He turned his head to the right to find a pistol uncomfortably close to his temple, and a stern-faced duchess on the other end of it.

"You always come through doors unannounced?" Sarah Black, the Duchess of Lofton, asked as she uncocked the gun and lowered it.

"Do you always leave doors unlocked?"

"When we're trying to catch a traitor, we do." Alec Black, the Duke of Lofton emerged from behind the glowing lamp. "Old family tradition," he added with a smirk.

"Why aren't you with Jane?" This was a rather thunderous question flung at him as the stairs erupted in stampeding feet with Nathan Black leading the charge.

"She's somewhere safe." It was true Peregrine was safe, but as to the number of guards, he truly only felt certain about Ben. He wasn't about to tell Jane's father that when he'd arrived in the middle of the night likely looking as if he'd just been run over by a coach-and-four.

But the occupants of Lofton House looked hardly better as they appeared from behind doors and down the stairs. They were each in varying states of undress as it was, again, the middle of the night, and he had arrived without notice. Nathan Black stood with sleeves rolled up and collar undone just as the Duke of Lofton. Samuel came from down the hall with cravat neatly in place but jacket gone, his rumpled wife trailing behind him.

Mrs. Black, Nora it was, appeared on the stairs behind her husband. She was still dressed but her hair had fallen down around her shoulders and dark smudges bruised the space under her eyes. She placed a hand on her husband's shoulder just as Lady Jane and Mrs. Seymour appeared at the top of the stairs.

He was aware of the professor arriving because the man barked at Lady Emily to shut her mouth and pay attention for once, but Austin's gaze remained fixed on Mrs. Black's hand on her husband's shoulder. In such a simple gesture lay the weight of a long and beautiful marriage. He had never been witness to such until now, and suddenly his chest tightened.

He needed to return to Jane. To fix what he had ruined. But what if he couldn't fix it?

But until then, he was still on a mission, and he lifted his gaze to meet Professor Mesmer's cutting stare. It was the murder of the professor's friend and mentee that had started all of this, and it was he who deserved Austin's attention when he said, "Lord Crawley."

There was silence then. The kind of silence that can only follow a proclamation with the power to utterly change one's life. Austin stood in the foyer of the grand house and watched each member of the family absorb the news. Each did it quietly, but in their own particular way. Quietly that is except for Lady Jane.

"That gutter snipe bloody bastard!" she cried as she clutched Mrs. Seymour's arm. "Did you know of this?"

There were tears in Mrs. Seymour's eyes as she shook her head. "I knew it was terrible, but I couldn't…I didn't fathom…" The sentence trailed away as her voice was lost in a sob. Lady Jane pulled her friend closer to her and turned her determined glare on him. "We must alert the authorities."

Samuel stepped forward immediately. "First we must secure the family." He turned to his uncle, the duke. "We must get as many of them to Bedford as quickly as possible. It will be safer there."

A cry erupted from the top of the stairs that had nothing to do with Mrs. Seymour's sobbing. Austin was not surprised to find it came from Lady Emily.

"We cannot leave now. The season's only just begun!" Her voice was shrill, but Austin ignored her as did the rest of them.

"We'll leave at daybreak," His Grace said as he looked to his wife who was already moving.

"I trust the servants are already awake. We'll get started on the packing." She swept through the foyer, and only then did Austin realize she wore trousers.

What a rather odd family the Blacks were behind closed doors.

"We'll need to go to the commissioner for this, and then, God, who do we go to for a treasonous earl who also happens to head the secret operations division of the War

Office?" Samuel looked to his father who was making his way down the last of the steps.

"Unfortunately, something of this nature requires we activate the failsafe." His voice was low and grave.

The duke stopped on his way out of the foyer to turn about quickly, his eyes wide. "You're going to the king."

Austin had spent the better part of the last twelve hours in the saddle. Stopping only long enough to switch horses and splash water on his face. But now, he came fully awake, his body alert, tense, ready. In his head, he heard the sounds of war, and his hands clenched into fists convulsively.

"We have no other choice. We don't know how deep this goes."

Mr. Black's words roused him long enough to extract the doctor's list from the pocket of his coat. He extended it to Mr. Black.

"This was a list the doctor made from what he could remember of the time he uncovered Crawley's secret. These are gentlemen of rank who have been coerced into doing his bidding. I'm afraid it's rather dangerous."

Samuel stepped closer to Mr. Black as did the duke as they peered down at the list.

Finally, the duke gave a low whistle. "It's astonishing we haven't all been killed by now with a list like that."

"Samuel, we're going to need Commissioner Mayne." Mr. Black turned to his brother. "Get the family to safety."

Austin turned back to the door. He didn't need instructions. He knew exactly where he was to be right now. Needed to be.

But a sharp voice stopped him dead.

"And where do you think you're going?"

He turned back to find Mrs. Black rushing down the stairs, her skirts caught in her hands so she could descend more quickly.

"I must get back to—" He nearly revealed the location of Jane and the doctor. He scrubbed a hand over his face, blinking as the need for sleep became apparent in the grit under his eyelids.

"Just as I thought. You're no good to anyone if you fall asleep in the saddle and fall off your horse. You must get some rest." Mrs. Black's slim hand gripped his arm with amazing strength.

He tried to shake her off but found she was either too strong or he too tired. Likely both. "I must get back immediately. I can't leave her—"

Samuel stepped into his line of vision. "I'm afraid my mother is always right, chap. A few hours of sleep are more important now. We have our man, and soon we'll have him in custody. The danger is over."

While his friend seemed to speak the truth, Austin's gut wouldn't settle, and he knew it wouldn't until he saw Jane again. Held her in his arms. Assured himself she was safe.

Mr. Black stepped forward then and lowered his head. "Now that the danger has passed, I think it's best that someone else know the doctor's location. In the event that it's necessary."

Austin hesitated for a moment, his gaze moving to the rest of the family loitering on the stairs as the duke tried to create some sort of order to get the family off to their country estate. "Peregrine Hall. It's the country estate of the Evanshire title."

Mr. Black nodded, and Samuel cuffed him on the shoulder. "We will forever be in your debt. Now off to bed."

Mrs. Black prodded him. "Listen to your friend. Now off to bed with you."

* * *

LORD CRAWLEY.

Professor Mesmer couldn't comprehend it. It was so simple.

Two words spoken so succinctly and yet they had the power to change everything.

For more than a year he'd hunted Bobby's killer. Had fled detection just to keep searching, the drive in him to find the culprit greater than anything he had felt before.

And now it was all over.

Samuel was right. The danger was over. The traitor had been unmasked, and he would be taken into custody. Dealt with.

The king.

God, these bloody British and their bloody monarchy. If he were home in Massachusetts—

Well, he would likely do exactly as he did now. Let the authorities handle it. While he may possess a good deal of courage, he possessed a greater amount of sensibility. There were those in place to handle matters such as this, and it wasn't for him to manage. His job was done.

He stepped aside as Mrs. Black ushered a nearly ashen Marquess of Evanshire up the steps to an empty room. She was right as well. They all needed a little more sleep. The past few of weeks had been tense to say the least. He was exhausted. Physically and mentally.

God, could he sleep now?

He hoped so.

He turned to ascend the steps after them but stopped, a movement catching his attention. He swiveled just enough to see what it was.

It was Lady Emily Black. The skirts of her gown clamped in her hands as she picked them up and scurried along the corridor toward the back of the house. Her rooms were on the floor above just like the rest of the family, so where exactly did she think she was going?

He sighed, flicking one last glance in the direction of the marquess and Mrs. Black.

It wasn't time for him to sleep. Not when Lady Emily Black was surely off to do something rash.

CHAPTER 21

Go to Bedford.

Was he utterly mad?

There was no way in God's teeth she was going to Bedford. Not now. She would be ruined. Utterly and irrevocably ruined. She would not be a deb entering her third season. *Third*. God, what could they possibly be thinking?

They weren't obviously. They never thought about her. How what they did affected her life. They only cared about poor plain Jane.

Well, she would show them. They no longer mattered. She had a duke on the line, and she wasn't about to let him get off. Who cared that he smelled like sour milk and stale tobacco? Who cared that his measly thin lips tasted like liver oil?

She would be a duchess. She would have the power to ascend above them all.

A twig snapped behind her, and she turned, hating herself for getting so lost in her own thoughts to forget where she was.

Dawn had just appeared through the branches of the newly budded trees where she often met Harlow. The dewy grass had already dampened her slippers by then, and she made a soft squeaking noise as she turned. He was just coming through the trees, and she pasted a brilliant smile on her face.

"Oh, Harlow." She painted her voice with just enough sadness to make the old sod feel needed before she rushed forward and threw herself into his arms. "You will not believe what has happened to me."

The old man teetered somewhat but caught her deftly enough to set her back on her feet. He still smelled of stale tobacco and liver oil, and she choked slightly, having forgotten to take a breath of fresh air before getting this close to him. She swallowed the cough under a soft mewl and leaned in closer, burying her face in his knobby chest.

"They are making me leave, Harlow. Leave London. Right now. Do you know what that will do to me? I will be utterly ruined, Harlow." She added some tears to her voice just at the end. She needed to sound weak, not hopeless. Harlow would want to save a damsel in distress. Not pick up a waif from the gutter into which she'd fallen.

"There, there, my dear." He awkwardly patted her back with a thin hand. It was more of a slap than the comforting gesture it was likely meant to be. "They surely don't mean to take you away when you have only barely enjoyed the pleasures of a London season. How do they expect you to embrace the full potential of your loveliness if you are not allowed to partake of what London has to offer?"

She drew back enough so he could see the tears in her eyes. "You understand me so well, Harlow. How can I ever go on with a family who is so…uncaring?" She heaped on a small wail with that last word and snuffled her nose into his cravat.

Another awkward pat of the back. "There, there, dear. You mustn't worry yourself so. Everything will work itself out. Surely, that horrid cousin of yours will return shortly, and all will be well."

She added a little sniveling now as she looked up again. "That's just it. She's not coming back. She's ruined everything!"

She'd made a misstep. She knew the moment the words left her mouth, and his face darkened instantly. His hooded eyes lit with a sneer as his mouth hardened into something vicious like she'd never seen before. She took a step back, but he had her arms now. His hands though thin grasped her with unbreakable strength, and she felt like a fly caught in a spider's web.

"What do you mean she's not coming back?" His voice had lost the soft lilt it had carried all of these weeks she had been meeting him.

She tried stepping back again with a silly shake of her head. She must appear weak. Hurt. Confused. But she kept her senses alert. She had missed something. Something important.

"Where is she?" He shook her now, and she tested her arm. He must have learned his lesson because she didn't have the room to get her palm up to his nose again. She hardly had room to squirm.

For the first time she felt real fear, but she swallowed it down. If her mother had taught her anything about this nasty business, it was to keep her head about her. "I don't understand, Harlow darling. Why does it matter—"

Her teeth rattled when he shook her then. "It matters a great deal, you little tramp. Now tell me where she is." He spit when he tossed the words at her.

You little tramp.

She was many things but tramp was not one of them, and

to hear such a base accusation tossed at her like it was deserved unnerved her enough to have her saying, "She's at Peregrine Hall, wherever that is."

"Emily, no!"

The scream came from behind her but it was too late. The words were out. Harlow let go of her so quickly she fell, her palms skidding against the wet grass. Only then did she see Professor Mesmer pushing through the snarling branches to reach the secret spot in the grove of trees. His eyes were frantic, his hands thrusting against the branches.

"He's Lord Crawley!" he shouted at her.

She looked up at Harlow, the disbelief likely clear on her face. Lord Crawley? The one they had been routing out? The traitor?

No, that couldn't be. He was her Harlow, the Duke of Merritt.

But—

"No, he's not," she shouted back at the professor just as he pushed through the last of the branches. "This is my Harlow. My darling, Harlow—"

She couldn't be wrong. She couldn't have wasted an entire season. She couldn't still be unwed with a third season looming over her. She just couldn't. She—

The professor did the oddest thing then. He picked her up bodily and put her behind him, shielding her with his body. The professor was tall for what he rather lacked in bulk. But for a stupid moment, she felt safe standing behind him.

"So I've been found out." Harlow's voice came as a sneer, and she pushed the professor aside to stare at him.

"How could you?" The words were useless, and she hated herself for saying them, but she hated herself more for falling for this old sod's dupe.

"I recognized the crest on the carriage you have waiting for you in the park," Mesmer said. "I shall warn you. The authorities are being made aware of your treasonous schemes."

What was this blasted nonsense Mesmer was babbling on about? Why didn't he clock the old bugger? What Mesmer lacked in obvious strength, he made up for in youth. Why wasn't he using it?

She made to step around him, but he held out a hand to stop her. She pushed against it. She couldn't let this happen. Her family. This man was a danger to them all, and she had—

She hated herself.

Standing there, pushing against the professor's arm, Lady Emily Black hated herself, and she had no one else to blame for it.

She had done this. She had let the secret out to the one man that could use it most dangerously. Just as the thought solidified, Harlow's face spread into a terrifying smile.

"Yes, that carriage is waiting for me. Along with these gents."

They didn't have time to turn before the branches cracked behind them. What happened next, she would never forget. Never. So long as she lived. Mesmer leaped in front of her as two burly men stepped from the trees.

It wasn't until after, when Mesmer fell to the ground at her feet, that she saw the knife. Blood streamed from his thigh, and a cry lodged in her throat as she dropped instantly to her knees, her hands going to cover the wound. That knife had been meant for her, and judging by where it had struck Mesmer, it would have gutted her.

"I'm really beginning to hate you bloody English," Mesmer ground out between clenched teeth. His face was void of color now, and she reflexively pressed harder on the wound. He sat bolt upright, his hands flying toward her ineffectually. "Hell and damnation, woman, are you trying to finish me off?"

"Shut up, you yank! This is no time for rebuttal." She pinned Harlow with a glare. No, Crawley. He was Lord Crawley.

He was a traitor.

She felt it the instant her blood ran cold, and for the first time in her life, she understood her family's legacy. She understood it all, and her world grew so far beyond herself in an instant.

She grabbed Mesmer's flailing hands and pressed them to the wound in his thigh.

"Hold this." She was already on her feet before the professor muttered any kind of response. Without hesitating, she swung. Surprise was on her side, and her fist connected with Crawley's cheek. It was a moment before his burly bodyguards were on her, but for one blissful second, she felt a surge of satisfaction.

Blood dripped from his nose as Crawley straightened to glare at her. "Leave her be. She isn't worth our time. We must get to Kent." He turned with a gesture to his thugs, and they dropped her immediately.

She landed in the wet grass next to Mesmer, her shoulder against his, and she wasn't sure who held up whom.

"Kent?" Mesmer had the sense to ask.

Crawley turned briefly. "Yes, you said Peregrine Hall, didn't you? I attended a house party there once. Enjoyed a bit of bed sport with the mistress of the house if I recall. Whorish woman." He turned about with a sneer and disappeared through the trees, his henchmen not far behind.

* * *

"Hoping to finish the job, eh?"

It would seem Lady Emily was attempting to pick him up, but as she was a great deal smaller than he, she had managed little more than to get his arm around her shoulders.

"I am trying to save your life." Her face was very close. Closer than he had ever been to her, and he realized her eyes had shards of green in them. A ridiculous thing to notice at a time like this. He was soon to join dear Bobby, and here he was romanticizing about a young deb's eyes.

"You are doing a terrible job of it."

She glared. "Well, you are not helping, are you?"

"I've been stabbed. In the leg. What is it exactly I can do to help?"

She wrestled some more with his arm and finally managed to slip her own arm about his torso. "Stand up on your good leg."

"Do I have a good leg left?" He knew making a joke of it was the only way to trick his mind into not concentrating on the blinding pain shooting through his right leg at that moment.

"Your sarcasm is not appreciated."

"It never is," he mumbled, and then God above, she was lifting him. "You're rather strong for such a little lass."

"Of course, I am."

"Of course? I wouldn't think feats of strength are on the finishing list for debs."

She shifted him and miracles of miracles he stood on his good left leg. She stood in the circle of his arms now, and for one blessed minute, he absorbed her warmth. He was so hellishly cold.

She peered up at him, her jaw pure steel. "The daughter of Sarah Black would be remiss in not having such strength."

He raised an eyebrow and enjoyed the fact that he still could. "I've seen your mother perform some rather courageous feats. I had no idea she passed such tradition to her daughter."

She angled away from him now and attempted a step. He nearly collapsed with the pain, reaching for a nearby branch so as not to take her down with him.

"Jesus Christ." He didn't normally take the Lord's name in vain. Not that he was a religious man, but rather, he carried fond memories of his devout mother. But just then, he would call in any help he could. "Leave me. You need to get to Lofton House and warn the others."

"I'm not leaving you." She pushed him forward, and the next step was just as blindingly painful as the last.

"Like bloody hell you're not." Fantastic. Now he was even picking up on their euphemisms.

"You Americans might turn tail at the sight of trouble, but us Brits never leave a man behind."

"That's poppycock." In for a penny.

She stopped as they had become wedged between two knobby trees and faced him awkwardly. "Do you wish to keep arguing or do you perhaps wish to save your strength for what is going to be an arduous journey back to Lofton House?"

He wasn't sure when it had happened but Lady Emily had suddenly turned into just that. A lady. Not a recalcitrant child. Not a spoiled deb. A rather fine young lady.

"Lead on, Wellington," he mumbled and then said nothing more as pain sliced through his body.

He didn't know how much later it was that he realized arduous was a rather banal term for what he had just endured. And judging by the sweat pooling along Lady Emily's bodice, it was likely the same for her as well.

"For such a skinny man, you're awfully bloody heavy." Her words shot through clenched teeth as they rounded the last bend, and Lofton House came into sight.

"When I figure out whether or not that was an insult, I will come up with a scalding retort."

They had passed no one between the park and Lofton House. It was too early in the morning for members of the ton to be out after a night likely spent attending social functions until the early hours of the morn. There wasn't even a street sweep or an urchin lurking, looking for a coin to earn.

So it was that Lady Emily Black, the daughter of a duke, carried an American professor clear from the park to the heart of Mayfair.

And she hadn't complained once except for that pithy remark about his size. He feared he was beginning to miss her whine.

The sun had broken clear of the morning fog, and weak webs of light fell across the still empty street. Where were the carriage and servants at Lofton House? Wasn't the house preparing to leave?

As if reading his thoughts, the door to Lofton House opened, and a row of footmen emerged each carrying a trunk or parcel. Lady Emily made a sound he thought was meant to get their attention, but as they were both short on air, it came out a bit grumbled.

"You're going to have to do better than that, deb," he said, forcing his teeth apart long enough to get the words through. His right leg was completely covered in the blood seeping from the place where he'd tied his cravat on his thigh. The pavement was getting a bit wobbly, stretching and contracting, and he no longer knew where to put his foot. "I wouldn't mind hearing the old Lady Emily scream just now." They needed help, or he was going to meet the pavement with his face.

He didn't know how she did it. Her breath was ragged in his ear, and he felt the sweat along her back. But suddenly, Lady Emily screamed with all the force he knew she possessed. The sound should have been soul shattering at his proximity, but there was an odd hollow sound in his ears now. Like an ocean roaring.

And just as her scream finished, his good leg gave out. They went down together. He and the great daughter of a duke to the filthy English pavement. He didn't care. It felt so good not to be upright any longer. He could just lay here forever. Just close his eyes…

"Don't you bloody fecking die on me, Yank!" She grabbed him so roughly his eyes shot open. And then she screamed again, and it was really better just to keep his eyes shut.

Footsteps. Running footsteps. Sweet baby Jesus, someone had heard her.

"Get a doctor!" There. There. Yes. That was the duke. Alex. Allen. Something…

"What's happened?" Ah. The sweet one. What was her name? Natalie. Nadine. Nargaret. No. That wasn't a name. But it definitely began with an N.

He opened his mouth not realizing he meant to speak. "S'my fault." That sounded like English, didn't it?

"No, it's bloody not." God, but the lady was growing fierce. "It's my fault. We must hurry. Lord Crawley knows where Jane is."

"What?" The duke again. They must be standing over him.

Fire shot through his leg, and he lurched upright nearly knocking that sweet Nargaret to the ground.

Nargaret was not a name. How many times would he have to remind himself of that?

"Easy, darling. Easy." See, she was sweet. He smiled at her. Or he thought he did. "You're losing too much blood. We need to staunch the wound. Can you tell me what happened?"

He thought she spoke to Lady Emily, but the smile on his face dragged the words from him. "The deb here got herself into a tryst with Lord Crawley. Rather unseemly if you ask me. He's far too old for her. She deserves a young bloke with a good sense of humor. It's the only way to handle that temper of hers."

"What?" The single word shot from the duke like a bullet, but God damn, if Lady Emily didn't cower.

In fact, she straightened her shoulders as if preparing for a firing squad.

"It was my fault. He made me believe he was a duke. I thought I was going to be a duchess. I didn't know who he really was."

Her voice never wavered. He sat on the ground, gazing up at her, and Jesus Christ, if he didn't find himself admiring her.

"He forced me to tell him where Jane was." She stopped. Shook her head. "No, that was my fault. I was weak. I was stupid. I made a mistake. I should have seen it."

Well, that was a bit harsh on herself, wasn't it?

She looked at him suddenly with something akin to disbelief in her eyes, and he wondered if he'd said that out loud. He might have.

"Professor Mesmer stopped Crawley's goons. He meant to have me stabbed but—"

More footsteps. More commotion. Someone was leaning over him.

"I hope you're a bleeding doctor. No, wait. I'm the one who's bleeding." Mesmer got his eyes adjusted to the new face. "Oh, it's you. Did you bring a doctor with you?"

The poor marquess. He'd ridden all night to get there. To unmask the traitor. Bobby's killer. He was a good man, the marquess. He'd told Mesmer who the killer was. He'd needed to know. Need to know...what?

Everything was getting a bit black.

"Crawley knows where Jane is. Samuel and Nathan have already left for the Office. You—"

There were no more words. Just pounding feet. The marquess. The marquess off to save his lady love. Mesmer smiled again.

At least something wonderful had come of all this mess. As long as the marquess made it in time.

What was it? What had happened?

It was all too confusing. The blackness was so much better, so he let it come.

CHAPTER 22

She had never dreaded the coming dark before now. As she stood by the window in the drawing room of Peregrine Hall, she felt it. Dread. Austin had left the night before. He had likely made London. Had revealed the doctor's secret.

What had happened?

Had Samuel alerted the commissioner? Had her father gone higher up the chain of command in the War Office?

She hadn't thought about that. Who was there to tell when someone so high ranking, so enmeshed in a government office, had turned? She turned away from the window, dropping the drapes to hide the coming dark.

"He's likely made it to London by now." The doctor's voice was matter of fact.

She studied him sitting in the chair before the fire, accepting a cup of tea from Mrs. Rowling. He appeared calm at the outset, but she didn't miss the telltale tap of his fingers against the saucer. He may have told his secret, but the damage Lord Crawley had wrought ran deep. Time was the only thing that could heal the poor man, and time was one thing he did not have left.

Jane wrapped her arms more tightly about her middle and returned to the window.

"If you keep staring, it shall never come."

She turned back at Mrs. Rowling's words. "What shall never come?"

Mrs. Rowling shrugged. "Whatever it is you're waiting for." The woman had been unusually reticent since Austin's sudden departure, but then, Jane didn't expect anything else.

It was as if the whole house sat waiting, poised, ready for whatever was to happen next. But that was just it. They didn't know what was going to happen.

If Austin had made it.

No, he had to have made it. She couldn't live with anything else. He must have made it to London. He must have told them.

But then what could be done? How did one go about accusing a member of the peerage with treason? Based on the ramblings of an old man escaped from Bedlam? Or on the loose retellings of a novelist and her one encounter with the man?

The darkness fell sharply now. The moment between light and utter darkness. It happened so swiftly she didn't notice it. But still, there in the dim, she could make out the drive winding itself up the hill through the trees. She kept her gaze fixed on it.

But what was she waiting for?

What if Austin did return? What would she say to him?

No, she mustn't think about it.

Movement at the window caught her attention, and she blinked. She was beginning to see things.

But then the movement happened again. Steadier this time. Real. She gripped the drapes.

There was a carriage coming up the drive. A carriage bearing colors.

She must have made a noise because Mrs. Rowling suddenly asked, "What is it, dear?"

Dear God, could it be? Had Austin made it to London and was now returning with a Lofton carriage?

God, please, say it was so.

The carriage made the final bend in the drive and as it turned, she caught the crest in full.

Her stomach dropped, and a cry spilled from her lips before she could stop it.

Crawley colors.

Those were Crawley colors. She would recognize the carriage anywhere from the number of times it had pulled up to her grandfather's house. Her stomach threatened to lurch, and she wrenched away from the window.

"It's Crawley. He's found us. We need to get you out of here." The words were out, but neither the doctor nor Mrs. Rowling moved when the door to the study banged open and Ben rushed in.

"There's a carriage, miss. Never seen it before. We need to get you to safety." Ben's words were stilted as he was clearly out of breath from running.

Jane shook her head. "It's too late. We need to get the doctor out of here while we form a distraction. Something to keep Crawley away."

Ben pounded one fist into his open palm. "I'd be happy to give him a distraction."

No, that wouldn't do. She'd witnessed Crawley's wrath. Had seen what his henchmen were capable of, and surely, Crawley would not have come alone.

Jane pushed forward, reaching to bring the doctor from his chair. "No, it's too dangerous. I need you to get the doctor to safety." She brought the poor man forward and passed him into Ben's hands as one would a small child. "You must keep him safe. I made a promise."

Ben's lips hovered on a smile. "I'm beginning to understand you take your promises seriously."

"I do at that." She turned about. "Mrs. Rowling, I must ask you to get the rest of the servants to safety."

"They're already headed out the back." They all turned to find Mary in the doorway. She swept forward pulling at the doctor's hands. "You're next, my good man," she said and pulled him from the room.

Ben gave one last weak smile and said, "I hope you know what you're doing. If anything happens to you, his lordship will have my head."

The words, although somehow pleasant, roiled her stomach further, because quite simply she had no idea what she was doing. She jumped when Mrs. Rowling laid a hand on her arm.

Her eyes were suspiciously moist when she said, "I can't leave you here. It will burn Puddles alive should anything happen to you. We must get away together."

Jane shook her head. Stopped.

She seized Mrs. Rowling's hands. "You're a genius, did you know that?" Mrs. Rowling's shocked expression said otherwise. Jane squeezed the woman's hands and pushed her to the door. "Out with you. I will create a diversion to get you away, and then I'm going for help."

"Help? But there's no one to help but what you see here." Mrs. Rowling wobbled to the door.

Jane shook her head again. "A true lady is never without an army."

Mrs. Rowling raised an eyebrow, but Jane scuttled her from the room without another word.

Jane backtracked through the drawing room and out the opposite door to the servants' stairs. It wasn't much longer before she broke through to the kitchens. She paused only long enough to grab the tin box over the stove and then hurried to the gardens beyond. Luck would have it the stables lay on the other side of the hall from the kitchens' entrance. But it also happened, this worked quite well with her plan.

The night air hit her as she rounded the side of the house, and the cold breeze swept over the lake. It was still that impenetrable dark before the moon rose, and she stumbled a few times until she got her bearings. The lawn swept around the front of the house uninterrupted from there, and she had a clear shot of the stables.

But it needn't matter if she made a good run of it if she did not capture her predator's attention.

She waited. Listening. Until the sound of carriage wheels became so distinct, her heartbeat matched their rhythm. And then she moved.

She slipped from the shadows of the house, hitched up her skirts, and bolted. The first shouts came as she cleared the front steps of the portico.

"Stop her!" The distinctly raspy voice of Lord Crawley made her stumble, but only for a moment.

She righted herself and kept going.

"Bloody sodding fools! Get out of my way!"

Something had happened, but she could not turn around now to ascertain exactly what, but she now knew this. Crawley had brought help, and they'd just tripped him up.

She was nearly to the stables now. She could see the sagging wooden doors. Smell the memory of hay. Only a few more feet.

The gunshot split the night so acutely, she fell to the ground as if her legs suddenly could no longer hold her. She rolled, losing her grip on the tin box. Her legs tangled in her skirts, and she skidded across the gravel of the drive in front of the stables, the rocks shredding the skin along her palms and arms.

"I wouldn't move another inch, Miss Black." Lord Crawley's voice was much too close. He couldn't have caught her. He was too old to match her spry run.

Ignoring the burning in her hands, she shoved to her feet, and heedless of Crawley's warning, she whipped around to find he hadn't caught up with her. Only, one didn't need to catch one's prey when one held a brace of pistols. He'd spent one of them though, and she was still a good deal away. She shuffled on her feet, swaying slightly.

"Ah, I see I've upset you." His sick smile shone through the darkness. "They never expect the quiet ones. Do they, Miss Black?"

She continued to sway, her feet shuffling through the grass. "I should say they never expect it of the stupid ones."

Ah, that had met its mark. Crawley's smile vanished, and the gun wavered.

"Where is that sniveling doctor?" His voice shook with rage. "Your family has done nothing to deserve the accolades it's received. Nothing! And I will not have my family—"

Her foot struck metal. She swept down and scooped up the box, dismissing Crawley with a flip of her hand.

"I'm really not one for long speeches, my lord," she said and ran through the sagging doors of the stables.

She wrenched the lid from the tin box even before she cleared the threshold, pulled out a match, and struck it. The small flame roared in the quiet of the dark stables, and for a second, she was transfixed by it.

Then she let it drop.

The small flame caught the dry hay and old timber with exuberant relish. Fire shot up, swamping the walls within moments. She didn't hesitate. She ran deeper into the stables toward the sound of a very faint neigh.

"You damned chit! What have you done?"

She turned only long enough to catch sight of Crawley standing amidst the flames at the main entrance. There was a sudden *woosh,* and fire shot up from the floor around him. He screamed and stamped at the ground before retreating back the way he came.

Jane was to Harold's stall by then.

"Ready for one last run, my handsome man?" she said, rubbing the startled horse's nose until he neighed in contentment. "Let's see what you've got left in you."

She unlatched the stall, taking time to grab a bit and bridle. They took the few steps to the west end of the stables, and she carefully prodded the doors. Through a slit, she saw nothing but the open fields of Peregrine and the darkness of a country night.

She slipped the bridle on Harold before bending to hitch up her skirts between her legs. She tied them in a knot at her waist, effectively making a set of trousers like Aunt Sarah had taught her.

"Nifty little trick," she muttered before smiling at Harold. "It really is rather handy to be raised by a family of spies."

She shoved the door wide and vaulted onto the old horse. She leaned down close to his ear, her eyes watching the horizon.

"All right, old boy, let's show them you're not done quite yet."

And with that, she gave him his head, his ears pointed toward Eaton Park.

CHAPTER 23

Smoke.

He saw it as soon as he crested the ridge from Maidenstone. His eyes searched through the darkness, but there was only so much he could make out as he pressed his horse harder. He'd swapped horses twice on this go as he pushed them harder, the drive in him to get to Jane reaching near insanity.

He rounded another bend in the drive, and this time, the night sky lit with an eerie orange.

Fire.

The house?

Jane?

He slowed the horse, and the animal wheeled at the sudden change in movement. Austin stayed there, hidden in the trees along the drive as he watched the sky above Peregrine Hall flicker in shades of red.

He could be riding into a trap.

He had reached a point somewhere beyond exhaustion, and he no longer trusted his thinking. Instincts were the only thing he could rely on, and right now, they were telling him to be wary.

Something wasn't right here.

If Crawley had reached Peregrine Hall, he would have simply killed Jane and the doctor. Wouldn't he? It was the doctor that could have traced him back to his past sins. Simply eliminating him would have been the easiest option.

So why was Peregrine Hall on fire?

No. Something was not right.

He eased the horse into a trot as he wound his way up the remainder of the drive. He kept close to the trees as he crested the last hill, turning the animal toward the front steps of the hall.

The stable.

The stable was on fire, not the house.

Jane.

He didn't know what it was, but something in him told him this was Jane's doing. It was a warning or a sign or—

He shook his head, exhaustion coating his brain in a fog. His thoughts reeled one into the next, and he needed to focus. He needed to keep his emotions tamped down and search out the truth of what he'd ridden into.

The hall was dark except for one or two windows glowing in soft light. The front door was shut. The steps empty. No servants ran to the stable to extinguish the fire, but then, there weren't that many servants left, were there?

He circled around the last copse of trees and came into the gravel drive at the front of the house from the east.

That was when he saw the carriage with the Crawley crest lit by the scorching flames of the fire.

He was too late.

The thought came zinging out of nowhere, and he pushed it away. He couldn't think like that. Jane needed him right now, and he needed to stay objective.

Think like a soldier.

That's what he needed to do. He'd spent enough years on the battlefields of India and Greece. Battle after battle had seen him cool, remote, calm.

But then the woman he loved hadn't been in danger.

He dismounted, letting the bridle drag as he crouched and skirted the carriage to the far side. He rose up on tiptoe, peering through the vehicle's window.

Empty.

He crouched back down. So where were they? And how many?

Gravel crunched, and he whirled toward the stable. He was hidden enough in the darkness behind the carriage wheel, but he wanted to maintain the element of surprise. It may be the only thing he had in his favor.

His hand slid to his side where Samuel's pistol lay nestled in the pocket of his coat. He'd only have one shot if he ever got into a position to use it.

"We didn't see the gel come this way. We swear it." The voice was rough, raspy, and carried an accent not found in Mayfair.

"That's all bloody well and good, but now she's in that bloody inferno, and we don't know where she's hidden the doctor." This voice was refined, cultured.

Crawley.

Austin knew it in a heartbeat because it was the same voice that had threatened Penelope Black the previous year at the Brownlow affair.

But it wasn't recognition of the voice that had rocked him. It was the words.

Jane was in the stable.

The stable that was on fire.

He surged to his feet, springing from around the side of

the carriage so quickly, the men he encountered faltered in their step, falling backward.

And Austin knew he'd made a mistake.

There were four of them. Crawley and three thugs.

He had thought it was Crawley and a single goon. He could have handled that. But three hired men. He didn't like those odds. His hand impulsively cradled the gun in his pocket.

"Well, you're not the bloody doctor, but I can't say I'm surprised to see you. Evanshire, is it?" Crawley's thin lips folded into a sneer. "You were only a boy the last time I saw you. Snotty nosed and smelling like sour milk. I can see much hasn't changed."

The three other men took up positions around Crawley almost reflexively. They were all varying shades of the same kind of mercenary. Tall, brawny, and sporting noses that had clearly been broken at some point. One bloody shot was not going to do him much good, and he resolved to save it for Crawley.

"What have you done with Jane?" he asked, ignoring Crawley's words. The man was only trying to incite a rise out of him, and Austin was far too well trained a soldier for such silliness.

Crawley made no visible reaction. "It is not what I have done to her. It's what the stupid girl did to herself." Now he gestured behind him at the burning edifice. "She's gone and set herself on fire." His tone dripped with acid.

No.

Not again.

It couldn't have happened again.

"I'm not sure what she hoped to accomplish by that, but in the mean time, that leaves me with only you to find out what's become of the good doctor."

Austin let his eyes stray to the stable for only a second but it was enough.

"Concerned about your lady love then, eh?" Crawley sneered. "Then I suppose you'd like us to allow you to pass so you can go rescue her or some such barbaric nonsense." He eyed his goons. "I'm afraid I cannot let you do that though until you tell me where the doctor is."

"I don't know where Dr. Seymour is." Austin was glad the words were true as his voice rang with authority. He didn't, in fact, know where the doctor was. Peregrine Hall loomed darkly over them, showing nearly no sign of life.

What had happened? Why had Jane set fire to the stable?

Crawley gestured to his men who began to surreptitiously ease toward him. "Now then. Enough with your nonsense. Tell me where the good doctor is, and you can save your lady love. Refuse to tell me, and not only does she die in that inferno but you will die as well." Crawley's smile was cold.

Austin traced the outline of the pistol in his pocket. How quickly could he draw it, and would it matter? He only had one shot.

That was when he felt it.

The ground shook under his feet. He knew it wasn't only him who felt it because Crawley's goons looked to the ground as if they expected it to slip out from under their feet at any moment.

"What in God's name—" Crawley never finished the sentence because then the shaking was matched with a noise.

Horses. It was a stampede. It had to be. But where?

Austin shot a look behind him, briefly so as not to turn his back on Crawley and his men, but it was enough.

Someone was coming.

Someones actually. And it was a whole lot of them.

An entire column of men mounted on horseback

streamed through the gates of Peregrine Hall at the bottom of the ridge. They carried torches and lanterns and lit the night sky like an explosion of fireworks to rival the stable fire.

They were still too far off to make out exactly who they were, but it was enough to know he wasn't alone. Now they just had to get here quickly enough to subdue Crawley and his men and allow Austin to get to the stables.

But just as the thought entered his mind an explosion tore through the darkness. The stable was collapsing. The roof fell in a shower of sparks, and flames roared from the abyss. He threw up a hand as the heat suddenly intensified. They were a good fifty yards from the building, but it was as if he stood directly in front of it.

Crawley had ducked when the explosion ripped through the night, but now he gained his feet and snarled. "Time is running out for your precious lady love, Evanshire. Will you let her die? Or will you tell me where the doctor is so you can save her?"

He couldn't force his eyes from the flames. Again, he pulled himself back, shoved exhaustion and fear away.

Not again.

Not again.

It kept playing over and over in his head, but along with it came the memory of Mrs. Rowling's words.

You've already given your entire self trying to save a mother that did not want you.

He shook his head, clearing it of the traitorous thoughts. Perhaps the riders were close enough that he could make a run for it. Dodge Crawley and his goons and save Jane.

But even as he thought it, Mrs. Rowling's words came roaring back.

It hadn't been his duty to rescue his mother, and he'd

spent the last fifteen years of his life running away because he thought it had been.

The thing that had plagued him for so long, that thing had been based on a lie. Watching the fire grow, it came back to him, and he suddenly understood how Jane had felt that day by the stream.

And his feet remained glued to the gravel.

He glanced behind him, and everything inside of him stopped. Just...stopped.

The riders were closer now. Close enough that he could make out each and every one of them. There were maids and footmen, obviously roused from their beds as they'd thrown on rumpled and half-buttoned uniforms. There were farmers with buckets and shovels. Townsfolk from the village. The milliner, the blacksmith, and even the vicar.

And leading them atop a horse that should have long been retired was Jane.

His Jane.

She held up her chin and met his gaze without flinching. The light from the fire struck her full in the face and lit her up like an avenging goddess.

"That's the funny thing about Jane Black," he said before turning back to Crawley. "The lady does not require saving."

* * *

SHE SLID from Harold as soon as they reached the top of the drive, unraveling her skirts as she did so. And then without another thought, she threw herself at Austin.

He caught her, his arms closing around her like steel bands, and she had never felt anything more wonderful in her entire life. So she shoved him away.

"I love you." She nearly shouted the words, and while shock registered on his face, she felt her own measure of disbelief at the words. But it was quickly overcome by a reeling sense of ease. Rightness. Truth. "We haven't the time for that, but I'm very pleased to see you alive," she rushed on. Later she would think about the sound of tears in her voice but right now, they had to save Peregrine Hall.

She spun about ready to bring her wrath down on Crawley and his men to find they had vanished. Beside her Austin swore, and she knew he had missed their exit as well. They spun in unison at the sound of a whip cracking to find Crawley scrambling to get into his carriage as one of his men had already set the horses into motion.

Austin took a step forward, and Jane's heart stopped.

He would go after them. He would seek out the danger, the thrill, anything that meant he could get away from Peregrine Hall and his past. The surge of elation she had felt upon seeing him dwindled to nothing.

She had thought it had changed his mind.

Being here at Peregrine these last few weeks. Seeing his childhood friends again.

Being with her.

But it hadn't, and it likely never would. He would always seek danger. The very thing she had planned her whole life to avoid.

She'd finally fallen in love, only it was with a man who wanted the exact opposite of everything she dreamed of.

He took another step and another, farther away from her, and it was as if she were watching him run away from her.

But then he did the oddest thing. He grabbed Harold's bridle and pulled the horse out of the way of Crawley's retreating carriage.

Jane stared, expecting any moment for him to fling himself on the poor animal's back. Harold had acted with great courage that night, but he was still an old horse, and he could not catch a runaway carriage.

She opened her mouth to protest when Austin did the damnedest thing. He pulled Harold's nose toward him and stroked the animal's snout.

"Well done tonight, old man," she heard Austin whisper before he straightened and called out to her. "I assume you have charge of this cavalry."

His words broke through her like a sharp wind coming off the lake.

He wasn't leaving.

He wasn't chasing after Crawley.

She watched as he walked back to her, shedding his coat and rolling up his sleeves. When he had been staring at her for several solid seconds, she finally managed to rouse herself.

"Yes." The word came out far too stammered. "Yes," she tried again and then turned, her heart warming as she met the intent gazes of the beloved servants from Eaton Park. "Anyone with a shovel, start digging a fire break around the perimeter. Those with buckets, set up a line."

People sprang from their horses and carts without hesitation, and Jane faltered. There. There in the instant response of these good people, when she had given orders, when she had arrived to rouse them out of their beds in the dead of night, and they had come to her call. That.

That was respect.

And that trumped beauty any day.

The farmers with their shovels went to work on the fire break while the maids and footmen with buckets trailed down to the lake, passing full buckets of icy water from one to the other as a return trail of children and old men and women set up a line for the buckets to be brought back.

It all happened within seconds just as she would have predicated, and it was only after she moved to step into her place in the bucket line that she realized Austin still stared at her.

"What are you waiting for?" she asked, proud of the goading in her voice.

He smiled at her through the smoke and flames and darkness, and she realized the thing she felt was happiness.

"You're right, Miss Black. We have a home to save."

CHAPTER 24

Dawn snuck up on them, spilling easily over the hills in the east until growing shots of light blanketed their shovels and overturned buckets.

He scooped another load of dirt onto the last of the dying embers and stepped back, resting a bent arm on the handle of the shovel.

"It's not how I would have gone about demolishing the place, but your lady has a keen way of going about things, eh?"

He turned, not realizing Ben had come to stand next to him. He eyed his friend, equally covered in dirt and soot as he likely was.

"When did you get here?"

The night had been filled with confusion and chaos even as the teams of farmers, servants, and village folk had formed up to battle the blaze. It had been a brutal struggle, but in the end, it was just as Jane had predicted. The stable was, indeed, burned to the ground.

Ben's laugh was warm. "I've been here nearly the whole

time, chum. Once we heard the commotion and knew it was safe to come out."

Austin faced his friend. "Come out?"

Ben gave a nod of his head toward the house. "Didn't the miss tell you?"

Austin followed the direction of his friend's nod to see Jane standing under the portico of Peregrine Hall, handing out food stuffs Mrs. Rowling had assembled for the volunteers.

"There hasn't been much time for idle chatter."

"It was Miss Black's idea to set the stable afire as a distraction, so Mary and meself could get Mrs. Rowling and the doctor away from the house." Ben's proud smile shown through the soot on his face.

"It was, was it?" Austin felt a pulse of pride as well.

"Oh, it was. I don't know how it would have turned out if she hadn't of thought so quickly. That's a smart woman you've got there."

Austin pulled his gaze away from Jane to eye his friend. "I don't have her quite yet. Would you mind holding this?" He handed his shovel to Ben and brushed at his shirtfront which effectively smeared soot along his ruined waistcoat. He didn't even know where his coat had gone. "Do I look suitable for courting a lady?"

Ben laughed again. "You don't look suitable for courting a privy, but I think the miss will let it pass on this count."

Austin swallowed his grin as he walked toward Jane. The dawning light had just struck the portico steps, and Jane lifted a hand to shield her eyes as the last of the volunteers trickled away. A soft smile came to her lips, and he wondered what it was she saw on the horizon.

He watched the lot of volunteers go and considered how it was he would ever repay them.

By staying in Maidenstone.

He knew the answer. Had known from the moment he decided to save the hall rather than chase after that damned Lord Crawley. It hadn't really been a choice though. When it came to Jane, there wasn't any other choice he'd care to make.

He reached the top step and stood beside her. She still stared out at the sunrise and hadn't noticed his approach as of yet. He didn't want to startle her. She looked so beautiful standing there on the stoop. Her hair hung around her sooted face in mismatched tangles, and her dress was long destroyed.

But she just looked so damned beautiful as she smiled and waved. The real mistress of Peregrine Hall.

"Are you going to keep staring at her or are you going to say something?"

Austin jumped as Mrs. Rowling walked past him, a glare thrown in his direction. He grimaced and turned to find Jane watching him.

Her expression was unexpectedly forlorn, and it hurt.

He gestured to the stable. "You were right. It should just be burned to the ground."

A weak smile came to her lips, and he thought she might laugh, but he realized with a jolt she was exhausted and trying very hard to stay on her feet.

So he simply opened his arms, and she walked into them.

She felt so slight and frail, but he knew she hid her strength well. He would never forget how she had looked on Harold as she had ridden to save his very life.

"It seems I owe the servants of Eaton Park and the folk of Maidenstone a great debt."

"I told them they were all invited to an assembly here at the hall once the stable was rebuilt."

"You did? Sending out invitations already? That's rather

bold of you." He nestled his chin on top of her head regardless of the fact she reeked of smoke.

She did laugh then, soft and cascading, and he liked how it felt, but then she grew quiet.

"How did you know?"

He tensed, but asked anyway, "Know what?"

"That Crawley had found us."

The knowledge lodged in his throat, but he forced it out. "Emily betrayed the secret." For all the animosity between the cousins, he knew Jane would still protect a member of her family.

But as soon as he spoke the words, Jane's shoulders sunk a little more. He thought she'd want to know more, but she surprised him by asking, "Would you have done it?"

"Done what?" He didn't like how quiet her voice had gotten.

"Gone into the burning stable after me?"

He eased her away to look into her eyes as he said one simple word. "Yes."

Her mouth parted, and he thought he may have shocked her. If he was going to ask, now was the time to do it while she was off her guard.

"Jane, I—" He didn't know what to say. There was so much inside of him. So much that he had to explain, but... not now. Now he just had to tell her the truth. "I want you to be my wife. I want you to be here beside me forever. I will do whatever it takes to convince you of that."

She shook her head, her disagreement already coming from her lips, so he spoke over her.

"Jane, I love you. Will you marry me?"

He didn't believe her eyes could get any wider, but just then, they did. They were so beautiful. She was so beautiful. He reached up, cupping her cheeks in both of his hands to push that blasted fringe from her face so he could see her.

"Please, Jane." He had never begged before. Never. For anything. But now, he would get down on his knees if she demanded it. "Please say you'll be my wife."

But she didn't say anything.

Because just then, the real cavalry arrived.

* * *

"WELL, I'm glad to see she's at least still alive."

Jane glared at her brother as he dismounted on the drive below them.

"*She* is quite capable of keeping herself alive, thank you," she returned, pulling free of Austin's grasp to set her fisted hands to her hips.

She had completed the mission and upheld her vow to her grandfather. She had unmasked the traitor and now Lord Crawley was on the run. She took the few steps down to the drive as a carriage carrying Lofton colors pulled to a stop. Of all the people she expected to emerge, Lizzie was the last one. But there she was, springing from the carriage in her ubiquitous trousers.

"Jane!" she cried and loped up the drive to capture Jane in a hug. "Whatever did you do?" the young girl asked, absorbing the damage around her.

"It was quite a battle," Jane said, proud she kept the laughter from her voice.

Penelope came next, wrestling her girth from the carriage as she gave a whoop of delight. "You must tell me everything. But not now!" She held up both hands as she rushed for the stairs. "This baby is stepping directly on my personal bits. You." She pointed an accusing finger at Austin. "Tell me exactly where the retiring room might be or forever regret it."

"I'll take you in, my dear." Mrs. Rowling stepped forward

and took Penelope's arm. "You must have had such a long journey. Come with me, child. We'll get you settled in with a nice pot of tea and some scones to start your day."

Penelope lit up. "Oh, and do you have any cream?"

Mrs. Rowling smiled. "We have the best clotted cream in Kent!"

The two disappeared through the front doors of the hall as if they were long lost friends.

Finally, her father stepped down from the carriage and strode swiftly to where they gathered at the bottom of the steps.

"He got away, I'm afraid," Jane said in response to the worried look on her father's face, but he didn't stop at her words. He simply pulled her into a strong hug.

"I don't care if he fell off the bloody edge of the map, my girl. I only care that you're safe." She had never seen her father this worried, and she suddenly realized exactly how much danger she likely had been in.

"Of course, I'm safe." She looked at Austin standing beside her. "The Marquess of Evanshire is a diligent nanny when he must be."

She had said it to lighten the grimace on her father's face, but instead, his expression turned to stone.

"I trust that my daughter was treated with the utmost respect while in your care," her father said to Austin.

Her father had always shown he loved her, but really this was too much.

"Father, I can assure—"

"Your daughter was treated in a manner deserving of her position." Austin returned her father's stare.

This was too much. "You are both being utterly ridiculous."

"Now you sound like Mum." Lizzie laughed.

Speaking of Mum…

Jane looked back at the carriage to see Mum handing down Lady Jane and Mrs. Seymour.

Mrs. Seymour peered about her as if she hadn't seen daylight in quite some time before her eyes stopped. Riveted. A smile came to Jane's lips because she knew exactly what Mrs. Seymour saw.

"Mitty!" the woman cried and launched herself from the carriage.

"My Bethany!" the responding cry came from the top of the stairs as the doctor rushed from the hall.

Tears pricked Jane's eyes when Dr. Seymour's arms closed around his poor wife. She started, but only a little, when Austin slipped his hand into hers. Only a few weeks ago, she would have pulled her hand back as if scalded, but right then, standing in the drive of Peregrine Hall, smoke still lingering in the air, the tension of danger and death slinking away, she let him hold her hand.

She had done a lot more than uphold a vow, she realized. So much more. She turned to her brother. "We must stop Crawley. He left several hours ago, so he has a lead on us, but if we move quickly—"

Her brother stilled her with a hand. "The authorities have already been alerted, and they sent word to all the ports."

"You think he'll make a run for the Continent?" Austin asked.

"Or America. There's really nothing else for him to do now that his secret is out." Samuel's face grew grim. "Jane, you should know—"

"Emily told our secret. I know," she said and squeezed Austin's hand. "Austin told me."

Samuel raised a brow. "Austin, is it?"

Jane had a stunning sarcastic remark planned but just then Lady Jane and her mother reached them. Jane smiled at her grandmother and then faltered.

"Are you crying, Grandmother?" Jane asked, incredulity soaking her voice.

"I'm just so proud of you," Lady Jane said and again, Jane was pulled into a crushing hug. "Did you do that?" the older woman asked when she finally pulled away, pointing to the smoldering remains of the stable.

Jane's face lit with a smile, and she nodded proudly. "I did."

Lady Jane crushed her in a hug. "I always knew you had it in you, child."

Her mum came next, but Jane didn't expect a hug from her and she didn't receive one. Instead she got a disgusted grimace. "I love you, and I'm proud of you, but you must get that filthy thing off if I'm going to hug you."

Jane laughed, her chest blooming in warmth at her mother's love. Her mother was finally here, and Jane could tell her everything. Except, now she wasn't so sure she needed to.

"You must be exhausted, child," Lady Jane said as she turned. "Eaton Park isn't far. You'll be settled in no time."

Her mum stepped forward to take her arm. "We'll get you a bath and tuck you into your bed. It will be good to be home."

They were taking her away, and she was so tired that for a moment she let them.

Let them pull her away. Away from Peregrine Hall. Mrs. Rowling, Ben, and Mary.

Austin.

She froze, her feet setting into the gravel. Everyone turned to look at her, puzzlement across their faces.

"I am home," she said, and never had she felt the truth of her words more.

Her eyes traveled to her father. She hadn't planned this part out. When she would accept a suit. Be married off. She knew her father was protective of her, and she steeled herself, ready to win his favor.

But her father didn't argue. Instead, a knowing smile came to his lips.

She took a step back and reached out for Austin's hand.

CHAPTER 25

Two Months Later

* * *

"You know what the funny thing is about plans?"

He was not listening to her at all. She knew that, but she continued when he gave a muffled mmm sound.

"Sometimes they go exactly according to schedule."

Now she had him because he pulled his face away from where he had been nuzzling her neck.

"I beg your pardon." A line of displeasure popped between his brows. "Are you saying I'm a suitable replacement for that inane Mr. Smith?"

Jane laughed and looped her arms more tightly around her husband's neck.

Her husband.

Although it had been little more than an hour since she'd been able to call Austin that, she was certain those were two words she'd never grow used to.

"I'm not saying that all," she said. "It's only that I had

hoped to live a quiet life of domestic simplicity, and here I am." She gestured about them. "The mistress of a beautiful estate."

His frown deepened. "Aren't you supposed to be spouting nonsense of love instead pointing out the practicalities of this arrangement? It is our wedding day after all."

It was her turn to frown. "Oh, please, don't remind me. Kiss me instead."

He did just that. Austin Peregrine, the Marquess of Evanshire, was turning out to be a dutiful husband. But the reminder that this was a stolen moment of privacy came with the shattering of an obnoxious laugh just beyond the study door.

They broke off the kiss to stare at the door in unison.

"I do think they're following us," she whispered.

"But we were so careful to evade detection."

She eyed him. "Clearly, we're losing our touch."

He eased her back to peer at her face. "Are you suggesting we require practice in the art of espionage?"

She shrugged and stepped toward the door, taking his hand in hers. "I'm suggesting no such thing. We've retired, remember?"

She liked seeing the smile that came to his face. He smiled so easily now when she made fun of what they had been through, but his fingers still tightened over hers.

Her entire family had come from the church in Maidenstone after the service for the wedding breakfast. Even Professor Mesmer was in attendance as his ship back to America wasn't to leave Liverpool for another fortnight. He and Lady Jane enjoyed comparing canes and seeing who had the best carved head to theirs.

And true to her word, her grandmother wore a spectacular hat.

But Emily was not there.

Jane felt a pang of sadness at that. Her cousin had still not emerged from a self-imposed sort of exile and remained ensconced at the estate in Bedford. Jane had tried to assure her cousin that there was no animosity between them. Emily had made an honest mistake, swept away by the allure of a title and an exalted position in society. She had been so young and trusting. That was not cause for a life sentence.

But still, Emily had decided it was.

Jane squeezed her husband's hand, pushing away the disheartening thoughts of her cousin.

"Shall we, my lord?" she said, moving toward the door. "It's best to get this over with, don't you suppose?"

"I'm afraid you're right, my lady," he said as he trailed behind her. "But I must ask for a favor."

She turned to him, an eyebrow raised.

"I hope you would grant me the honor of watching your back as we embark on this mission." His lips turned up in a mischievous grin.

She smiled back. "I wouldn't have it any other way." And with a wink, she turned and opened the door to face the rest of their lives.

Together.

ABOUT THE AUTHOR

Jessie decided to be a writer because the job of Indiana Jones was already filled.

Taking her history degree dangerously, Jessie tells the stories of courageous heroines, the men who dared to love them, and the world that tried to defeat them.

Jessie makes her home in the great state of New Hampshire where she lives with her husband and two very opinionated Basset hounds. For more, visit her website at jessieclever.com.

Printed in Great Britain
by Amazon

56893807R00177